Debating Darcy

SAYANTANI DASGUPTA

SCHOLASTIC PRESS/NEW YORK

All rights reserved. Published by Scholastic Press, an imprint of Scholastic Inc.,
Publishers since 1920. SCHOLASTIC, SCHOLASTIC PRESS, and associated logos are
trademarks and/or registered trademarks of Scholastic Inc.

The publisher does not have any control over and does not assume any responsibility for
author or third-party websites or their content.

This book is a work of fiction. Names, characters, places, and incidents are either
the product of the author's imagination or are used fictitiously, and any resemblance to
actual persons, living or dead, business establishments, events, or locales is
entirely coincidental.

Library of Congress Cataloging-in-Publication Data available

ISBN 978-1-338-79769-5

10 9 8 7 6 5 4 3 2 1   22 23 24 25 26

Printed in Italy 183
First edition, February 2022

Book design by Abby Dening and Elizabeth B. Parisi
Handlettering by Maeve Norton

For all the brown girls who dreamt of gossamer gowns
Only to realize we were already wearing crowns

(And for Colin Firth. For reasons that I hope are obvious.)

CHAPTER 1

THE FIRST TIME I saw Firoze Darcy, I was standing on the top of a cafeteria table in a high school I didn't even go to, a borrowed tie around my head like a bandanna, belting out show tunes into a wedge platform heel I was using as a microphone.

In other words, I was not at my dignified best.

To be fair, what normal sixteen-year-old girl wouldn't have been a little punchy in the same situation? I'd woken up far too early on a Saturday morning to ride in a freezing bus to a school that should have taken fifteen minutes to get to but took forty-five due to a very confused (and possibly very myopic—sorry, parked Toyota with new yellow racing stripe) bus driver. Then I'd used up all my nervous energy in three back-to-back rounds of what was basically competitive acting against a bunch of fellow teens of variable thespian skill. Lunchtime was my chance to rest my jangled nerves, unwind with my friends as we waited to see which of us speech competitors had broken into our final rounds, and basically let my inner theater nerd have her way with me.

I was on the aforementioned cafeteria table, in the middle of performing my favorite song from *Hamilton* with my friends Tomi and Jay, when I saw him. A boy I'd never seen before. He was suited and booted, as my cousins in India would say. He was tall, dark, and handsome, like the cliché hero from an eighteenth-century British romance novel. Also, I realized with a weird skip of my heartbeat, he was Desi. Like me.

And maaan, could the guy wear a suit.

Of course, pretty much every other teenager in the Hartford High School cafeteria on that September afternoon was wearing a suit. Because that was the generally accepted uniform at speech and debate competitions. (Except Tomi, who actually made her own clothes, but that was a whole other crafty situation.)

But while most of us looked like awkward adolescents wearing cheap, off-the-rack imitations of adulthood, this guy looked like somebody had cut and molded his dark blue blazer to his not-inconsiderable shoulders. And don't even get me started about the fit of his slacks. That description would be quite shockingly NSFW.

What I mean to say is this: He was, at least by appearance, just what a young man ought to be.

So, logically, I entirely blame him for what I did next. Which was to look straight down into the boy's dark eyes from my perch on the wobbly cafeteria table, crook my non-manicured finger at him, and start singing at him like he was a beautiful woman and I the future murderous vice president of the United States: "Excuse me, miss, I know it's not funny, but your perfume smells like your daddy's got money!"

The entire cafeteria, already hopped up on nervous competition energy and vending machine snacks, exploded in laughter. The boy made an incoherent noise, half clearing his throat and half protesting.

"I'm . . . sorry?" he managed to say, blinking at me. His voice was deep and chocolate-molten-cake yummy.

His delightful voice, combined with the uptightness of his expression, somehow egged me on. I winked, hamming it up. "Why you slummin' in the city in your fancy heels? You searchin' for an urchin who can give you ideals?"

Next to me, Jay laid a hand to his forehead and sang in a dramatic falsetto, "Leela, you disgust me!"

"So you discussed me!" I stared at the handsome boy, my body humming with mischief. "I'm a trust fund, baby, you can trust me!"

Everyone in the cafeteria went bonkers at that, howling and pointing. When the boy realized the entire high school cafeteria was staring at him, his body grew tense, his expression changing rapidly from surprised to shocked to glowering.

"She's got you there, man," said a blond dude I hadn't noticed before next to the Desi hottie. "You do have that fat trust fund, don't you, Darcy?"

Blond boy was smiling and nodding at us, or rather, should I say, smiling and nodding at Jay, a flirtatious smile playing at his lips. But as much as he seemed to be enjoying our performance, his friend clearly wasn't.

"I hope you're happy, Bingley." The Desi boy named Darcy knocked his friend's arm off his shoulder. "This kind of . . . immature behavior is exactly why I didn't want Netherfield Academy joining the public school forensics league in the first place."

Everyone in earshot—who, as it happens, almost all attended public schools—shouted in outrage. Someone threw a wadded-up page of homework in his direction. Giving the crowd an imperious look, Darcy turned on his heel and stalked away.

"What in the actual Marie Antoinette?!" Jay asked, and the team at the next table cheered.

Jay was always able to come up with a good line, even at a tense moment. One of the many reasons I loved him. That, and the fact that we'd been neighbors and best friends since my dad had lost his old job and I'd moved to our town in the sixth grade.

Even Tomi, who normally did not stoop to insults, snapped her finger in the air like she was one of the Schuyler sisters. "Seriously. Off with his head!"

"'This kind of immature behavior!'" I mocked in a voice loud enough to carry. "What an elitist jerk!" Then, a beat or two too late, I added, "I mean, let them eat cake!"

"The moment's passed, Sofia Coppola." Jay patted my arm in mock sympathy as he jumped off the table.

"I'm still working on my timing vis-à-vis spontaneous quippery," I admitted.

"That Marie Antoinette comment was so good, though," said Tomi.

"I know, right?" Jay said in such a self-satisfied way that I laughed. Our Longbourn High teammates, along with the next-table-over Meryton team, clapped, and Jay took a wavy-handed, Shakespearean-style bow.

"Why are the good-looking ones always such turds?" I asked with a dramatic sigh.

"Beyond the obvious explanation that the cis hetero-normative patriarchy tells them the world should revolve around them?" replied Tomi. "Oh, no reason at all!"

Tomi gave me a hand as I clambered awkwardly down from the table, my bandanna once again becoming a borrowed tie and my microphone transforming back into a slipper. Cinderella turning back into a pumpkin after the ball, as it were.

"Only the good-looking straight ones are turds, my darlings." Jay waved across the cafeteria at the blond boy Bingley, who actually waved back. Not that I should have been surprised. With light brown skin, dark eyes, and a jawline that could double as a rapier, Jay was way too handsome for his own good.

"He is cute," Tomi offered with a twinkle in her long-lashed eyes. "I give you leave to like him. You've liked many a stupider fellow."

"But his cuteness manifests in a very Chip and Muffy/ Martha's Vineyard/Hamptons beach house sort of way, wouldn't you agree?" I clenched my jaw for extra elitist emphasis.

"Oh, I'll shake up his little country club life, don't you worry!" Jay assured me airily.

I would have gone on, scouring my brain for more witty ways to tease Jay about Bingley, if the acoustics of the cafeteria had been different. If the acoustics in that cafeteria had been worse, in fact, a lot of things would have gone down differently. But, as it was, Hartford High's cafeteria doubled as its theater, and the two boys from the Netherfield team were standing right next to the stage at one end of the room. Whoever had constructed the space clearly knew what they were doing, architecture-wise. Because just then, in one of those natural lulls in the volume of the conversation nearby, Darcy's and Bingley's voices bounced back to us from across the cavernous room.

"Oh, come on, man, don't be like that!" Bingley was cajoling his friend. "It was a joke!"

"Mentioning a trust fund here, with these kids? Not funny!" Darcy responded.

"Loosen up, dude," Bingley went on. "It's not like it's every day you get serenaded by a beautiful girl on a table!"

"Beautiful? If you say so." Darcy's scornful voice rang out across the cafeteria, clear as a bell. "Certainly not beautiful enough to tempt me!"

My entire team, and the teams around us, got even quieter then, and I could feel their eyes on my back. Somebody went "ooooh" and somebody else snickered but was quickly shushed. Even as the volume of conversation rose again around us, people repeating what we'd all overheard, Darcy's words and their implication hit me like a crashing wave, washing me in a painfully familiar sense of humiliation.

"What the *actual* fork?" hissed Tomi, her worried eyes searching my face, her hand reaching for mine. "You okay, Leela?"

"Sure, no, what do I care what that jerk thinks?" I managed a wobbly smile.

I let her twist her fingers through mine but only felt worse for it. I wished I could melt into the sticky tiled floor, or maybe pull on a magic ring of power and make myself invisible. The crummiest part was I hadn't felt this way in years, not since I'd moved out of the almost-all-white town in which I'd grown up. There, among the Bingley-like blonds with their matching polos and polo ponies, I'd been convinced that my brown skin made me intolerably, horribly, disgustingly ugly. It had taken me years to unlearn those cruel lessons, but to be perfectly honest, I wasn't 100 percent there yet.

It was Jay, predictably, who saved the day, not by giving me sympathy but by making clear he didn't think I needed any.

"I don't care what you haters say." He ran his hand over his spiky black hair, smoothly continuing our conversation from before. "I'm planning on giving that Bingley my number. That is, as soon as I can get him away from his evil idiot buddy—the one with the shockingly terrible eyesight. Guy's clearly overdue at the optometrist."

I turned back to my friends, trying to maintain control over the muscles of my face, trying to stop the boy Darcy's comments from echoing again and again through my brain. But my heart was beating uncomfortably fast and my mouth felt full of ashes, like all the silly joy of being young, carefree, and theatrical had been burned to dust by his scorn.

With his brief, hard words, Darcy had stuck me in a time machine, sending me back to the schoolyard bullies who had mocked elementary school me with pseudo Native American "woo-woo-woos," who had rubbed my dark brown skin to see if my "tan" would come off, who had taken ostentatious sniffs in my direction and complained that I smelled like curry. Back then, I had been sure someone like me could never be considered pretty, heroic, or worthy of being a protagonist, even of my own story. I had been convinced I should try and erase myself from every social situation, from every public space, from the very narrative that is America.

My forensics teammates kept chattering around me, but I couldn't get Darcy's mockery out of my head. Because what made it worse, of course, was that he was Desi. Unobtrusively, I tried to straighten my out-of-control shag of a hairdo, noticing for the first time how rumpled my skirt suit was. And, egads, what was that stain near the waist? Ketchup? My mind drifted to my aunts in India, who made such a fuss about me staying out of the sun, whispering to my mother that it was too bad I'd inherited my father's complexion and not hers. I thought of how in my American Bengali community, people always said I had a "pretty face," adding, in a lower voice, "for a dark girl."

As if my subconscious manifested her, right then, I looked up to see a blonde girl standing in front of our table, her smooth straight hair hanging like a model's around her impossibly perfect features. She was wearing a blazer the same style and color as the two other boys had been wearing. On the breast pocket of her blazer was a golden N—undoubtedly for Netherfield Academy. She reminded me of every girl I'd gone to ballet class with when I was little, the ones whose "nude" tights and shoes actually matched their skin, the ones who always got picked to be the ballerina princess over me because they looked the part, whereas I never would.

"Honestly, Firoze Darcy's right. I mean, I don't see the lie." The girl gave a sour-lemon twist to her perfectly lipsticked lips, and I couldn't tell which of Darcy's comments she was talking about—the one about Netherfield joining the public school league, or the other, more terrible one?

Tomi seemed to be thinking along the same lines, because she stood up from her seat and confronted the girl, blocking me from sight with her body. My friend crossed her arms. "How exactly do you mean?"

"You public school teams . . . !" the blonde girl said, without fully finishing her thought. "I mean, are you people even here to be serious about forensics, or just be clowns?"

"Oh, the clown thing, obviously," deadpanned Jay, standing up now, next to Tomi.

"Funny." The girl narrowed her eyes at my bestie. "And by the way, just some friendly advice, kindly meant? Don't even bother giving my brother your number, my dude. You're so not his type."

Jay opened his mouth, then shut it again, at an uncharacteristic loss for words. Tomi made some incoherent sounds of protest, but I just sat there, my brain empty of an appropriate comeback.

The girl rolled her eyes and clip-clopped away on her perfect heels.

"I take it back," Jay said in a weirdly strangled voice, straightening the tie I'd just returned to him. "I'm going to give that Bingley guy my number, make him fall hopelessly in love with me, and then marry him and live happily ever after, just to get back at that evil shrew of a sister."

"Revenge is an excellent reason to choose a life partner," Tomi

9

agreed, even as she lightly touched my shoulder, like she was making sure I was okay.

I cleared my throat, trying to get ahold of myself. "Also, the 'my dude'? I mean, what *was* that?" I said as lightheartedly as I could.

"I have absolutely no idea." Jay shook his head. "Clearly, our education is too limited at our sad public school to make use of such sophisticated vocabulariage."

The shame I'd been feeling before as a result of Darcy's words was fast hardening into anger. I wasn't that little bullied elementary schooler anymore. Finding my voice through speech competitions, and finding community in my forensics team, had changed all that. I mean, who were these snotty Netherfield Academy types to put us public high school kids down, suggest we weren't good enough to compete with them, laugh with them, date them? They were obviously so privileged, they couldn't even see beyond their own hateful patrician noses, their own exclusive, gated-community lives.

It was settled. Firoze Darcy was, without a doubt, the most disagreeable, horrible, nasty, evil, conceited person I had ever met. I quite detested him.

CHAPTER 2

I T IS A truth universally acknowledged that there are two kinds of people in high school forensics: speakers and debaters.

We speech-type forensicators (yes, it's a real word, and no, it has nothing to do with criminal science) value interpersonal connection, the written word, and emotion. Whether we're performing a ten-minute piece of prose or poetry, or a humorous or dramatic interpretation of a play excerpt, we are all about the art. High school sports teams may get all the public glory, but there's nowhere to find such pure, unadulterated teenage passion as weekend tournaments of competitive acting.

Debaters of all genders, on the other hand, are the mansplainers of the forensics world. What speech competitors are to nuance and emotion, debaters are to speed-talking, ham-fisted point grabbing. They are, on the whole, pen-twirling jerks. If we speakers are the equivalent of football, soccer, basketball, and fencing teams all rolled up in one, debaters are the equivalent of verbal wrestlers—minus the tight onesies and weird helmets. They are all arguing, no artistry. (Also, don't be offended or anything if you're a wrestler—it's just a metaphor, okay?)

Which is why I wasn't surprised at all by the news passed on by one of our team coaches, Mrs. Bennet, who bustled up to us in the cafeteria just as Bingley's sister was walking away. A frustrated community theater actress, Mrs. Bennet now threw all her passion for acting into coaching our team.

"Forensicators, gather round!" she chirped, wedging her flower-dressed form into the cafeteria bench.

We all obediently did so. Our forensics team consisted of seniors Oluwatomisin Lucas—or Tomi—who was an original oratory speaker, and Colin Kang, who did extemporaneous speaking. Even though brainiac Colin had the entire National Forensics Association rule book practically memorized, or maybe because of that, we'd elected Tomi president of the club, and Colin vice president. Then there were Jay Galvez and me, Leela Bose, juniors who did dramatic and humorous interpretation respectively. Our other team members included one sophomore, an emo/goth reincarnation of Wednesday Addams named Mary Stewart (I jest you not). And then there were two new, kind of silly ninth graders named Lidia Rivera and Kitty Cho, who were doing prose and poetry interpretation, although what they really seemed to be interested in was flirting with boys from other teams.

"Do you want to hear the news?" Mrs. Bennet was all gleaming eyes and whispered intensity.

"You want to tell them, and I imagine they can have no objection to hearing it," said a calm voice. It was Mr. Bennet, our other coach, as pinched and calm as his wife was messy and excitable.

12

He had been an accountant before he'd retired early and joined his wife in forensics coaching, and he still looked the part.

"Netherfield Academy has come at last!" chirped Mrs. Bennet. "They've finally broken down and agreed to be a part of our local state forensics league!"

"Oh, we know, Mrs. B," I said with a dramatic sigh. "Their private academy is probably slumming it with us public schoolers to get more practice for all those fancy invitationals."

At their end of the table, Kitty whispered something about "invitationals" to Lidia and giggled, to which Lidia gave out a honking snort.

"We just had the inordinate pleasure of meeting some of their team." Jay indicated the far table by the stage, where the two blond Bingleys and Mr. Disapproving Desi Darcy were now sitting. The only team anywhere near them were the red-uniformed boys from Regimental, the all-boys military academy. I'd noticed Kitty and Lidia swooning over some of their competitors before, and made a mental note to warn the baby forensicators away from those Regimental dudes, who had a reputation for being bad news.

"So that golden-haired chap is Charles Bingley and next to him is his sister, Caroline, or Ro, as I believe she is called," Mrs. Bennet was saying. "This is the first of our tournaments they've attended and already the judges' room is buzzing with what a remarkable public forum debate team they are! A creative, quick-thinking duo. They *crushed* their morning opponents, from what I heard!"

Mary let out a little squeak, her pale face turning a kind of purple.

"You all right?" Tomi looked up from her knitting. (Yes, I said knitting. I told you she was crafty.) "What's up, hon? Did your first day of LD not go well?"

Mary had just started competing in Lincoln-Douglas, or one-on-one, debate, against everyone else's better judgment. It was heavily philosophical, something that no one but Mary thought was her forte. Not that I knew too much about debate, but LD was different from either what the Bingley siblings did, public forum debate, or the more intense and rigorous policy debate, which were both teams of two each. Also, our Mary wasn't exactly the most polished public speaker, having bombed in all the speech categories she'd competed in as a ninth grader. But since Tomi and Colin had helped her formulate her arguments before today's tournament, there was no way it could have gone that badly.

Unless, of course, it had. Like Mary, Queen of Scots, decapitation-level badly.

"Don't worry, my dear." Mr. Bennet sat down next to Mary, patting her hand in a fatherly way. "No one remembers what happened!"

"Oh, I beg to disagree!" said Colin seriously, his mouth half-full of some delicious-looking dumplings he was eating from a Tupperware. I mean, really, would it kill him to offer us some? "From what I heard, I am assured that no one who was there could possibly ever forget!"

"Colin!" Tomi clicked her tongue as she dropped a stitch.

"I'm being descriptive, not pejorative!" Colin took a slurp of a fizzy purple soda. "No offense meant whatsoever indeed, Mary!"

Mr. Bennet gave Colin a mildly disapproving look before

going on. "My dear Mary, it was unlucky, that's all, that you got paired up with such an experienced LD debater for your first competition in the category!"

"It was *horrible!*" Mary had slammed her face dramatically into her folded arms, so her words were a little muffled. "He completely *destroyed* me!"

"Oh, it can't have gone that bad—" I began, but Colin cut me off.

"Do you recall that time last year when Mary was doing a dramatic interpretation of *Saint Joan* and screamed so loudly during the burning at the stake scene she made the judge vomit?" he asked.

"Colin!" Tomi put down her knitting, her face twitching as if she was trying her hardest not to laugh. "Seriously! What a thing to bring up now of all times!"

Colin took another drag of his soda. He was good-looking enough, I guess, but his slicked-back hair, patchy mustache, and precise manner always made him seem like a Korean American Hercule Poirot or something.

"I mean, yes, I acknowledge the woman was pregnant," Colin went on. "But Mary's acting surely did not help her hyperemesis gravidum . . ."

"Colin!" This time, both our coaches joined Tomi in the rebuke, even as Kitty and Lidia—having not been around last year to witness Mary's infamous making-a-judge-vomit incident—shrieked with laughter.

"What?" Colin's eyebrows rose in confusion. "All I meant to say was that today wasn't nearly as bad as that time, since there was no emesis involved! And definitely it was nowhere near as bad as the time that Mary had the wardrobe malfunction while she was doing that scene from *Our Town*. I was sure our entire team was going to be disqualified for that disgraceful incident!"

Lidia was laughing so hard now she was hiccuping, and Kitty had practically fallen off the bench from mirth.

Mary whimpered, pulling violently at the reddish roots of her goth-black dyed hair, as Jay and I added our voices to the chorus of "Colin!"

I tried to turn the conversation, making my voice artificially upbeat. I didn't want anyone to think I was still upset from before. "So, Mary, were you arguing the affirmative or negative today?"

But instead of answering, Mary wailed, "He's an absolute monster! The guy's got a heart made of ice!"

It took me a moment to understand Mary wasn't referring to Colin, who was irritating but hardly a monster. And then, suddenly, I realized exactly who Mary's debate opponent had been. Of course the guy was a debater. Of course he was. It made perfect sense. (Refer to my earlier treatise on the truth universally acknowledged, yada, yada.)

"His name is Firoze Darcy, and he's the president of the Netherfield forensics team," Mr. Bennet explained, looking significantly at the Desi boy. "He's, um, a bit more experienced than our dear Mary in LD debate."

"If he's so good, how'd he get paired up with Mary?" Jay blurted out. Then, turning to Mary, he added, "No offense, Mary." To which Mary gave a little miserable nod of her head.

"Our local league is so small it's never made the distinction between novice, junior varsity, and varsity debaters." Colin jammed some more dumplings into his face. Just the smell of them was making my mouth water. "Although I believe they should reconsider that decision."

"Mr. Darcy is the son of the president of Pemberley University, don't you know," Mrs. Bennet added in a conspiratorial whisper.

Tomi let out an involuntary gasp, clapping her hand to her mouth.

"Pemberley University?" Colin sat up a bit straighter. "Well, that *is* interesting news!"

"Darcy's dad is the *president* of Pemberley?" I clarified.

"No, his mother is!" Mrs. Bennet corrected me. "Honestly, Leela, I would have thought you of all people wouldn't make such gendered assumptions!"

"And you call yourself a feminist!" Lidia waggled her finger at me as Tomi still held her hands to her throat, looking dazed.

"He's the son of the president of *Pemberley!*" Tomi breathed, like that fact made up for all the guy's nasty behavior. "Imagine— growing up on the campus at *Pemberley!*"

I couldn't be angry with her for gushing. I knew as well as anyone that Pemberley was Tomi's dream school. She was applying there early decision and had been fretting about her application all summer. Even though her mom was a high-powered lawyer from *Hah-vahd* (Tomi said it was a legit rule, it had to be pronounced like that) and her dad was a high-powered lawyer who'd attended Howard (which had to be called *The Mecca*, according to Tomi), Tomi had her heart set on Pemberley. She'd been low-key wearing Pemberley colors to school all the time, and even made the

17

Pemberley fight song her ringtone. It had an amazing African Diasporic Studies department, with some rock-star professors Tomi really admired and wanted to study with. She'd showed me so many online photos, waxing on about Pemberley's beautiful grounds, that I'd started to want to attend myself. But I had kept that a secret, one of those fragile, yearning wishes it was better not to speak out loud, lest it never come true.

Now I felt a pang of regret as I struck it off my mental college list. It had been an ill-thought-out pipe dream anyway. Even if I probably had the scores and grades to have a shot when I applied to colleges next year, how could my family ever afford to send me somewhere like Pemberley?

And now there was no way I was even applying. Not ever, under any circumstances. I wouldn't want to give Darcy the satisfaction.

CHAPTER 3

BESIDES HAVING GROWN up on such an elite college campus as Pemberley," Mr. Bennet was saying, "young Mr. Darcy made it fairly far in nationals last year. If I'm not mistaken, he might have won the Phillips College invitational, if not a few others! It's just some darn bad luck that poor Mary was paired with him this morning."

"Round one!" Mary bit at her blue-black nails. "I got obliterated! I'm totally quitting LD and taking up the piano!"

"You can't quit after your first tournament ever!" Tomi mother-henned.

"Besides the fact that piano playing isn't a category in forensics," added Jay with a teasing smile.

"Also, we've all heard you sing, Mary." Colin pushed his product-goopy hair back from his face. "It would be generous to call you tone deaf. I can't imagine you'd fare much better with an instrument, regardless of training."

I gave Colin a withering glare across the table, but he just nodded back at me. Really, the guy was utterly unfamiliar with subtlety.

I turned back to Mary. "So what were you arguing? Did you get stuck with the negative?"

The LD topic for the September-October debates across the state was the same: *Resolved—Immigration is a human right.* Negative was that same statement, only with a "not" in it. In other words, *Resolved—Immigration is NOT a human right.*

"No!" moaned Mary. "I was arguing affirmative! Which is so much easier!"

"So Darcy won against you arguing that immigration *isn't* a human right? Like, that we should close off borders or something?" I glanced over at the guy I'd only just been thinking of as the most handsome boy I'd ever seen. Now I was pretty sure he was one of the vilest. "I mean, he's probably a kid of immigrants, right? But he made that kind of ignorant argument?"

I felt a bubbling sense of outrage begin. When I was a civil rights lawyer/award-winning writer/inspirational teacher/Broadway actress/president in the future, I would make sure that ugly arguments like that never got to stand. And guys who made such arguments? Off with their heads, indeed.

"I didn't even understand what he was saying!" Mary was all red-faced and snuffly now, which made a serious dent in her emo vibe. "Or rather, what he was saying actually made a lot of sense to me at the time, so instead of cross-examining him, I started agreeing with him!"

"Oh no, honey, you didn't!" Tomi exclaimed.

"Oh, from what I heard, she did!" agreed Colin, his mouth

full of dumpling again. "Which is quite against league rules!"

"Yes, thank you, Colin, we are all aware of that." I was shocked that Tomi didn't impale the team vice president with one of her knitting needles as she said this.

"That Darcy's really good!" Mary rubbed at her eyes, making her non-waterproof eyeliner smear everywhere. "I mean, I couldn't keep up! Even with all that stuff you guys helped me with!"

Mrs. Bennet handed Mary a tissue from her purse. Mary blew her nose and handed it back.

"You keep it, sweetheart," Mrs. Bennet muttered, looking pained.

"This guy is obviously evil—to be able to argue that immigration is *not* a human right?" I fumed. "I mean, what about refugees? People fleeing war and persecution? What about wanting a better life for your kids?"

"As the Somali-British poet Warsan Shire would say, 'No one puts their children in a boat unless the water is safer than the land.'" Colin got up from his seat and came over to squish between Tomi and me. "Leela, you were brilliant when you performed that piece last year for poetry interpretation."

"Well, thanks, Colin." I had adored that poem. Even now, one line from it, "no one leaves home / unless home is the mouth of a shark," brought me to tears. Why couldn't poets and writers be in charge of everything? The world would undoubtedly be a better place.

I was brought back to reality by Jay, who ostentatiously looked from Colin's beaming, slightly sweaty face to me and back again. Then he gave a loud snort. I glared at him, and behind

Colin's back, Jay wiggled his eyebrows, and put his hands in a little heart shape. The moment Colin was looking away, I stuck out my tongue at Jay.

"Arguing the negative was literally Darcy's job," Tomi said, continuing the conversation from before Colin's interruption. "Mary would have had to do the same thing had she been assigned neg."

"Don't even, sis. You're just feeling soft about him because of the Pemberley thing!" I shot back.

Tomi gave me a half grin around Colin's head. "I know he's a jerk, but maybe we should pretend to make friends with Darcy anyway? I mean, if it would help my Pemberley package at all?"

"Ooh! Your package!" Lidia squealed, sending Kitty into a fit of giggles.

"She's talking about her college admission package, which perhaps you aren't familiar with as mere freshmen!" Colin said, eliciting loud protests of "we knew that" from both Lidia and Kitty.

"Yeah, sure, I'll romance him posthaste, just to improve your chances of getting into his mom's college," I said sarcastically over the hubbub.

"I didn't say anything about romance," said Tomi, raising her eyebrows.

I made an irritated sound with my throat.

"I don't mind sliding into Bingley's DMs, if it'll help," said Jay.

"What if we date some of those boys from Regimental?" squealed Lidia. "Would that help us get in anywhere?"

"Only into their uniforms!" snickered Kitty, throwing some

Flamin' Hot Cheetos at Lidia, which Lidia tried unsuccessfully to catch with her mouth.

"Or maybe their packages!" Lidia shook out her hair, raining a few Cheetos to the ground. Then she started pelting Kitty with kettle corn, in response to which Kitty squealed and ran around the table, Lidia in hot pursuit.

"That is very inappropriate!" Colin's cheeks and ears were creeping with red. "Madam President, I demand you reprimand them!"

"Cut it out, girls!" Tomi banged on the table in frustration. "And you too, Colin!"

"Me?" Colin's eyes gleamed with hurt behind his glasses. "What did I do? I'm not the one referencing 'packages'!"

As all this was going on, Mary continued having her one-person pity party next to our coaches. "I choked! I was a total disaster!" she howled, her voice echoing now through the cafeteria. "I mean, I'm only doing this dumb club anyway because my parents want me to be engaged in more freakin' wholesome activities!"

"There, there, dear!" said Mr. Bennet awkwardly.

Mrs. Bennet rubbed at her temples, groaning, "My nerves! Mary, have some compassion for my poor nerves!"

That's when I heard the cruel snicker and realized that the team from Netherfield was passing by our table, having probably overheard everything we'd been saying.

"Um . . . it was nice to meet you!" said Charles awkwardly, giving Jay a little half wave.

"What a delightful team you have!" said his sister, Ro, a smug smile on her face. "Very classy!"

"Oh, no!" I shot up from the table, standing face-to-face with

23

Firoze Darcy. Or face-to-neck anyway. I realized how tall he was, particularly as I was no longer standing on a table.

"The pleasure's definitely all ours," I spat out, my voice entirely contradicting my meaning.

I noticed a little muscle twitch painfully in Darcy's cheek as he regarded me, his dark eyes scanning my face. Then he made a little adaab gesture with his hand to his head, like some Moghul emperor of old, bowing to me before turning crisply on his heel and walking away.

CHAPTER 4

I HATE FIROZE Darcy!" I screamed, banging back into my seat with a little more force than necessary.

My speech and debate family all turned around to look at me, and I waved apologetically up the aisle. It was the Friday after the Hartford High competition, and we were on our way to Phillips College, our one away, all-weekend invitational meet of the year. As opposed to private schools like Netherfield, which could afford to attend all the expensive college invitationals, our team at Longbourn was on a strict budget. Just to get to Phillips, we'd had to do extra fundraising on our own, including a bake sale. Luckily, Tomi was an excellent baker as well as crafter, or else we probably would have had to forfeit this entire trip.

We were on another bus this time, a proper, full-sized coach we were sharing with the Meryton and Regimental teams. Usually, when local teams shared buses like this, every team kind of kept to its own area. But Kitty and Lidia had, of course, chosen to sit right next to some Regimental guys, and I could hear their giggles clear in the back of the bus. The team coaches were mostly gossiping or sleeping in the front. Colin, who'd at first seemed eager to sit by me, had then gotten distracted by his vice presidential duties.

"Mary, let's work a bit more on your argument on the way down," he'd said to the sophomore in his serious way. "I don't like how easily you were swayed by your opponent. Let's build up your self-confidence in your own argumentation, shall we?"

Mary had shot Tomi a desperate look. I didn't blame the girl. She probably just wanted to zone out to some music or look at her phone, but instead she'd be talking about LD debate strategy with Colin all the way down the New Jersey Turnpike.

But Tomi was no help to Mary. "Thanks, Colin, that's great. Let me know if you need me to help too."

"Indeed I will!" Then Colin corralled Mary into some seats up near the coaches.

That left Jay, Tomi, and me spread out on the two rows of seats in the back. And I was looking forward to talking to them about my favorite new topic: how much we all hated the team from Netherfield Academy. I'd only just been reading something online about them joining the local league and how their team was favored to win states in both LD and team debate. Next to the article was a picture of the team president, smiling out at me from my phone screen. The smug expression on his face made me feel like he, even in his inanimate, two-dimensional state, was still judging me and finding me lacking.

"Firoze Darcy is the worst," I said with grim emphasis.

"Darcy's nothing compared to that wench Caroline—oh, sorry, *Ro*." Jay stretched out his long legs on his seat, adjusting his hipster wool hat on his head. "I mean, what is that, like a reference to caviar?"

"Oui, dahling!" I purred, my fake accent dripping with fake fanciness.

Tomi cleared her throat. "Ro Bingley actually might not be that bad," she said in a strangled voice, not lifting her eyes from the fingerless gloves she was making.

"Say what?" I whipped around in my seat to look at her so fast, I made myself a little carsick. The humming drone of the moving bus was constant, and as it was early October, it was already growing dark outside. Tomi had her reading light on to knit by and was bathed in its weird glow.

"I thought she and Charles looked familiar," Tomi explained as her fingers continued to fly over her creation. "And then last Sunday, when I went to my SAT prep session, I realized we've all been in the same class a couple weeks now. Me and the Bingley siblings, I mean."

"And you decided to keep this from us until today?" Then, after a couple of awkward beats, Jay added, "Charles Bingley didn't, uh, ask about me or anything, right?"

Tomi shook her head, making her twists shake a little. "Well, I mostly talked to Ro. Who was very nice, actually. I think she was embarrassed by how she behaved last Saturday. Anyway, it turns out her top choice is *Hah-vahd*, and she had a number of questions about how my mom liked it there."

"And you don't think her being nice to you had anything to do with her wanting to somehow get in good with your mom, an alumni interviewer, right?" I clucked my tongue at Tomi. "Oh, you poor sweet innocent Bambi of a lambykins."

"Hardly! I'm nice, not stupid. Anyway, my mom can't interview during a year when I'm applying." Tomi arched a dark eyebrow at Jay. "And guess what, even though I didn't have a chance to talk to him too much, right as we were going back into the testing room after break, Bingley did ask me if my whole team was coming to the Phillips College tournament this weekend."

"Your whole team?" Jay's eyes were dancing with excitement under the bus seat spotlights.

"Indeed!" Tomi grinned. "I told him I wasn't sure if you were coming . . ."

"You didn't!" Jay practically leaped across the aisle into Tomi's lap.

"Hey, careful of my knitting, loverboy!" Tomi giggled, pushing Jay off her. "Yes, I told him we were all coming."

"Wait." I paused, listening for a minute to the whirring of the bus engine as I gathered my thoughts. "The Netherfield team's not staying in the same hotel, are they?"

"All the forensics teams are pretty much in the same hotel," Tomi was saying as her phone buzzed. She carefully put her half-knit gloves in her bag before peering at the screen. "Well, gee whiz, speak of the bourgeoise."

"Ro?" Jay tried to grab her phone. "What does she say?"

"All right, Sir Grabbyhands, wait a moment and I'll tell you." Tomi batted him away. "Ro wants to know if we want to meet up in the hotel lobby. They apparently just got there."

"We're supposed to have dinner with the team." My voice sounded slightly more shrill than I intended.

"So we'll tell Ro that we can meet up after dinner," Jay said. "Come on, Leela. If you and Tomi distract the others, maybe I can actually get to know Bingley."

"Except for the tiny problem that you hate Ro Bingley?" I pointed out, with what I thought was a great deal of self-restraint. *And the fact that Darcy hates me*, I added in my head.

"I can still hate her and get to know her brother," Jay said as if it was the most reasonable thing in the world.

"But what about the classist way Darcy treated us?" I tried to lay out the argument as if it was me who was the debater. "Like just because we go to a public high school we're somehow clowns."

"I think it was more the fact that we were standing on a cafeteria table, acting like actual clowns," Tomi observed. "Although that thing he said about you later was pretty unforgivable."

Jay pursed his lips, studying me dramatically. "To be fair, he didn't say you weren't beautiful. Just not beautiful enough to tempt *him*."

"Because that's ever so much better," I said dryly.

"It was very wrong of him," Tomi said, and again, I felt the weight of her sympathy. Did she think Darcy was right? She was so striking—curvy and stylish, smart and confident—next to her I sometimes felt like a grubby little twerp.

Jay grinned, activating his superpower of making every difficult situation a little easier with humor. "You know, Leela, to be fair, you may have some responsibility for what he said. You did serenade him in kind of a sexist, street-catcally sort of a way."

"And made observations about his perfume and his daddy's money," Tomi added, matching Jay's flippant tone. "Which could have felt emasculating to someone really tied to his assigned gender role."

"Or alternately, someone worried that he had BO." Jay leaned over at me across the aisle, smirking.

"That too," Tomi agreed gravely. "Nothing more emasculating than a girl on a table singing into a shoe to an entire cafeteria about your potential BO."

"Although I imagine with all those valets and butlers and such scrubbing his back and pits on the daily, Darcy probably doesn't actually have BO." Jay elaborately pantomimed the aforementioned pit-washing.

"It's more the suggestion of it than the actual possession of the BO in question." Tomi nodded, acting professorial.

"For the love of all that is sweet-smelling!" I put up my hands in mock surrender. "Please, you two, stop talking about body odor already!"

"So will you do it?" Tomi batted her not-inconsiderable eyelashes at me. "Maybe help me ask the monstrous Mr. Darcy a question or two about Pemberley?"

"I cannot believe you are actually expecting me to spend my precious downtime during the most important tournament of the fall talking to that . . . that . . ." I tried to think of a word vile enough to apply. "Pile of prideful pomposity."

"Nice alliteration, but not your best work." Jay put his hands together in a begging gesture, putting on the fakest puppy dog eyes I'd ever seen. "But will you indulge me in this, my dearest boo-som friend?"

I snorted at Jay's pronunciation of the word *bosom*.

"Fine!" I muttered through clenched teeth. "I'll come to your stupid post-dinner hangout with Richie 'unobtainable beauty standards' Rich and his capitalist gang."

"Thank youuuuuu." Jay bounced over to my two-seater to give me a hug. "I thank you! My future husband thanks you! All ten of our future children thank you!"

"All right, all right!" I hugged him back. "Just promise that when I'm an old maid I can move in with you and teach your ten children to play the piano and embroider cushions or something."

"How very cottagecore of you." Tomi squinted at me with curiosity. "Can you actually embroider cushions?"

"Very badly," I admitted, thinking of how many times my mother had tried to teach me all the seamstress skills they had mandated at her beloved all-girls school in Kolkata. Ma would have done a lot better with Tomi as a daughter on that score.

Jay bounced out of my seat again and back over to Tomi's, giving her a long list of instructions about how to phrase her text back to Ro Bingley. There was an elaborate discussion about punctuation—would an exclamation mark sound too eager, was a period too mean—followed by one regarding the appropriateness of emojis, interspersed with lots of laughter, and finally, I tuned them out.

I turned my head, looking out at the lights of the passing cars on the highway. All the happiness I'd been feeling about the tournament was squashed at the thought of having to see Firoze Darcy again. Should I pretend I hadn't overheard his comment, or confront him about it? And how in the world did someone bring up something like that—"I am offended you didn't find me tempting"? Besides which, why did I even care?

I stared into the vague reflection of my own face in the bus window, touching my forehead to the cool glass. My dark skin barely showed up, but my huge eyes, the whites stark against my brown pupils, were a bright contrast to my face. I looked pinched, and kind of scared, and very young. I looked down at my sweats and sneakers, touched my pulled-back-into-a-bun curly hair, and wondered what I might look like if I had a team of people to work on me. Not butlers and housemaids, necessarily, but, like, the stylists that those influencers on social media were always talking about. I let my mind drift off, imagining myself dressed for a ball like a girl in a novel, my gossamer gown brushing the tops of my delicate dancing slippers. I'd have one of those dance cards hanging from my gloved wrist so I could write down the names of all the partners who would stand up with me.

I sighed, pressing my forehead into the cold glass once again. Who was I kidding? One of the last vestiges of my childhood torments was my reluctance to dance in public—onstage, or even at parties. I wasn't sure if it was about how girls like Ro Bingley had heckled me in ballet class, or just about how I'd learned to make my brown-skinned body as invisible and inoffensive as possible. The sad thing was, I loved to dance in the privacy of my house or bedroom. But dancing seemed a very public and unapologetic way to move one's body through the world, and I just wasn't that confident yet.

Anyway, I told myself, if I really was ever transported back into the time of any of those novels, I would be a scullery maid, not a heroine dancing at a ball. Those times and those stories weren't made for brown girls like me.

I stuck my hands up the sleeves of my sweatshirt, scrunching up in the seat with my feet under me. Jay and Tomi were still giggling, one obsessed with a new boy, the other with a new college connection. All of a sudden, I felt too young to be going away on this weekend tournament to a hotel in a faraway city. I wanted, with an aching pang, to be home, in the safety of the same house I'd lived in for years now, eating a familiar dinner of rice, daal, and fish curry and watching silly Bengali movies with my parents. The feeling was so intense it took my breath away.

CHAPTER 5

Excuse me?"

"Yes?" I looked up, confused. There was a boy standing in the bus aisle. A brown Desi boy in jeans and a Regimental Track Team sweatshirt. His hair was short-short, like all the Regimental guys, but it suited him. He grinned, and something flipped in my stomach.

"May I sit down?" he said in a soft voice, indicating the seat next to me.

I glanced back at Tomi and Jay, who were still yammering on about text etiquette. "Okay, I guess?"

The boy scooted into the seat, and I could smell the detergent he'd washed his sweatshirt in. It was the same one we used in my family. I could also smell something else on him—cloves and cardamom and the spices of home. I looked at him suspiciously. He felt far too close. How were his eyes so brown, his cheekbones so sharp?

"I'm Jishnu," he said. "I'm on the Regimental team."

"Hi," I ventured cautiously, trying not to seem freaked out

and therefore uncool. "I'm Leela. From the Longbourn team. Have we met before or something?"

"No, we haven't," said Jishnu. "I was just talking to your teammates Kitty and Lidia"—he pointed up the aisle, in the direction of a lot of high-pitched giggling—"and Kitty mentioned that maybe you were Bangali?"

He said the word like only a Bengali would. I felt the muscles in my jaw relax a little. "Oh, so you're Bangali too?"

Jishnu nodded. "Now I feel dumb for coming back here and bothering you, but I was excited to hear about you. I mean, there aren't many Bengalis in my school, not many Desis either. I've never met anyone who speaks the same language outside of week-end functions and community events, that kind of thing."

"I know." I nodded, feeling more like myself now. "Everyone thinks that just because somebody else is Desi that we should speak the same language, eat the same foods, wear the same clothes. Um, hello? There's a huge ton of variety among us." I couldn't help think of Firoze Darcy as I said these words.

"Thumi Bangla bolo?" Jishnu asked, his accent not half bad.

"Nishchoi!" I grinned in the half darkness of the bus two-seater. I forgot about the rest of the bus, even Jay and Tomi, who were talking nearby. It felt like Jishnu and I were transported to a little bubble of reality, with only the two of us inside. "Of course I speak Bangla. I spend almost every summer with my grandparents in Shantiniketan."

"Shantiniketan!" he exclaimed. "Home of our Nobel Prize–winning poet!"

"You like Rabindranath?" I turned myself so I was facing him in the seat, my back to the cold window.

35

"How can I not? Isn't every Bangali kid raised on Tagore's poetry and plays?"

"I did 'Where the Mind Is Without Fear' my ninth-grade year for poetry-reading competition," I said.

"I love that poem!" said Jishnu. "'Where the mind is without fear and the head is held high; where knowledge is free.'"

"'Where words come out from the depth of truth,'" I said, hopping forward a little in the poem to my favorite lines. "'Where tireless striving stretches its arms towards perfection!'"

"I heard they take away your Bangali identification card if you can't recite and sing at least fifty percent of our Kabiguru's poems and songs." Jishnu made a little motion and cracked his neck. I tried not to get too distracted by the gesture.

"And ban you from eating any rashogolla for the rest of your life! And ilish maach! Fuggetaboutit!" I laid on my Jersey accent thick, making Jishnu laugh.

He leaned toward me, turned now in such a way that we were almost nose-to-nose. For a moment, I wondered if he was leaning forward to kiss me. But then he said, in an extremely serious voice, "Do you have any idea how many dance dramas I've been forced to perform in?"

Balmiki Pratibha?" I guessed, naming Tagore's play about Balmiki, the poet said to have written the first epic poem of *The Ramayana.*

I remembered, with a twist of my gut, how Ma had begged me to dance in that play when I was in about the seventh grade, but I'd flat-out refused. Over the years, there had been other dance dramas, but I'd never agreed, much to my parents' bewilderment. Of course, I'd never told them why.

"Do you know how hard it is to be a boy with three older cousin-sisters and always get wrangled into community dance dramas?" Jishnu was asking.

"Well, you were doing your part for the culture!" I patted him bracingly on the arm. Which was solid and muscle-y. I pulled my hand back quickly.

"The culture would probably be fine without me being forced to wear eyeliner and a dhuti onstage," Jishnu laughed.

"It's part of the reason I joined forensics," I admitted in a mock whisper, seriously fudging the truth. "I'm not really one for hanging out in some auntie's basement all weekend long learning dance choreography."

"I can't believe we've never met at some pujo or function or something?" Jishnu asked. "I mean, we can't live that far apart."

"My family usually goes down to the pujos in central Jersey," I explained.

Durga Pujo, the biggest festival of the year for Bengali Hindus, was actually right around the corner. I imagined in my mind's eye meeting Jishnu at a pujo—me decked out in a Benarasi sari of my mom's and him in a sparkling white pajama-panjabi. The image took over my previous daydream about gossamer dancing dresses and gentlemen in breeches. Who needed other cultures' ideas of flirtation and finery when we had our own?

"My mom's brother, and all my bossy cousin-sisters, live in Jersey City, so we go to those pujos," Jishnu was saying.

"So no wonder we've missed each other." I felt something warm and comfortable lighting up my insides. We were talking about our common childhoods, but we were also talking about home. Our similar familial homes, and also our common home of the Bengali immigrant community. And in the middle of a school trip. What a surprise. I grinned at Jishnu, and he grinned right back. From his expression, he didn't seem to find any problem with my appearance.

This time, when he leaned toward me, I felt my pulse speed up. And I didn't mind the feeling.

But then the bus lurched, downshifting as the driver veered off the highway and onto an exit. The noise level on the bus rose significantly.

I squinted out the window. "We must be almost there."

"Looks like it." Jishnu peeled his long limbs back up out of the seat. He grinned, shrugging awkwardly in an incredibly endearing way. "It was great talking to you. Save me a dance this weekend?"

I froze for a second, frowning. Could this boy read my mind?

"My dance card is entirely free," I said as lightly as I could, remembering with warmth the gossamer gown, the slippers, the Benarasi sari.

Jishnu nodded, grinning in a way that made my heart flip. "I'm very happy to hear it!"

And then he loped off, back up the aisle to get his things, leaving me staring after him.

CHAPTER 6

AFTER WE CHECKED into our rooms—I was with Tomi, Jay with Colin, and Mary, Kitty, and Lidia were all together—the Longbourn team met in the hotel restaurant for dinner. It was one of those American casual chain places, with old-timey signs for COCA-COLA 5 CENTS! and fake-rusty rooster weather vanes.

Jay and Tomi had their heads together, planning our after-dinner meeting with the Netherfield team. I didn't have the stomach to listen to their excited conversation, so I turned toward Kitty and Lidia for distraction. When I realized they were still gossiping about the Regimental boys they'd sat with on the bus, I leaned across the slightly sticky brown table toward them.

"Listen, you two. You're here to compete in your speech categories, not flirt with military academy guys who for some reason or another couldn't hack it at a normal school."

"That's rich. You didn't seem to have any problem flirting it up with Jishnu Waddedar." Kitty pointed her fork accusingly at me as Lidia used the opportunity to swipe the pickle from her plate.

"I wasn't flirting!" I said defensively.

"Sure you weren't." Lidia grinned through a mouthful of pickle. "You didn't think he was cute or anything!"

I thought about Jishnu's face, how funny he was. How easy it was to talk to him. Did I think he was cute? Of course I did. But I wasn't about to admit that to these ninth-grade ninnies.

Lidia, disturbingly perceptive, must have caught a change in my expression. "Ohhhh, you do think he's cute! I knew I was right sending him back to you!"

"Stop. This isn't about me." I tried to right my facial features. "This is about you two."

"I heard you say something about dancing with Jishnu!" Kitty took a big sip of iced tea through her straw. "Which I didn't get, since there's no dance this weekend. Were you saying you'd dance with him, like, as some kind of metaphor?"

"A metaphor? For what?" When I saw Lidia about to answer, I put up my hand. "No, never mind, I don't want to know. Listen, I was just talking to Jishnu because he's Bengali."

"And yet, you never wondered once why a nice Bengali boy like Jishnu got stuck in a military academy by his parents?" Lidia asked, her eyes round with feigned innocence.

"That's not the point! Jishnu was nice, but I talked to him for like three minutes." I felt a French fry I'd swallowed too fast get a little stuck in my throat. I took a swallow of water to help wash it down. "Unlike you guys, I wasn't sitting with him and his buddies for an entire bus ride, giggling it up."

"Don't be like that, Leela." Kitty started playing with the salt and pepper shakers, pantomiming like the bottles were kissing.

"We were just having a good time. Making new friends. Denny and Carter are really nice."

"I mean, we're new on the team." Lidia took a big bite of hamburger before going on. "You, Jay, and Tomi are all so tight you don't have time for anyone else. And Colin's so bossy. He's always trying to make us practice and improve our scores. So who are we supposed to hang with? Mary?"

Kitty gave a rude snort to that, and even though I shot her a "keep it down" look, I couldn't exactly disagree.

"Besides, it's hypocritical," Lidia continued. "What, you're worried we'll look like 'loose women' or something just because we were laughing with some guys? I mean, would you be policing our behavior so much if we were dudes?"

"I don't mean it like that." I sighed. Lidia somehow always knew just which buttons to push on me.

"Or is it that we're not white girls so we have to toe the line more?" she asked. "Are you going to be policing our outfits next? Like no bras showing and no shorts, lest we distract the boys with our unfettered primal sexuality?"

"Unfettered primal sexuality"? Where did this girl come from? I rubbed at my aching eyes. "It's just that you're both in ninth grade, okay? This might be a good time to focus on your-selves first."

Kitty seemed to be taking me a bit seriously, but Lidia just rolled her eyes at me, throwing up a peace sign. "Whatever, Abuelita."

I shook my head, suppressing the impulse to give Lidia what my mother would call one tight slap. "Fine. You two do your thing. Just don't say I didn't warn you."

The servers had just cleaned up our plates when Mrs. Bennet pulled out her folder from the giant handbag next to her. It was the folder covered in silhouettes of empire-waisted ladies in bonnets that she always used at competitions. But because Phillips was an away meet, with two full days of competition, the bonneted ladies folder was stuffed to overflowing.

"Does everyone have their campus maps for tomorrow?" Mrs. Bennet fussed through a stack of papers until she found some maps and handed them around. "I don't want anyone getting lost getting from one round to the other."

"There's a Phillips College map online." Mary held up her cell. "It's on the app the tournament organizers sent around."

"An app!" Mrs. Bennet said in a horrified voice, as if Mary had suggested the tournament organizers and Bill Gates were somehow implanting chips into high schoolers' brains. Mrs. Bennet waved the paper map under Mary's face until she reluctantly took it.

Our coach went on, "I know I have all your cell numbers written down here someplace in case of emergency, but do you all have our numbers?"

"We have your numbers in our phones." This time it was Kitty holding up her phone, a sparkly bedazzled affair.

Mrs. Bennet angrily waved her off.

"Phones can lose battery! Phones can be lost! Or worse still, stolen!" Mrs. Bennet shrieked like she was in some melodramatic community theater production. She flapped her arms, and a huge stack of papers flew out of her folder and onto the floor.

"I've got it, Mrs. Bennet! No worries whatsoever!" Colin

jumped to pick up what she'd dropped, only he dropped everything again the second he'd gathered it. Then, on the second time bending down, his glasses fell off his nose, and then, in an attempt to grab them, he kicked them out of his own reach. All of which sent Kitty and Lidia into hysterics. Colin reddened, beads of sweat popping up on his forehead. Sometimes, I really felt for the guy.

In the meantime, Mr. Bennet was trying to reassure his wife. "I'm sure the kids know to be careful with their phones," he said in a soothing voice. "They'll charge them all night and take their chargers with them to campus tomorrow too!"

"But I can't help but worry." Mrs. Bennet looked alarmingly like she was about to burst into tears.

"We'll be fine, Mrs. Bennet. Everybody's got a good head on their shoulders, and they all promise to be responsible." With these words, Tomi gave a meaningful glare down to our end of the table, pointing at Lidia and Kitty.

"Uck, whatever," muttered Lidia under her breath.

"Thank you, my dears." Mrs. Bennet gave us a wet-eyed look. "I know you all think I'm ridiculous, but I am responsible for you when you are away from home, and I take that responsibility seriously!"

"We know you do, Mrs. Bennet," I said soothingly. "You and Mr. Bennet both."

"We're grateful for all the time you take away from teaching ninth-grade English," Lidia said blandly. Mrs. Bennet beamed, but I knew Lidia better than to take her words at face value. I glared at the girl. It took all my self-control to keep my temper in check.

Mrs. Bennet riffled through her folder and pulled out a stack of yellow Post-its. "Now, no arguments! I want all of you to write down each other's numbers! And ours! Here, on these yellow sticky pads."

Without a word, I handed everyone a pen and a yellow sticky paper from Mrs. Bennet's stack. Kitty and Lidia started snickering, but I jammed the paper and pens into their hands. Even though she didn't trust newfangled things like cell phones, Mrs. Bennet meant well. And I wasn't going to be the one to explain to her that everyone would undoubtedly lose these Post-its long before tomorrow.

"I know if my cell phone loses battery, I will be very happy to have these phone numbers in written form," said Colin in a serious way, causing Lidia and Kitty to snicker even more.

"All right, now, I'm expecting you all to be in your rooms by eleven p.m. at the latest!" Mr. Bennet clapped his hands together jovially. "Big day of competition tomorrow and we want you all to be rested! We'll be coming by to make sure you're all in by curfew!"

"Shouldn't we send them up now?" Mrs. Bennet asked worriedly. "Wouldn't it be safer?"

"Mrs. B, it's just seven thirty," Jay said gently. "You can't expect us all to go to bed now."

"Well, I suppose not," burbled Mrs. Bennet, absentmindedly patting her helmet of a hairdo. "Although I'm ready for a nap, I'll tell you. Maybe some of that home decoration channel on the cable television!"

"We'll all be in our rooms by eleven, we promise verily," Colin assured our coaches.

"Eleven!" Lidia gave her characteristic snort. Kitty giggled in agreement. "As if."

"Eleven, Lidia," Mr. Bennet said in a surprisingly firm voice. He was usually such a softy. "Mary, you too."

"It's not a problem for me; I'm going to our room now. I don't want to be awake when these two get in." And with that, Mary stomped off in the direction of the elevator banks. "Plus, I'm not sharing a bed with either of you," she shot back as she departed.

"We're outta here too!" said Kitty, getting up and picking up her bag. "We got places to go and people to see!"

"Where are you two going?" Tomi asked suspiciously. "No leaving the hotel, okay?"

"Oh, we don't have to leave the hotel." Luckily for us, Lidia was not a big one for subtlety. If her tone didn't give away her intention, her wiggling eyebrows did.

"No going to other people's hotel rooms either," I said. "Especially not those boys from Regimental."

"Oh, come on! We were just going to see if we could catch those Regimental guys Denny and Carter in their pajamas!" Kitty burst out. There was a serious amount of food in her braces. "If they even wear pajamas, that is!"

Lidia frowned, practically stomping her foot at her friend. "You said the quiet part out loud, goofball!"

"Who are you calling a goofball?" Kitty sniffed.

"You, you goofball!" Lidia swatted at her.

"Hey, stop that!" Kitty swatted back. "You're the goofball! Plus, you stole my pickle before without asking!"

"You're the goofball!" shrieked Lidia. "And if you didn't want me to take the pickle, you should have said something! Ever heard of claiming your voice?"

"Girls!" Mrs. Bennet squawked, looking around at all the other teams now staring at us in the restaurant. "How many times have I asked you to have some compassion for my poor nerves?"

"Actually"—Colin stepped in between Kitty and Lidia, effectively stopping their rapidly escalating slap fight—"I think it might be a good idea for you two to go over your pieces before we let you go for the evening. I think that there are a few things both of you could work on to improve your performances. Your diction, for instance, is rather poor. Both of your voices drop at the end of your sentences, and I really have quite a lot to say about how you articulate your consonants!"

"Now?" Lidia shrieked. "You want us to work on our pieces now?"

"I agree with Colin. There is no time for articulating your consonants like the present," Mr. Bennet said with a benign smile.

Kitty and Lidia shot me dirty looks, as if this were all a giant plot on my part, as I stood up to go.

"We were actually going to do some . . . prep for tomorrow too." Jay looked at me, then made a not-so-subtle head gesture toward the hotel lobby.

"Do you need me to stay, Colin?" Tomi sounded hesitant.

"No, you go, my lady," he said with a ridiculously formal bow. "I've got this under control, Madam President. I will have these young competitors projecting, articulating, and diaphragmatic breathing by the end of the evening."

Kitty and Lidia utterly collapsed at Colin's use of the word *diaphragmatic*. They were so completely predictable.

"Thanks, Colin," Tomi called over their ruckus. "You're my rock."

Colin gave her another bow, looking rather pleased with himself.

"We don't have to go just yet, do we?" I felt my stomach drop. I'd promised, but I really didn't feel like dealing with Firoze Darcy.

"Yes, we do," Tomi said sternly.

"Come along now," said Jay, actually steering me by the shoulders. "A promise is a promise."

I sighed. There was no getting around it. I was going to have to go face Firoze Darcy again.

CHAPTER 7

I HEARD THE piano playing before I saw him. If I'd known he was a piano player, I would have guessed he'd play some kind of very serious classical music. Probably Beethoven, one of those composers with all those heavy, sonorous, and sorrowful notes. I certainly wouldn't have guessed he would be into playing the lighthearted jazz I heard trilling through the lobby, like laughter put to song. The music poured through the high-ceilinged space, making the mood seem more champagne pillars at a Gatsby soiree than fading campus hotel on the eve of a speech and debate tournament.

"Nice! That sounds great!" Tomi was snapping her fingers and doing a little your-weird-uncle-at-a-family-wedding move-your-shoulders thing just to make us laugh. "Who's playing, I wonder?"

"Probably just some overachieving forensicator!" Jay gave Tomi a little twirl and then a dip.

Before he could try to do the same to me, I blurted out, "It must be Mary, coming through on her promise to quit LD and take up the piano!"

Making people laugh had been my way of deflecting for so long, it was a well-honed skill. As my friends chuckled, I went on, "Although if it was her, it would be a few less parts roaring twenties and a few more parts Edward Gorey funeral dirge."

"All right, all right." Jay clapped his hands for me. "Completely decent quippery. Ten points to Ms. Leela Bose!"

I dropped into a graceful curtsy. Well, as graceful as one can be in an oversized sweatshirt, jeans, and sneakers. "I dedicate this award to my adoring fans," I said, holding a throw pillow from one of the lobby sofas like it was a trophy. "I couldn't have made that quip without your steadfast support."

There were a number of people crowded around the lobby piano, which is why we saw the Bingleys before we recognized the piano player. It wasn't until Charles tapped him on the shoulder and he stopped playing that I realized that the person was none other than Firoze Darcy himself. He turned slowly around on the bench, caught my eye, and nodded without moving a single solitary facial muscle.

To which I could only think: What a complete and utter weirdo.

"Nice playing," offered Jay. It was testament to how much he must like Bingley that he didn't say anything snippier.

"Thank you," said Darcy.

It didn't escape my notice that he was staring straight at me. What, because I was so hideous he had to memorize my grotesque appearance? Was I like some sort of car wreck he couldn't look away from?

I had a brief impulse to stare right back at the infuriating debater, but knew, as if by instinct, that in a game of unwavering persistence against him, I would not be the winner. And so I turned my head away from him, purposefully, obviously. I had to use so much mental effort to do so, it was as if his stare had some kind of magic tractor-beam pull. I felt my heartbeat speed up at the feeling of his eyes still on me and hated him even more.

My gaze fell then on Ro Bingley, who, unlike Darcy, seemed like a completely different person than the last time we'd seen her.

"So pumped we could meet up." Ro walked up to Tomi and handed her a coffee cup. "I remembered from SAT class you drink tea, right? This is a chamomile."

"Thank you, that was very thoughtful." Tomi took the cup from Ro with a smile as Ro Bingley held her phone up above the two of them.

"Selfie or it never happened!" the blonde sang out, making fishy faces with Tomi as she took the picture.

I exchanged a look with Jay. This Bingley girl was the definition of transparent! Did she really think kissing up to Tomi could somehow help her get into Harvard? Or did she think making a coffee date with three brown people from a public school somehow marked her as less of an elitist snob?

As she put down the phone, Ro Bingley looked over at Jay and me. "I didn't realize you'd be bringing your friends, Tomi. I'm so sorry I didn't get any extra drinks." She took an ostentatious slurp of her own coffee.

Okay, there went my theory about her trying to kiss up to at least two out of three of us.

Next to me, Jay muttered, "Didn't realize, my arse! We texted her it would be all three of us from the bus."

Catching his expression if not his exact words, Charles Bingley made a little gesture. "Um, Jay, would you like to go get some coffee or whatever? I think the shop's still open for a little bit." The poor boy looked so uncomfortable, hands jammed into overpriced jeans pockets, face pink with embarrassment.

"That sounds absolutely wonderful," said Jay with an enormous, thousand-watt smile. "Let's go!"

Bingley froze in place, as if Jay's smile had put him into a trance. I didn't blame the guy; Jay's movie-star looks did sometimes have that effect on people.

"Charles?" his sister prompted, her voice shrill. I could tell she was less than pleased by the fact that her brother was crushing on someone.

"Bingley? You good?" Jay raised a perfectly arched eyebrow.

"Of course," he said, the tips of his pale ears turning from pink to bright red. I saw Jay's eyes soften at Bingley's shyness and knew that my friend was smitten.

Bingley started walking toward Jay, only to stop, turning toward me. "Um, it's Leela, right? Do you want to come with us to the coffee shop?"

I guess I couldn't hold it against the guy that his blue-blue eyes were like the color of a polo shirt out of a Vineyard Vines catalog. He couldn't help that he looked like all my childhood torturers. Unlike those kids, though, Charles Bingley seemed kind. I remembered how he had laughed at us singing *Hamilton*. How he had called me beautiful. I guess I wouldn't completely hate it to have him as a friend-in-law.

"I'm good. You two go ahead." I gestured toward the coffee shop. "Have fun storming the castle!"

"Sorry?" Bingley squinted at me with a perplexed smile, looking a bit like someone who was wondering where he'd parked his yacht.

Oh dear. Bingley was going to have to pick it up in the wit department if he had any hope of keeping Jay's attention.

"Don't worry about it." I smiled at a still-flustered-looking Bingley. "It's just a line from one of my favorite old movies, *The Princess Bride*."

Jay winked at me. "You want me to bring you something, babe? A decaf Earl Grey?"

"Sure, why not?" I said, digging into my backpack for some money.

"I'll get it," said Tomi smoothly, and I knew she must be annoyed at Ro for getting her the chamomile and us a big fat nada.

"It's good, I don't need money from either of you. I'll add it to your tab, Leela," Jay said merrily. "Although, as a disenfranchised public school student, I might have to sell a kidney for it."

Bingley looked alarmed. "I can get it . . . I mean . . ."

"He's joking," Tomi assured Bingley, giving Jay a death-ray stare. "He tends to do that a lot."

"Although I did hear a rumor there's a black-market kidney operation to the left of the bellhop stand," I added with a grin. "So be careful out there, all right?"

"I always am!" singsonged Jay.

I watched Bingley and Jay walk away through the crowded lobby toward the distant coffee shop. There were groups of forensicators loudly practicing their pieces, pouring through their debate research, or just trying to catch up on homework. But, regardless of gender, most looked up as Bingley and Jay strolled by. Light and dark, both equally tall but good-looking in such different ways, they really were eye-catching.

"So I heard your mom is the president of Pemberley?" Tomi said abruptly. All righty then, no verbal foreplay at all. Right to the chase.

Darcy stood up slowly from the piano. "That she is," he said.

"Did you grow up on campus? That must have been a great experience," Tomi nudged. "It's the most beautiful place I've ever seen."

Before Darcy had a chance to answer, Ro jumped in. "His parents were masters of one of the residential colleges, so he totally grew up on campus. Had students babysitting him, the whole thing."

"Heads of college," Darcy corrected her, looking uncomfortable. "They don't use that 'master of college' expression anymore."

"A little too slave-owner-y for them?" I said pointedly.

"Absolutely." Darcy nodded in my direction. "Although they didn't change the title until after a lot of student protests."

I was a little flabbergasted by how normally he was behaving with me. Did Darcy really not realize I'd overheard him saying what he'd said? Was he seriously just going to pretend it never happened?

"There's protests going on now about how a couple of the residential colleges are named after people involved in the transatlantic slave trade," Tomi was saying. "I've been reading about it."

Tomi looked at Darcy, but if she was hoping for a civil answer, she'd be waiting a long time. Because just then, something buzzed in his pocket, and he turned away from us.

"Excuse me for a second."

Tomi nodded, looking only a little deflated. As he walked away from us to answer his text, I wondered again at how rude Firoze Darcy was. If there was a speech and debate category for pomposity, he would be the undisputed champion.

"Is that Gigi texting you?" Ro walked up to peer over Darcy's shoulder. "Tell that silly billy she shouldn't have quit the team if all she was going to do was text us every five minutes."

"I'll tell her you said hello." Darcy turned slightly away from Ro's peering eyes.

The girl faced Tomi and me, talking to us as if she were the narrator in some play that we were both watching. "Gigi's Darcy's sister. An adorable little sophomore who went to states last year as a freshman in LD! Quite the talent."

"But she quit the team?" Tomi asked. "Why? Sounds like she had a promising future in forensics."

"I have no bloody idea." Ro tossed her blonde hair unnecessarily dramatically. "Something about her little piano lessons coming in the way."

"She's at a Saturday piano academy, Ro," Darcy explained in an over-patient way. "I believe I told you that. It's why she can't make any Saturday meets."

"Well, still, it seems ridiculous, to give up a promising career in forensics," Ro continued. "Not that I know anything about speech events. Debate's the real deal."

"We both compete in speech events." Tomi's voice was tense as she pointed at me, then herself. "We're the real deal."

"No, girl, I didn't mean it like that! I heard that Gloria Anzaldoza piece you do is way powerful."

I saw Tomi's eyebrows go sky-high at Ro Bingley's inability to remember the poet and legendary feminist Gloria Anzaldúa's name, not to mention her use of the word *girl*, and had to stop myself laughing. Now *that* was a serious mistake on Ro's part. Tomi did not tolerate overfamiliar fools gladly.

Sensing Tomi's change in mood, Ro burbled, "I'm so sorry! I didn't mean anything by that." She linked her arm through Tomi's. "Come on, let's take a turn around the lobby. I need to stretch my legs after that long ride, plus I want to ask you some more questions about your mom's experience at Harvard. And I can tell you what I know about Pemberley."

Wannabe Barbie Bingley shot me a look from under her lashes, like—what?—she was stealing my BFF from under my nose? Ugh. I seriously wanted to give her the same treatment I'd given my childhood Barbie—after raggedly chopping off the doll's hair with some kindergarten scissors, I'd promptly lost her in the backyard and forgotten about her. That is, until the neighbor's dog was found dragging her around by a leg.

With Tomi and Ro walking in circles around the perimeter of the lobby, and Bingley and Jay still at the coffee shop, I was stuck with Darcy. Who was busy texting his sister and seemed to have forgotten about my not-beautiful-enough-to-tempt-him existence. Oh, goody. This was just my lucky day.

CHAPTER 8

I SAT DOWN in one of the lobby's overstuffed winged chairs and pulled out a novel from my backpack. It was a comedy of manners from a past century that I'd read so many times, the paperback cover was tattered and torn. It was, in fact, the book from which I'd pulled my current humorous-interpretation piece. You'd think I'd be sick of the book, after having memorized and performed parts of it for competitions, but I would never get sick of it. I guess that's just the way it is with favorite novels, stories that are so familiar they feel like a part of yourself.

I was just getting settled into my reading when a deep voice to my right said, "You like humor, right?"

Outside the hotel, there was a loud crack of thunder. One of the competitors who had been practicing her piece near us let out an overdramatic scream, and I practically jumped out of my seat.

"Sorry, I didn't mean to startle you," Darcy said from the wingback chair adjacent to mine.

I looked up from my book and out the lobby's front windows at the sudden storm. "I didn't realize it was supposed to rain."

For a moment, neither of us said anything, listening to the lashing storm hitting the hotel walls and ceiling.

"What I meant to ask was if you enjoyed it?" he asked in a rushed voice.

"The storm?"

"No. Humor, like in that novel." Darcy pointed at my book, leaning forward so I could hear him over the noise outside. "Or . . . competing in humorous interpretation and performing someone else's words. Is it . . . freeing to have someone else's ideas to say?"

I stared at him. That was exactly why I'd begun forensics, for the joy of being able to hide behind someone's else's words, inhabit the body of a character who wasn't me. It was a different form of hiding, but one that felt healing too.

"I'm not sure I'd describe it that way. I'm acting out a brilliant writer's words, but adding my own interpretation." I tried to avoid looking directly at him as I spoke, like he was a solar eclipse or something. "And yes, I think humor's a brilliant way to talk about serious things."

"Debate is too," Darcy countered.

"I wouldn't know; I've never done debate." The storm was pounding the walls of the hotel, echoing the way that my heart was pounding inside me as I tried to have a conversation with this horrible boy.

"No, you shouldn't ever try debate. You'd definitely hate it." Darcy sounded so sure of himself, I felt my hackles rise.

"Why would I hate it? I'd probably be great at debate, if I tried it." I had a sudden, wild desire to join LD debate just to have the immense pleasure of proving Darcy wrong.

Darcy's mouth twisted a little, like he wanted to smile but wasn't letting himself. I stifled the impulse to haul off and smack him. But he didn't explain what he found so funny, simply saying, in an over-polite way, "Oh, I'm absolutely sure you would be."

I felt my blood boiling. I held up my book, pretending to start reading again, when he said, seemingly out of nowhere, in a pressured voice, "The thing is . . . it's just that . . . I mean, to be honest, I don't like *Hamilton*."

Okay, what? That wasn't exactly what I'd been expecting to hear. "What's your issue with *Hamilton*?" I asked heatedly.

"It's so popular. Everyone seems to think it's so edgy." Darcy had his legs crossed, ankle over knee, and his fingers tented under his chin. All he was missing was a smoking jacket and he'd look like a brown-skinned host of *Masterpiece Theater*. He was talking in that strange, flat way, and not really meeting my eyes, despite being only inches away. "In actuality it's just a weak apologist play that lets a bunch of racist enslavers off the hook, makes them seem palatable and cool."

"Did you read that hot take on social media, or did you come up with it yourself?" I snapped. I mean, we were talking about my favorite play here. What kind of a monster didn't like a clever hip-hop musical about America's founding fathers?

"Oooh! Thomas Jefferson couldn't have been a rapist, the guy who plays him is hot and he can rap really fast," Darcy said in a scornful voice.

The guy who played Thomas Jefferson *was* really hot, but Darcy clearly didn't know what he was talking about, because that actor was playing Lafayette and not Jefferson when he rapped fast. But all of that was beyond the point.

"It's a legendary moment in musical theater history, in which brown and Black folks got written into the story of America for once. In which we got to see ourselves as the protagonists," I argued. How could he not think that was a good thing?

"Why do we need to co-opt the majority's stories and insert brown and Black faces into them?" shot back Darcy. "Why can't we just write our own?"

"Why can't we do both?" I demanded. "We've been silenced for so long. Can't we find multiple ways to express ourselves, speak, and have our voices and stories heard?"

"*Hamilton* is revisionist and puerile." Darcy dismissed me as if he were debating me on the LD stage.

"It's revolutionary—theatrically, musically, and narratively. Besides being a whole lot of fun." I felt as furious as the storm raging outside. "Something you obviously don't know a lot about."

"Is that what you think of me?" Darcy's eyes flashed, and for the first time, I realized that the guy might not just be a robot inside. "That I'm not *fun*?"

"I don't know anything about you, except the fact that you apparently think immigration isn't a human right," I snapped. When he looked confused, I clarified, "At the tournament last weekend? You were debating my teammate Mary Stewart?"

"I was assigned neg. It was literally my job to argue the

negative." Darcy's eyes were wide with surprise, reflecting the twinkling chandelier lights of the lobby ceiling.

"Do you enjoy that?" I parroted his earlier words. "Arguing opinions not your own, I mean, is that freeing?"

Darcy puffed up with irritation. "Did your teammate tell you what I was arguing? Did she actually have a problem with what I was saying?"

"You apparently argued so well, Mary found herself agreeing with you." I felt like hitting him over the head with my book. "I can imagine what you were arguing."

"No, you probably can't. Because they weren't someone else's words or thoughts I was just using—they were my own. I wasn't playacting, I was saying things I actually believed!" Darcy's accusations hit deep, stinging as they found their target. "Maybe you should come hear me debate before deciding what you think about my arguments. But you probably won't, because if you did, you couldn't snap to some kind of prejudiced judgment."

"Prejudiced judgment!" I glared back at him, feeling barbed-wire sharp and dangerous. "How dare you! You don't know anything about me!"

"Oh, that's where you're wrong." Darcy smirked. "I know plenty about you."

"What are you two arguing about?" Suddenly, Tomi was standing in front of me with a concerned look on her face. I could see her brain whirling, wondering if I was somehow tanking her chances to get into Pemberley. Which, to be honest, I probably was. Over her shoulder, Ro was smirking at us.

"We're not arguing," Darcy and I said, at almost the same time.

"We were discussing something," he added, giving me a tight-lipped smile.

"What in the world were you discussing in such, uh, passionate tones?" asked Ro, her voice dripping with fake honey.

"Leela's witty novel." Darcy pointed at my book.

"Ha, ha," I added dryly.

"We were dis . . . talking about the benefits of expanding our minds through extensive reading," Darcy went on as if I hadn't said anything. "After all, there's no enjoyment like it!"

"Indeed." I shot him a look and quoted the book I was reading. "'How much sooner one tires of anything than of a book.'"

"Charming." Darcy gave me a bland-faced smile. "And you do so love to laugh."

"You're right, I do love to laugh." I was smiling now through clenched teeth. "In fact, I've just been teasing Mr. Darcy here, laughing not *with* but *at* him."

Darcy made a choking sound but said nothing.

"Laughing at Darcy?" Ro asked in a weirdly sexy voice, like she was a heavy-lidded femme fatale from an old-fashioned movie. "I don't think that is even possible. How can you laugh at perfection?"

Then the girl actually *winked* at Darcy! I mean! Gah. I felt the bile rising in my throat.

"Perfection?" I snorted. I caught Tomi giving me a big-eyed "stop it" look but plunged on anyway. "Seeking perfection, always needing to be right—well, that seems like a sad way to live your life."

"Don't be ridiculous, Caroline," spluttered Darcy. "That's hardly an accurate description of my character."

"Don't be falsely modest! You're so accomplished! You speak multiple languages; you've traveled the world!" Ro asserted with a feline smile. Wow, this girl obviously had it bad for ole Firoze. "And you have something extra about your manner, your air, the way you speak . . ."

"Are we talking about Darcy, then?" It was Bingley coming up now with Jay to join us. Important to note: They were both completely drenched, with no coffee to be seen between either of them.

"What happened to you two?" I exclaimed, taking in their drenched clothes and hair, their rain-splattered faces.

"Were you attacked?" Ro sounded like she was about to call the hotel manager and get him fired for allowing it to thunderstorm on her brother.

"The coffee shop was actually closed, and so we thought we'd take a walk," Bingley said sheepishly. "We didn't realize it was going to start raining like that."

"You could have come back sooner," Tomi pointed out as the two boys dripped onto the lobby carpet.

I squinted at my friend, who looked a little paler than usual. "Jay, what about your asthma?"

"It's completely under control!" Jay wiped water out of his eyes and onto the floor. "I'll go take a hit of my inhaler when I go upstairs!"

"I didn't realize you had asthma!" Bingley started peeling off his sopping-wet jacket, as if offering that to Jay was going to be any measure of protection.

"I'm fine!" Jay waved him off. I could tell he was cold, though, because he kept rubbing at his runny nose. "I want to hear what you all were talking about when we came in!"

"Oh, just about what an accomplished man Darcy is!" I said airily. "How he's a polyglot and can cover screens, embroider cushions . . ."

"Cover screens?" repeated Bingley, confused. His hair looked darker all slicked down, his features even sharper.

"Again with the embroidering cushions," Tomi muttered under her breath. "What is with you and the embroidering cushions?"

"Well, Darcy, you're obviously quite the model of a modern major general." Jay was shifting from foot to foot now to keep warm.

"*The Pirates of Penzance*," said Darcy unnecessarily loudly as he leaped up from his chair.

"The what of who?" Ro looked flustered, which was obviously a state in which she didn't like to be.

"*The Pirates of Penzance.* The musical that quote is from," Darcy said, answering Ro but looking straight at me. "It's from a song. A funny song. A song that makes me laugh from a musical that's not trying too hard to be something it's not."

I smiled venomously. "And Darcy does so love to laugh."

We stood there for a moment like actors in the middle of a movie, at that point when everything else fades, when there's no more extras swirling in dance around them, but only the two characters, tied together with some electric, invisible energy. I felt my palms and cheeks growing warm, something prickling at my hairline and on the back of my neck. Darcy too was frozen in place, his serious face etched in concentration, like he was trying to decipher some secret from the lines of my face. My breath caught, and I could swear I heard music all around me.

It was Jay who broke the spell. By sneezing. Like five times in a row in rapid succession and with increasing volume.

"That's it; it's absolutely ridiculous for us to be standing around here talking nonsense while the two of you get pneumonia," Tomi announced firmly. "I think it's time for everyone to get up to their respective rooms and dry off."

I batted at Jay's drippy arm. "You still owe me an Earl Grey, yo."

As we all moved toward the elevator banks, I couldn't help but notice Ro Bingley slip her arm through Darcy's. My face got even warmer than it had been, and I knew I must be glowing like I were radioactive.

There was no wait at the elevators, and while the Netherfield trio got into one car, we three from Longbourn got into another.

"Good night!" Bingley called out as we separated.

"Parting is such sweet sorrow," returned Jay, then added, "I'll text you when I'm out of the shower!"

I couldn't help noticing that he was already sounding a bit congested and wheezy.

Before I entered the elevator, I caught Darcy's eye again. He was looking strangely upset, his mouth twisted grimly.

Man, I thought yet again, *what a complete weirdo.*

And with that, I walked into the elevator car, letting the door shut behind me.

CHAPTER 9

I DON'T THINK Darcy was mocking you," Tomi reassured me for the fifth time. She was sitting on one of the two double beds in our hotel room, in a pair of comfortable sweats, her SAT study material spread out around her. "Or challenging you to join LD just to debate him."

After we'd gone upstairs and gotten ready for bed, I'd told her about my conversation with the infuriating debater.

"I don't know, Tomes," I muttered. "He kept telling me that speech categories were somehow *fake*, like we were lying because we spoke other people's words."

"I write my own speeches in original oratory, thank you very much." Tomi stifled a yawn.

"Inspired by the greats like Gloria Anzal*doza,*" I said with a laugh.

"What can I say," quipped Tomi, *"girlfriend* is not up-to-date on her feminist poets of color."

I laughed, getting back to my original topic. "And then Darcy connected it to *Hamilton,* like he was implying I consistently liked things that were just inserting myself into other people's stories. As if he was saying I was addicted to lies."

"I still don't understand how you could have gotten into such a heated argument about musical theater, of all things." Tomi squinted at me through her thick-framed glasses since she'd just taken out her contacts. They made her look like an inquisitive owl.

"He's a jerk." I angrily fluffed the pillows behind me, against the headboard of my bed. "A wanker. A pile of prideful pomposity."

"Is he, though?" Tomi mused. "Or did he just hurt *your* pride?"

I felt myself swelling up with indignation. "Tomi, you heard what he said." I couldn't even bring myself to repeat Darcy's words.

She thoughtfully tightened the scarf around her head. "Leela, you're absolutely sure that comment we overheard him making last weekend wasn't him playing the opposite game?"

I knew what she meant, but didn't want to admit it. "Whatever can you mean?"

"That he wasn't saying you weren't beautiful because he actually thought you *were* beautiful but was mad at his friend for yanking his chain?" Tomi made an exasperated noise. "Leela, please tell me you don't not realize how beautiful you are?"

"There are too many double negatives in those sentences for me to understand them." I pretended to busy myself with my calculus homework.

"First impressions aren't always the right impressions." Tomi yawned. "Don't be so attached to an opinion you've formed about someone that you don't have room to change your mind."

"Sure, whatever, Abuelita," I said with a dramatic sniff. Sometimes Tomi was way too honest. It made me miss Jay and his habit of heaping his friends with overflowery compliments.

"Abuelita or not, I said what I said." Tomi organized her SAT materials together and put them on the nightstand. "I wanted to study some more but I'm exhausted. Although I know my cousins in Nigeria are taking bets on my score this time."

I snorted. Cousins in India weren't all that different. "Don't stress about your SAT retake. You'll do great. Besides, Pemberley's going to be lucky to have you."

"I hope you're right." Tomi stretched, cracking her back. "I don't want to have even darker eye circles tomorrow when I see—" She broke off her sentence.

I stared at her. "Wait, when you see *who?*"

Tomi had already laid down and turned her head toward me on her pillow. "It's a miracle! Are you actually able to focus on somebody other than Darcy for a second?"

"I'm sorry." I had the grace to feel embarrassed. "I was ranting about him so much I was being a bad friend. So, what's going on? Is there someone you like at this tournament?"

Tomi rubbed her eyes before exchanging her glasses for some sleep shades. "Maybe."

"Tomi!" I bounced up on my knees. "Who? What? Where?"

She peeked out from beneath her mask. "I'm not ready to talk about it yet, but when I am, I'll tell you."

I knew Tomi better than to press any further. Unlike Jay and me, she had a pretty strong sense of privacy, and when she said she wasn't ready to talk about something, she really wasn't.

"Whenever you're ready to talk, I'm here," I said, itching with curiosity. Who did Tomi have a crush on? Was it Jaime, that top-ranked original-oratory kid from the Meryton team? Alex, the Leonardo DiCaprio look-alike from Hartford who was always up against Jay in dramatic interp? Or maybe it was that spoken-word poet Riley, from Purvis High? I realized that Tomi was so private, I really didn't have a sense of what kind of guy she was attracted to. I mean, apart from fictional characters like Heathcliff or T'Challa. But let's get real, who didn't have their share of fictional boyfriends?

I cleared my throat, hoping to say the right thing so that she'd open up to me. "Just like Pemberley, anyone you're interested in would be so lucky to even be associated with you."

"Love you too, sis," mumbled Tomi, turning off her light.

Okay, then. I guess I wasn't learning any of her secrets tonight.

Within minutes, she was lightly snoring. It always unnerved me how quickly Tomi could drop into a full slumber. Probably on account of how overtired she always was, running pretty much every club in the school and all.

I was still thinking about who her mystery love interest might be when I got the text. I looked at my phone. It was Colin.

> Might I ask that you come over
> for a moment, Leela? Tomi isn't
> answering her phone

I sighed. Colin really was too much. Did he want to complain to us about Kitty's and Lidia's diction or something? This late at night?

I stretched out under the hotel covers. I'd literally just been planning to turn the lights out. Why hadn't I put my phone on sleep mode like Tomi obviously had?

Tomi's asleep, and it's late,
Colin. Can it wait?

I looked at my phone, feeling impatient and sleepy. Colin wasn't replying right away, but then finally he did.

I hesitate to disrupt your rest, but it
is rather important. Can you come
over immediately, please?

I sighed. Why couldn't he just text me what it was? At least Jay and Colin's room was right across the hall. I'd pop over and be back in bed within five minutes.

I slipped on my jacket over my pajamas, sticking the room key into one pocket, my phone into the other. Without even bothering to put on shoes, I padded across to Colin and Jay's room.

"Thank the forensics gods you are here." I knew something was wrong as soon as Colin opened the door. "I'm afraid I can't get in touch with the coaches." Colin's hair, usually so slickly smoothed back, was sticking out in all directions, as if he'd been pulling on it, and his eyes looked panicked behind his unusually smudgy glasses. "They must have turned their ringers off. I wanted to go down and get them, but I was . . . well, concerned about leaving him alone."

"Leaving who alone?" I pushed past him into the room and stopped in my tracks.

Jay was sitting on one of the double beds, clutching his chest and coughing. His eyes were closed, and his lips looked a pale blue color.

CHAPTER 10

G O GET MR. and Mrs. B," I ordered Colin. "Now!"

"No, I'm okay . . ." Jay began, but started to wheeze and cough even more.

"Stop, you're obviously not okay," I interrupted, running over to sit beside him on the bed. "Where's your inhaler?"

"He can't find it. He looked everywhere," said Colin grimly. "And it's not like anyone else has an inhaler since no one else on our team has asthma. I checked the health forms, which I have, for accessibility reasons, scanned into the online team portal."

"You shouldn't have done that!" I said, distracted for a second from Jay. "That's super invasive of everybody's privacy!"

"I considered the ethical implications, I assure you," Colin huffed. "But I was a bit afraid he was going to die!"

"He's not going to die!" My heart was beating wildly in my throat. I turned to Jay. "Are you?"

"I'm fine!" Jay wheezed. He was hacking and struggling to get in breaths between coughs. He was on the thin and tall side, but hardly skinny. Yet, as I put my hand on his heaving back, I could feel how hard his muscles were working.

Instead of leaving the room, Colin just stood there, watching me with a panicky look on his face.

"Colin, just get the coaches already!" I ordered. "Please!"

"Are you going to be all right alone?" he asked, even as he opened the door.

I looked worriedly at Jay. "I don't think we have any choice."

Without any additional protest, Colin bolted out of the room.

I scooched aside the scratchy hotel coverlet, sitting closer to Jay and looking him in the eyes. "Jay, look at me. You can do this. You've had asthma attacks before. Just slow down. Slow down and take bigger breaths."

"Okay," Jay managed, nodding. "Okay." His eyes were wide with fear, and I felt myself beginning to panic too.

I was about to look up *how to treat an asthma attack* on my phone when there was a knock at the door. Was that Colin and the coaches already? He'd only been gone a minute. But when I yanked open the hotel room door, it was Bingley and Darcy standing outside.

"You heard Jay was sick?" I asked, letting them inside the room.

"We were FaceTiming, and suddenly he was coughing a lot and hung up," Bingley said. He was in some kind of fancy designer sweats with his hair still wet from the shower. "I got worried when he wouldn't text me back."

All right, this was not the time to be gushing or anything, but Charles Bingley was definitely growing on me. I saw his blue eyes widen with concern as he strode over to sit next to Jay on the bed.

He may have been born with a silver spoon in his mouth and a closet full of weird designer sweat suits, but this dude just might actually be worthy of Jay.

"Does he have an inhaler?" Darcy asked. He was still in the pressed jeans, button down, and V-neck sweater he'd been wearing in the lobby. Then, looking down at my feet, he blurted out, "You don't have shoes on."

"I forgot. What does it matter?" This guy really had no sense of priorities. "Jay didn't bring his inhaler. Colin's already gone to get the coaches, but I don't know what else to do in the meantime."

Darcy frowned, looking at Jay. "Do you have any of your other medications on you?"

Jay shook his head, struggling to get the words out. "I. Forgot. The. Entire bag. At home."

"Here, put this on." Darcy was rolling up one of his sleeves and taking off a fancy-looking electronic watch. Without waiting for Jay to respond, he began fixing the watch to Jay's wrist.

As he did this, Darcy frowned over his shoulder at me. "Go turn on the shower in the bathroom as hot as it goes."

"What?" I balked. "Why?"

"Don't ask questions, I'm trying to help your friend," Darcy snapped, looking up from where he was still fiddling with Jay's wrist. Then Darcy sighed and said in a calmer voice, "Sometimes steam helps during an asthma attack."

At the word *steam*, Jay looked up. He couldn't manage any words, but he nodded.

"Well, you don't have to be so bossy about it," I said, even as I ran to the bathroom and turned on the hot water.

"You have to shut the door," called Darcy, and I slammed it behind me.

Within a couple of minutes, we had Jay sitting on the closed toilet seat lid in the now-steamy bathroom. Bingley was rubbing his back, and he seemed to be breathing a bit easier, so Darcy and I left. It was too small a bathroom for so many people. Plus, even though he was sick, Jay and Bingley had an intimate chemistry between them that felt awkward to intrude upon.

"How did you know to do that?" I pushed back my damp hair from my face. It had curled into a wild mess in the steam.

"My sister, Gigi, has asthma," Darcy explained, casting a worried look toward the closed bathroom door. I noticed his thick hair had gotten a little curl to it as well. "And Jay's oxygen saturation levels weren't great."

"Is that what you were doing with your watch?" I'd gotten so hot in the bathroom, I'd taken off my jacket, so now I crossed my arms over my chest with more than a little self-consciousness. I was wearing a T-shirt over my checked pajama bottoms that said CHAI TEA = TEA TEA / NAAN BREAD = BREAD BREAD, and while I didn't think it was see-through, I definitely didn't feel like taking any chances.

Darcy nodded, focusing on some speck on the wall over my shoulder. I wasn't sure if he was being gentlemanly or just clueless, but he didn't seem to notice my clothes at all. Which was strange, since he had definitely noticed my lack of shoes. "My watch is the latest model, which has an oxygen saturation monitor on it."

"Of course it is," I muttered. "And of course it does."

Now Darcy looked down, like he was studying my bare toes again. I curled them self-consciously against the carpet, and he looked away. I wondered about what Tomi had suggested, about him having said the opposite of what he actually thought about me last week to Bingley. Could she be right? Or did this guy just have some creepy thing about bare feet?

I was thinking of a way to thank him for what he'd done for Jay when, true to form, he pulled out his phone. "Excuse me," Darcy said, walking away from me and straight out the hotel room door into the hall.

Wait, what? Okay, I guess Tomi was wrong, then. Even my toes didn't seem enough incentive to have Darcy stick around for more than three seconds.

But before I had a chance to check on Bingley and Jay in the bathroom, there was a light knock on the door, and I jumped up, assuming it was our coaches at long last.

Only, it wasn't. It was just Darcy, who had been in the hallway, finishing whatever phone call was so important to make at 11:30 p.m. But when I stepped out of the room, completely prepared to tell him off, I heard the elevator ding and saw Mr. and Mrs. Bennet, as well as Colin, scrambling out toward us. The coaches had obviously gotten dressed in a hurry and looked frantic.

"What happened?" Mrs. B breathed. Her daisy-print blouse was buttoned entirely off-kilter. "Leela, how is he? Oh, that dratted phone! It always turns off when I don't mean it to!"

"He was wheezing quite a bit. He's forgotten his asthma medicines," Darcy explained, before I could answer. "So we're giving him some steam treatments. But his oxygen saturation wasn't terrific, so I hope you don't mind that I called the ambulance."

"Well, I never . . ." began Mrs. Bennet. "Who are you, pray tell, to be so high and mighty and call the ambulance before we, his coaches, have even had a chance to get here?"

I felt a rush of embarrassment at Mrs. Bennet's lack of gratitude. Darcy was high and mighty, yes, but he had also just helped Jay's breathing when the rest of us couldn't.

Mr. Bennet shot me a look, then put his thin hand on his wife's shoulder. "Let's go see how Jay is doing, and then we can decide what to do about the ambulance."

CHAPTER 11

I T TOOK MR. and Mrs. Bennet about two minutes talking to Jay and Bingley to make up their minds.

"Son, thank you." Mr. Bennet shook Darcy's hand. "You did the right thing. Let me call down to the lobby and see if the ambulance is here yet."

It was, and while Jay said he felt well enough to walk down to the lobby, Mrs. Bingley put her foot down and made the paramedics come up. It was a little chaotic when they got to the room, and they asked the rest of us to leave so they could take care of Jay properly. All of us, including Darcy, Colin, Mr. Bennet, and me, stepped out into the hallway. Only Mrs. Bennet and Bingley refused, sticking by Jay's side in the room until he was brought out to the hall on the stretcher.

"I feel ridiculous," said Jay through his oxygen mask. They had the stretcher cranked so he was sitting up in it, and he was holding Bingley's hand. He looked, and sounded, far better than he had when I'd first come into the room.

"You'll feel better when you get a few treatments at the

hospital," the paramedic assured him. She was young and smiled when she saw all of us hovering around. "I think it's better without the crowd, though. Your boyfriend can ride with you, and maybe your teachers can follow in their car?"

"I'm not . . . I mean, we just . . ." mumbled Bingley, getting very pink around the ears.

"Yes, my boyfriend's riding with me." Jay grabbed on to him even tighter, to which Bingley just grinned and nodded. Jay looked over at me, meeting my eye. "Okay, Leela?"

My smile was a bit strained. I couldn't help but be a little hurt that Jay would want Bingley and not me with him, but I understood too. "You take care of him, all right, Bingley? Text me when you get there so I know what's going on."

Then for a second, Mrs. Bennet looked like she was going to protest the arrangement, until Mr. Bennet cleared his throat. "We'll follow the ambulance to the hospital," he said firmly.

Mrs. Bennet was already sniffling, twisting her hands with worry. "I'll call Mrs. Galvez from the car," she said to no one in particular.

At this, Jay tried to pull his oxygen mask off, but Bingley stopped him. "What is it?" Bingley asked, gently rubbing Jay's arm. "You don't want your mom to know you're in the hospital?"

"She'll just worry," Jay said between coughs. "And she won't be able to leave my brother and sisters."

Jay's mom, Mrs. Galvez, was a single parent and worked long shifts as a nurse at our local hospital. As the oldest, Jay helped her out a lot with the little ones.

"I'm sure my mom won't mind going over and babysitting so your mom could drive down," I told Jay.

"Why don't we cross that bridge when we come to it?" Mr. Bennet said soothingly. "Let's see what the doctors say at the hospital."

The paramedics wheeled Jay off, Bingley trotting alongside and Mr. and Mrs. Bennet bringing up the rear. Even as the elevator door closed, Mrs. Bennet shouted a stream of instructions for Colin and me to tell the team.

And then it was just Colin, Darcy, and me in the empty hotel hallway with its terrible lighting and fading wallpaper.

Instead of just saying good night like a normal human being, Colin stepped forward and stuck out his hand to Darcy. Darcy looked startled.

"Thank you, old chap," said Colin in a slight British accent. Or was it just his ridiculously crisp consonants that made him sound British? I noticed there were beads of sweat on his upper lip and near his temple. "On behalf of the entire Longbourn team, I thank you for your invaluable help."

"Don't mention it." Looking bewildered, Darcy took his hand. "Old . . . chap."

"There was one other matter I wanted to discuss with you," Colin said in the same formal tone. "I understand you are acquainted with Professor Catherine de Bourgh, who teaches now at Rosings College, but is formerly of Pemberley University's theater department? I am lucky enough to be under her tutelage— she is my diction coach."

Trust Colin to start talking speech and debate in the middle of an actual crisis.

"Aunt Catherine? Yes, she's a family friend," Darcy said, looking even more confused. He forcibly took his hand back from Colin. "She knew my father well."

"She told me that herself," Colin said with all the formality of someone not standing in the middle of a hotel hallway in his flannel pajamas. "If you have not sought her help professionally, I would recommend it highly. She could assist you with your diction, I'm sure." Colin paused. "I notice that, in your speech patterns, even outside of debate, you sometimes hesitate and rearrange your word choice—"

"Thank you for the advice." Darcy interrupted a little coldly. "I will take it into consideration."

Colin nodded seriously at him, started to move toward his door, but hesitated.

"Leela, don't you want to return to the privacy of your room?" he suggested. "You still have to compete tomorrow."

He raised his eyebrows, looking first at me and then at Darcy, as if it was inappropriate for me to be standing here talking to a boy in the hallway. Or as if he was worried Darcy would try something underhanded.

"I'm fine, Colin," I reassured him. "I'll go to bed in a second."

"As the vice president of the team, I feel a certain sense of moral obligation to assure myself of your well-being and, as a female, although it is not fair that it should be so, you are perhaps aware of the unequal threat of—" Colin began, but I cut him off.

"I'm fine, Colin."

"Well, then, if you're sure." My annoying teammate hesitated another minute, before adding, "I'm right behind that door if you need me." He pointed at his hotel room. "You wouldn't even have to scream. Simply call loudly and forcefully."

"Loudly and forcefully. Sure," I mumbled. "Thanks, Colin."

"Your servant," he said with that bizarre British accent again, bowing a bit to Darcy, then me. "Leela."

"Colin," I said, trying not to jump over and strangle him.

When he finally left, I looked at Darcy, feeling awkward. "I'm sorry about him."

"He seemed very concerned about your virtue," Darcy said mildly. "Also, in unrelated matters, my diction."

I decided to ignore the part about Colin worrying about my virtue. "I don't know where all that diction stuff was coming from. Your diction seems fine. More than fine. Your diction seems great."

Now that the word had tumbled from my mouth so many times, I realized that *diction* was kind of a weird thing to keep saying. I felt my cheeks heat up. What was wrong with me?

"Don't worry about it." I noticed a muscle working painfully in Darcy's cheek. "I'm sure Colin meant well."

We stood in silence for a few seconds, listening to the buzzing of the yellowish overhead lights, the distant clink-clink of an ice maker. Finally, I blurted out, "I kind of want to go to the hospital, make sure Jay's okay."

I expected Darcy to persuade me out of it, to tell me that the coaches and Bingley were there, so I shouldn't worry. But instead, he looked up and smiled gently. "I have my car. I can drive you there if you want."

That smile was distinctly unnerving. What did he mean by it? I could hardly guess. So instead of answering him, I asked, "How did you know to call the ambulance?"

"My sister used to have really bad asthma attacks a few years ago." Darcy was looking down at the psychedelic hotel hallway carpet as he spoke, as if studying for some kind of surreal interior decoration quiz. "It was right after my dad had died, and my mom was kind of a mess. I was usually the one who had to decide that it was time to call the campus paramedics."

This was the same mom who was the college president, I realized. It was a little shocking to hear him describe her that way, but I guess who wouldn't be a mess in such a situation. "You must have been pretty young yourself."

Darcy rubbed at his neck, scowling at the carpet like it had done him a serious wrong. "It wasn't an easy time all around."

I nodded, not sure what to say. Finally, I sighed. "It's probably not very helpful for me to go to the hospital now. That's what the paramedics said, right?"

"Jay was talking comfortably on the oxygen." Darcy looked stern, speaking more like a doctor than a high school senior. He cleared his throat, taking on an even more serious tone than normal. "You know, if he had his medicines with him, he would have probably been fine. Your friend really should be more careful."

That got my back up. What was he implying? "This isn't Jay's fault."

"I'm not saying it is, just that he should be more careful about bringing his medicines with him," Darcy returned, scowling. "My sister, Gigi, has backup inhalers in every purse, every backpack . . ."

"Oh, and that's something everyone can afford, right?" I had no idea, actually, if Jay had to pay anything for his asthma medicines, or if his mom's health insurance covered them, but I just couldn't stand Darcy's supercilious attitude.

Unsurprisingly, he backed down. Rich people sure hated talking about how much things cost. "That's not what I . . . of course it's easier when you don't have to think about the money . . ."

"Exactly." I flung on my jacket over my T-shirt, feeling suddenly chilly.

"I should probably let you go to bed." Darcy looked at me with a surprising intensity. "You look exhausted."

"I want to stay up until I hear from one of them," I said stubbornly. I'd been thinking we could wait up together for a text from Bingley or the Bennets, but now it felt like I couldn't get away from Darcy soon enough.

"You can do that from your room." He pointed at my bare toes. "I mean, look at you, you don't even have on shoes."

"What does that have to do with anything?" I peered down at my multicolor-pedicured feet. "Of course I'm barefoot, I was about to go to bed."

Darcy rubbed at his eyes, as if trying to rub away a mental vision he wanted erased. "Preplanning doesn't seem to be something anyone on the Longbourn team is particularly good at, is it?"

"Sure, that's us," I said, "just some barefooted, asthmatic, public school idiots." Firoze Darcy really did talk a load of rubbish, as my cousins in India would say. "Never mind we actually had to fundraise and save to come to this fancy invitational, unlike some people who have everything handed to them on a silver platter."

"You're purposefully misunderstanding me," Darcy retorted.

"I don't think I am," I snapped back.

Something crackled in the air between us. Something other than the sound of the terrible fluorescent lights overhead. I felt myself leaning forward, off balance, everything feeling louder and brighter.

"Anyway, it's late, and we might as well both get some rest." Darcy glanced at his watch, the same one he'd put on Jay's wrist just minutes earlier.

I felt inexplicably hurt and irritated. "You'll tell me if you hear from Bingley?"

"Of course." Darcy gave me a little bow. "Get some sleep if you can."

And with that, he walked swiftly away.

CHAPTER 12

I DIDN'T GET very much rest that night. Almost as soon as I'd fallen asleep, my phone buzzed with a text from Mr. Bennet. The doctors had decided to admit Jay to the hospital for overnight observation. Bingley and Mrs. Bennet were coming back to the hotel, and Mr. Bennet would wait with Jay until his mother arrived. Mrs. Galvez's sister was apparently visiting for the weekend, so Jay's younger siblings had someone to watch them. For a moment I considered texting all this information to Darcy, but then decided against it. He probably didn't care, and he would hear what he needed to from Bingley anyway.

Then, in the morning, I had to recount everything to Tomi. It was testimony to how hard the girl pushed herself that she'd actually slept through all the overnight drama. By the time we went down to meet Mrs. Bennet and the rest of the team for breakfast in the hotel lobby, I was already exhausted.

The old-timey American restaurant we'd eaten in the night before was converted into a breakfast bar, with long rows of covered stainless-steel dishes on either side of the room. With pretty much all the competing forensics teams eating breakfast at the same time, it was crowded and super noisy. People were loudly practicing their pieces at their tables, or arguing the nuances of their debate topics, and the air buzzed with that pre-competition frenetic, nervous energy.

At our table, Mary, Kitty, and Lidia were all listening with bated breath to Colin's account of the night. Tomi and I put down our bags on the far side of their gaggle. As Tomi huddled up with an exhausted-looking Mrs. Bennet, coming up with a team plan for the day, I dragged myself to the buffet.

I was just getting myself a spoonful of scrambled eggs when I realized that a familiar face was staring at me from the other side of the plexiglass buffet dome.

"Good morning, good morning! It's great to stay up late!" sang Jishnu Waddedar. He was wearing his red-and-gold Regimental uniform and looked, I freely admit, pretty dashing.

"I love *Singin' in the Rain*." I smiled at Jishnu over the unappetizing, slightly worse-for-wear melon salad. "But I must say, I disagree with that song's premise. It's really not that great to stay up late."

I suppressed a giant yawn.

"I heard one of your teammates had an asthma attack and went to the hospital last night." Jishnu scooped himself a generous helping of the slimy fruit. "Sorry about that."

"How did you hear already? I mean, we only just came down to breakfast." Then I followed Jishnu's eyes to see who he was looking at. It was Lidia, buzzing like a little bee from table to table, spreading the gossip like it was verbal honey.

"Ah, of course." I shook my head, sighing. "That girl is something else."

"She's a trip," Jishnu agreed with an appreciative grin. "A force of nature."

We scooted down the offerings, gathering this and that, until we came together on the other end, by the drinks.

"I think I'm going to break down and have as much caffeine as possible," I admitted. "The under-eye concealer I'm wearing isn't going to do the job all by itself."

Jishnu laughed, offering me a coffee mug. "You're not like most girls, are you?"

"Ehhhhh." I made a "wrong answer" buzzer sound even as I accepted the mug from him and went about selecting some black tea. "Don't do that thing."

"What thing?" Jishnu looked surprised as he poured the hot water into my mug for me.

I nodded my thanks. "That thing where you put down other girls to compliment me. It's so old-school old boys."

"Touché, Ma Durga," Jishnu said, referring to the ferocious mother goddess. He poured himself some black coffee, which he then saluted me with. "I stand corrected."

I squinted at him, unsure whether he was being sarcastic. Jishnu gave me a huge, zillion-watt grin. "Hey, you should come see me debate in the LD semifinals this afternoon."

"That's pretty confident of you." I looked around for some

milk for my tea. "Plus, how do you know I won't be in my own semifinal speech round?"

Jishnu blanched, like it had never occurred to him I might be pretty good at speech and debate. "Oh, right, no. I'm sure you will."

Sensing my need without me saying anything, Jishnu poured a little milk into my mug, turning my tea milky brown. "But if you come by afterward, maybe we can go out to coffee or something. I can tell you how my round went. I hear you already had a close encounter with the douche I'm hoping to humiliate in debate today."

I winced internally but let his gross use of the word *douche* go unremarked upon. "Who?" I asked.

"Firoze Darcy!" Jishnu announced, wiggling his fingers like he was talking about the boogeyman. "Both your and my archnemesis!"

I took a sip of my tea, resisting the incomprehensible impulse to laugh. "I didn't realize I had an archnemesis. Makes me feel like Batman."

"Girl, let me just tell you," Jishnu said, grinning roguishly at me, "you are plenty beautiful enough to tempt me."

I almost choked on my tea. All righty then, Jishnu didn't seem to believe in verbal foreplay either. Right to the point, this one.

"So you heard about what Darcy said about me, I guess?" I asked, hoping my dark skin covered up the hot blush now spreading across my face.

"Hasn't everyone?" Jishnu spread out his hands to indicate the whole dining room full of breakfasting forensicators, and suddenly, I felt very exposed. Were all these speech and debate folks discussing my attractiveness, or lack thereof?

"So you'll come find me after semis?" Jishnu repeated.

"If you make it," I said in as carefree a tone as I could muster. "If not, *I* can tell you how *my* round went."

"Just the knowledge you're coming to see me will be enough motivation for me to break into the next round," Jishnu said with a cheeky grin. "And believe me, if I get to debate Darcy, I'll obliterate him."

"Don't let that big head of yours explode or anything," I called as he went back to his team of red-coated high schoolers. "It'll be a mess to clean up."

"I make no promises," he called out without turning around.

I had to admit, the guy was charming.

When I returned to the table, Lidia and Kitty were all over me. "How's your soldier boy?"

"Leave her be," Tomi warned.

"Inquiring minds want to know," protested Lidia.

I sprinkled salt on my eggs and took a bite. "He's not my soldier boy, and you both know that perfectly well."

"What was it like last night, when Jay got sick?" gushed Kitty.

"Enough, Kitty," Mrs. Bennet warned.

"It's just a lesson that health is a precious and delicate thing," pontificated Mary. "We think we're invincible, but in truth, our bodies are like fragile eggshells. One misstep and *crack*!" She widened her eyelinered eyes ominously. "It's all over."

Colin frowned at her. "While I wouldn't normally agree with

that grim framing, Mary, I must say that's exactly what I was thinking last night, when I was alone with Jay as he struggled for each and every inhale, each and every exhale. When I was the only one between him and certain death."

Mrs. Bennet rubbed her forehead. "Mary, Colin, is this entirely necessary?"

"I tried to respect and honor his wish to be independent," Colin went on seriously. "But at some point, it became impossible. Morbidity demands, and we must listen."

"Yes, thank you, Colin," Tomi said seriously. "We are all very grateful that you texted Leela when you did."

Everyone turned back to me. "So he was near death, huh?" Kitty breathed.

"More importantly, did Bingley kiss him back to health?" Lidia waggled her eyebrows.

"I'm too tired for this right now," I snapped, pushing my plate away.

"Don't be such a snot, Leela," Lidia said. "You're not any better than us."

"Good luck with your rounds, everyone," I said as I got up. My head was pounding from lack of sleep. "See you at lunch."

"I'll come with you, sis," said Tomi, but Mrs. Bennet stopped her.

"I want to just go over a few more things with you, as president of the team." Our coach yawned hugely. "You're sure now you can check in on everyone if I go take a nap for the first round?"

"Of course, Mrs. B." Tomi made a head motion to me. "Go ahead, Leela. I'll catch up."

I would have waited for her, but I was so tired, and getting so irritated by Kitty and Lidia, that I couldn't stand it there for one more moment.

As I turned to go, a voice called out from behind me. Colin.

"Leela? Might you have a moment to spare?" Despite his lack of sleep, Colin looked as chipper as always. "I have a matter on which I'd like to ask your advice."

I tried not to roll my eyes. My head was pounding. I wished I could be like Mrs. Bennet and wail about my nerves. "Can it wait, Colin? I want to grab some headache medicine before my round."

"Oh." His face fell; then he forcibly smiled again. "You are in pain. Of course I would not want to disturb you when you are unwell. Is there anything I can do for your present comfort?"

"No, I just need some medicine. But thanks." I forced myself to smile at him.

"How is Jay doing? Has he improved sufficiently to be discharged today?" Colin peeked at his phone, inducing me to look at mine.

"I'm not sure, but I'll text him to find out." I began to walk away, back toward the elevators up to my room.

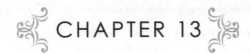

CHAPTER 13

As I HEADED back down from grabbing a bottle of headache reliever, my phone buzzed. A return text from Jay.

Mom's here. They're going to release me in a couple of hours probably. I'll drive home with her after getting my stuff at the hotel

How're you feeling?

Better. Stupid

Stahp. Why? Because you have to forfeit the tournament? There'll be others

Just in general. Your Darcy boy was right. Should've had my meds with me

Not my boy

Should've had my inhaler with me.
Could have prevented this whole
thing

Or . . . you could have just not gotten
drenched in the rain like some kind of
heroine from a novel. Dramatic and
romantic, but always goes wrong

So worth it tho

WHAT? I demand details!!!!!!

Not exactly the way I envisioned
spending the night with a boy for
the first time

The ER not high on your list of romantic
first date places?

I didn't say I didn't make it work! Sadly the hospital gown is

so not my color. Totally washed
out my glowing Filipino-Dominican
complexion

If anyone can pull off an ugly hospital
gown, it's you, babe

Stop with your dirty mind! Bingley
didn't pull off my hospital gown!
We were in public! As your mama
would say, chhi chhi chhi!

LOL. You are too much. Have a safe ride
home. Just remember to bring your
asthma meds next time? I don't think I
can take another night like that

Sorry, sorry. Thanks for your help.
Thank your big hunka burning love
Darcy too. That steam idea saved me

Told you, not my big hunka anything. I'd be
happy never to speak to him again in my life

Methinks the lady doth protest too
much . . .

＊　　＊　　＊

It was therefore a bit like out of that old Alanis Morissette song (the one about irony that lists a bunch of things that aren't really ironic) when, shortly after this text exchange, who should I find standing right before me but the man in question, Firoze Darcy himself.

He looked like he'd been standing there a while, leaning against a random hotel lobby table, staring at me.

"Did you sleep well?" he blurted out as soon as I looked up. We were standing in front of some elevator banks, each next to a giant floral arrangement.

"Not really." I blinked at him, feeling a rush of mixed emotions. It was mostly annoyance, to tell the truth. "Did you sleep well?"

He stared at me for a second, the muscles of his face working. "No." Darcy pulled at his white dress shirt collar. He was wearing that amazing-fitting jacket again, the one with his school insignia on it. "Your friend Jay—is he all right?"

I shot him a surprised look. "How did you know who I was texting?"

Darcy ran a hand through his damp black hair. "You were smiling in that way you smile with him. You seem very close."

"We've been best friends since middle school," I admitted, wondering if my smile really was particular to each friendship relationship. More importantly, I wondered why Darcy of all people had noticed such a thing. "He's doing all right. I think they're going to let him go home from the hospital this morning."

"Good, good." Darcy nodded, biting at his lip. "Bingley seems to like him very much, even though they're such opposites. He's very outgoing, huh?"

"Jay?" I paused as one of the elevators dinged open, letting out a few laughing forensicators, giddy before the first day of the big competition. "He's a complete goof."

"Goof?" Darcy frowned. "What do you mean? Like he's insincere? Changeable?"

"No!" I protested, remembering his comments about Jay being irresponsible for having forgotten his asthma medications. "Not like that at all! I just meant he's one of the funniest people I've ever met."

"But you're the one who does humorous interpretation," Darcy pointed out.

"I do love to laugh." Then I paused, feeling the uncontrollable urge to shake up that unflappable demeanor of his. "But, you know, you've gotten me thinking, about relying on other people's words and all that. I'm considering quitting HI and trying debate, like you suggested."

Darcy's eyes widened. He shook his dark head. "I'm . . . I'm not sure I told you to quit your category! Or start doing debate in your junior year?!"

"Oh, really?" I stepped forward, reducing the distance between us. "I'm pretty sure I remember you belittling me for being fake and not speaking my own thoughts, using my own voice."

"You know I didn't . . ." he began, then stopped himself, his expression growing irritated. I felt a surge of joy at having succeeded in bugging him. "I thought you loved your category. And I've heard you're quite good at it too."

"I can excel at anything I set my mind to," I assured him. "And now that you've shown me the error of my ways about debate, I'm sure I can excel at that too."

As if by instinct, he stepped forward as well, so there were only a couple of feet between us now. "Well, I see my words have had an impact. You never struck me as being so easily impressionable."

"Oh, but you're so authoritative, so all knowing," I said sarcastically. "It's very hard not to take your wise words to heart."

"Tell me, Leela . . ." He let out a gush of air, and I wasn't sure if he was exasperated, or trying not to smile. He looked down at me, his dark eyes meeting mine in such a way it did odd things to my equilibrium. "Are you always this irritating?"

"Oh, wait till you get to know me—I'm much worse," I assured him with what I hoped came off as confident self-deprecation.

"Duly noted," Darcy said in a soft voice, taking two steps even closer to me.

There was an awkward pause during which neither of us said anything. Darcy's eyes were disconcertingly fixed on my lips, as if he was preparing for me to launch some complicated verbal assault. I felt my cheeks grow warm, and I opened my mouth and closed it again.

"Leela," Darcy said, then stopped, frowning.

"Yes?" I moved forward myself, until there was less than an arm's distance between us. I felt a magnetic, swaying pull toward him, as if my body were urging me to take the first steps of a dance.

Three of the elevators around us dinged one after the other, and a bunch of different forensics competitors rushed out. They were laughing and talking about their pieces, their arguments, and the latest forensics gossip, a sea of high schoolers sweeping by us and between us. We both stepped back, allowing them to separate us, me on one side of the hall and Darcy on the other.

After they finally passed, Darcy looked down at his watch. Did I imagine that he looked regretful? "I guess I should let you get to your first round."

"You should go too." My voice sounded breathy to my own ears. "Happy arguing."

Darcy paused, taking in my comment. Then he ducked his head in a totally endearing way that threw me off balance even more.

"Happy laughing," he said before striding off.

CHAPTER 14

KILLED IT at my semifinals. I was shocked at how well it went, judging from the fact that I'd gotten so little sleep. But I was on fire. My voices were spot on, my timing was impeccable, I got laughs where I wanted to and rapt attention otherwise. Better still, my fellow competitors shot me little resentful looks and my judge even smiled and gave me a little head nod when I was done.

But I didn't feel as happy as I should have been as I left the room. I felt deflated, bored. Did it all come too easy? Was there no more challenge left? I blamed Darcy for somehow planting that poisonous seed of doubt in my mind. I'd begun competing in speech as a way to find my voice, claim my space but in a safe way, within the confines of another person's words, a different character's body. Now that I'd figured out how to do that well, it didn't feel like enough. For the last year or so, I had been kind of coasting on my speech skills—doing well at tournaments, breaking into finals consistently. But, I now realized, I'd stopped growing, learning—getting better not just in my category, but in myself. The realization made me feel so frustrated, I wanted to kick something as I walked across campus in search of the LD semifinal rooms.

I'd never had so many negative thoughts after a successful round, and I knew exactly who was at fault. I don't know why, but the entire time I performed my comedy of manners about a family of marriage-minded sisters and their social foibles, all I could think about was Darcy's face. What would he have said or thought had he been there? He probably would have scoffed about the lack of depth or meaning in my topic, saying that it didn't have enough real-world or modern-day impact. The question was, did I believe that too, or was I just letting the guy get into my head?

With the help of the college's app, I made it to the rooms where the various LD debate semifinals were occurring. I was tired, and honestly, not in the mood for hanging out. But maybe coffee with Jishnu would lift my spirits. He, unlike Darcy, was so uncomplicated, charming, and easy.

One round was just finishing as I walked into the hallway of the chemistry building, where the debate semis were being held. As if by fate, the first face I saw coming out of the room was the one I was looking for: Regimental's own Jishnu Waddedar, all five foot eight of lanky track runner dressed in a military uniform; cute smile, cute face, friendly and fun demeanor.

"Jishnu!" I waved enthusiastically, kind of stage-whispering since I knew there must still be other debates finishing up. "How did it go?"

He squinted at me, smiling wanly, and before he'd even loped his way over to me, I knew exactly how it had gone. Badly, at least for him.

The air was heavy with the smell of chemicals. We walked together down the hallway, beyond the last closed semifinal door, before he spoke.

"You won't believe who I was debating." Jishnu grinned ruefully down at me. "My wish came true." We were standing in a hallway crowded with carts of discarded Bunsen burners, beakers, and other equipment.

"Not Darcy?" I felt breathless. "Were you aff or neg?"

"I was affirmative, arguing that immigration *is* a human right. You would have thought it would be a slam dunk, but not so with that asshat." Jishnu leaned up against the tiled wall in a posture of frustrated defeat, kind of mock banging the back of his head against it even as he propped one foot up. His pose looked so familiar, in fact, I started to wonder which teen movie I'd seen it in.

"This morning you said you wanted to debate him," I teased. "Humiliate him, is I think how you put it. Or was it obliterate him?"

"He's such a dick," Jishnu muttered darkly. "Not worth my talents."

"So he actually argued that immigration *isn't* a human right?" I remembered how Darcy had told me that when he argued neg against Mary, he had believed what he was arguing. "I mean, what was he saying, that people who lived in a particular place had more rights than refugees or immigrants to that place?"

Just saying the words made my blood boil. I had an ugly image pop into my head of the endless numbers of times in my life that I'd encountered xenophobes and racists screaming at my family to "go back" to where we "came from" or demand that my accented but fluently-English-speaking parents "speak American." I was sick of having to hear people say that immigrants were taking jobs from "real Americans." The assumption was that some Americans were "authentic" and others interlopers. But could Darcy, a brown Desi guy himself, really have made such an argument in good faith?

"I'm glad you didn't make it to watch." Jishnu rubbed his hand over his eyes. "I mean, at first, I made totally good points about America being a country built by immigrants. You know, 'immigrants, we get the job done,' the American dream and all that."

I smiled at his *Hamilton* reference. It was part of the reason I loved the musical so much—it was about the hardworking-immigrant dream. "Sure, of course."

"But then that ass Darcy said something about how that was the myth of American exceptionalism, and how the story of America being a country built by immigrants only covered up for the genocide of Native Americans by European colonists, or, like, the enslavement of African Americans," Jishnu scoffed. "And erased immigrants who struggled and *didn't* make it."

I frowned. Why was Jishnu scoffing at settler colonialism and chattel slavery, neither exactly things to take lightly? "And then what happened?"

"I just couldn't believe him," Jishnu huffed. "I mean, I was talking about immigrants fulfilling the American dream— a dream that allowed us to grow up here. It's only the story of America!"

"Or at least *a* story of America," I said, hearing the echoes of

Darcy and my argument over *Hamilton* in my head. That musical, like the story of America being built by immigrants, was a comfortable one, and an uplifting one for me as a daughter of immigrants. But when I thought more deeply about it, I could recognize it wasn't the whole truth of America.

Just as I was thinking this, I turned my head and saw someone coming down the hallway. There he was, Firoze Darcy, neat and perfectly fitting suit below a grim expression, and dark brows in an unusually fierce scowl, even for him. In fact, his face was downright thunderous. As he approached us, he gave Jishnu such a look of murderous hate I thought he was about to punch him in the nose.

"What are you doing talking to *him?*" Darcy growled. Wow, if his animosity was anything to go by, this debate was ugly. Darcy seemed so hot and bothered, I was surprised he didn't spontaneously light one of the Bunsen burners around us.

"Sore winner, bud?" Jishnu eased off the wall and ever so casually-not-casually flung his arm around my shoulder.

"Seriously?" Darcy narrowed his eyes, shaking his head. I got the impression he was somehow disappointed with me. My stomach fell, and I felt the strange urge to explain to him that there was nothing going on between Jishnu and me. But without another word, he stalked off down the heavy-aired hallway.

"Nice round!" called Jishnu to his retreating back. "Jerk-off!"

Without knowing why I was so uncomfortable, I shrugged Jishnu's arm off my shoulder. "What the actual toxic masculinity is going on between you two? It is obviously more than just debate."

Jishnu sighed sheepishly. "Yeah, I guess it is."

I stared down the hallway in the direction I'd seen Darcy go. I clearly wasn't going to get any answers from him. I felt the frustration bubbling inside me. Why was Darcy so blasted changeable? Hadn't we just been having a semi-pleasant conversation at the hotel this morning? Well, if he didn't want to stick around and talk to me, I didn't want to run after him either.

"Buy me a coffee and tell me about it," I said to Jishnu, linking my arm through his.

CHAPTER 15

JISHNU AND I walked out of the campus building and down the sidewalk. It was a perfect fall day. The rain of the previous evening had left everything clean, crisp, and brisk, with the multicolored trees just starting to lose their leaves. Trying to erase Darcy's disapproving expression from my mind, I jumped over a small puddle and filled my lungs with fresh air.

We walked by groups of college students studying, hanging, and playing Frisbee on the green. They were dressed in jeans and flannels, casual boots on their feet. They gave us passing glances as we walked by, some even waving. I felt very young and very overdressed in my suit and very conspicuous next to red-uniformed Jishnu. They were all only a couple of years older than us, but their lives seemed a world of cool intellectual hipness away.

In a few minutes we got to a coffee shop on the main drag that went through the center of Phillips College. There were more forensicators here, so we didn't stand out as much in our formal clothes.

"What are you guys all doing here? Is this like a religious

thing?" a nose-ringed college girl locking her bike in front of the coffee shop asked us.

"We do speech and debate," I explained, feeling embarrassed.

"Forensics!" the blue-haired guy next to her exclaimed. "Man, I miss those competitions!"

"Good luck!" called the nose-ringed girl as they walked away.

The line inside the coffee shop was ridiculously long, and full of fellow high school students. As Jishnu and I waited to get our drinks, I noticed how friendly he was, and how many people from different teams he knew. People called out his name as he smiled, high-fived, or fist-bumped them all.

"So I take it you're kind of shy, huh?" I said as we finally made our way to the counter to place our orders.

Jishnu's eyebrows shot up. "You noticed?"

"Your adoring fans are hard to ignore," I said, gesturing to a gaggle of skirt-suited girls farther down the counter who were whispering to one another and waving. Well, all but the one girl who was giving Jishnu some kind of stink eye. *What was her problem?* I wondered.

Jishnu waved back to girls, making all but Stinky Eye titter. They reminded me of Kitty and Lidia.

As we left the coffee shop with our drinks in hand, Jishnu led me to a high-top table on the sidewalk between two giant potted palms.

"So tell me about you and Darcy," I said, trying to ignore the college couple at the table next to us who were starting to casually make out.

"I know you met him at the Hartford High competition,

when he was oh so charming to you." Jishnu took a slurp from his drink, grimacing at the heat.

I forced myself to keep looking away from the kissing couple, who had their fingers entirely entangled in each other's hair now. "Very true."

"So what's your impression of him?" Jishnu cracked his neck from side to side.

"I'm not sure." I took a sip of my Earl Grey, feeling it warm me up even as I warmed up to my subject. "For the most part, I've found him cold, and proud. Like a robot, hard to figure out."

A brightly colored van drove by us, honking. The kissing couple broke apart and waved. Then they promptly launched into an argument about a philosopher named Foucault and something called biopower.

Jishnu snort-laughed at my words, then stretched out his long legs under the table, knocking my foot off the stool perch by mistake. "So imagine growing up with him."

"Get out!" I exclaimed. "You grew up with Darcy?"

"Yup, on Pemberley campus." Jishnu nodded. "Although you wouldn't guess it by the way we act around each other."

"You're kidding me." I was, as the British would say, gobsmacked. "But also, Pemberley, wow! My friend Tomi is dead set on going there. Keeps showing me pictures. It looks amazing."

"It is," Jishnu said. "But don't get the wrong idea, I'm no professor's kid."

"So how did you grow up there?" I took another warm slurp of tea.

"My mom was a housekeeper in the fancy residential college

that Darcy's parents were the 'masters' of. Can you believe that language?" Jishnu made air quotes with his fingers. " 'Masters' of the college. Like they're slave owners or something."

"Yeah, I heard about that." I remembered my conversation with Ro Bingley and Darcy in the lobby the night before. "But they changed all that, right? They call them heads of college now or something?"

"Well, sure, *now* they've changed it," Jishnu agreed. "After a bunch of student protests. But it always bothered me. My mom too, of course. But it didn't really seem to bother the Drs. Darcy at all. They were living high on the hog as co-masters of Derbyshire College."

"And that's how you and Firoze were friends when you were little?" I was still not getting my head around all this new information.

"Firoze's dad's name was Dr. Fitz Darcy. He was this totally legendary professor of linguistics. A really kind and amazing man." Jishnu's face grew soft at the memory. "My parents split up when I was young, so Fitz was like a father figure to me. He's the one who taught me how to ride a bike on the college green."

"That's so sweet." I remembered how my own parents had taught me together, holding on to either side of the bike and running alongside me until, without me even noticing, they each slowly let go and let me ride on my own power.

"He was British, you know," Jishnu said. "Firoze isn't like us; he's only half Desi."

"Oh?" I wasn't sure why this was relevant. Plus, I'd learned to hate calling multiracial people "half" of anything. Jay always said

110

he was 100 percent Dominican and 100 percent Filipino too, and that categorizing people as "half" of anything had its history in racist things like the "one-drop rule." (Google it, seriously.)

"Anyway," Jishnu went on smoothly, "Fitz wore a bow tie and Union Jack socks and the whole deal. But he was obsessed with American things too. He loved American candy, root beer, hot dogs. It was him who bought me my first baseball glove, took me to my first ball game. Said he preferred it to cricket."

I laughed. "Don't tell that to my parents. My dad plays on a weekend cricket team with all the Desi dads from our town. They are very serious about it."

"I can imagine." Jishnu grinned, making something flip in my stomach.

I leaned forward, staring into Jishnu's eyes. Why in the world should I continue to be bothered by Darcy when there were other cute boys like Jishnu in the world? In fact, why should I even waste another minute of my precious teenage life worrying about Firoze Darcy?

Easier said than done, of course. "And so you and Firoze were friends?" I asked eagerly.

"Like brothers," Jishnu amended. "We were in the same grade at the campus elementary school. I saw him all the time. I would hang out in their residence while my mom cleaned. I'd play with Firoze's toys. Fitz would help me with my homework as I grew older."

"He passed away, though, right?" I remembered Darcy mentioning it.

Jishnu nodded sadly. "He was the best of men, Leela, he really was. I loved Fitz Darcy like a father. And I'm not embarrassed to say that I know he loved me back."

"I'm so sorry." I reached out awkwardly to pat Jishnu's hand.

"Thank you." To my surprise, he stopped me from pulling away, instead gripping my hand in his own. His hand was warm and his skin soft. I wondered, fleetingly, about what sort of skin cream he used. He didn't let me go for a few seconds, seemingly unembarrassed to be holding my hand in the middle of the crowded street outside the coffee shop. I tried to judge how I felt about it. It was surprisingly thrilling and nice.

Finally, letting me go, Jishnu went on. "Fitz wanted big things for me. You know, he actually promised me full tuition coverage to Netherfield Academy for all four years of high school."

"But . . ." I hesitated, glancing at his red Regimental jacket. "What happened?"

"Well, I went there for ninth grade," Jishnu said. "Got a partial scholarship and everything. Fitz helped with the rest."

"You were in school at Netherfield? With Darcy? And the Bingleys?" I had a hard time picturing Jishnu there, with all those snobs.

"Yeah, I was, for a year. And I loved it. It was hard, but man, it was a really good education." Jishnu frowned. "But then, after Fitz died, the money disappeared and I had to change schools."

"Netherfield made you drop out because you couldn't pay?" I was shocked. "Wasn't there any financial aid? Or couldn't they increase your scholarship or something?"

"All I know is that Dr. Khan-Darcy, Firoze's mom, wasn't

112

really interested in keeping her husband's promise." Jishnu folded up his plastic coffee stirrer and flicked it angrily off the table. "Maybe because we're Hindu Indians and Darcy's mom's a Muslim Pakistani. I always thought she was prejudiced against us."

"You really think it was because of that?" I asked skeptically.

I mean, I knew that historically, and even into the present day, India and Pakistan had a lot of conflict. And I knew that some Hindu and Muslim communities were violently prejudiced against each other, despite actually having so much in common. But would Darcy's mom be so small-minded? Especially since her husband had loved Jishnu so much, and Jishnu had practically grown up inside her home?

"I don't know, maybe. Maybe not. Who knows." Jishnu scratched his chin. "Suddenly, the money was gone. Even though Fitz had put the money away in a separate bank account and everything."

"That seems super unfair," I began, but Jishnu cut me off.

"It wasn't even his mom, you know. I know it was him."

"What do you mean?" I gripped my tea tighter. "You mean, it's Firoze Darcy's fault you couldn't keep going to school at Netherfield?"

"That's exactly what I mean." Having crumpled up his coffee stirrer, Jishnu now took his frustration out on his coffee lid, taking it off the top of his drink and crushing it. "He was always jealous of his dad's relationship with me. Firoze was always more of a mama's boy, you know? Always going to the mosque with her and all that."

I was seriously not a fan of Darcy, but there was something about Jishnu's statement that rubbed me the wrong way. A year ago, I might have just nodded and let it pass. But I'd been working on being better at speaking up when I heard something I disagreed with. Even if it was out of the mouth of a boy I thought was cute.

"So . . . I'm sorry, but what's wrong with going to the mosque?" I asked. "Or being close to your mom?"

"Nothing!" Jishnu said, his hands up in surrender. "Nothing wrong with any of that!"

I chalked Jishnu's comments up to his sorrow at losing his only father figure. "But how could Darcy stop you from getting to the money that his dad had put away for your school?"

"He's always been a drama queen," sighed Jishnu. "He made up stuff about me to his mom. Turned her against me."

"How did he do that?" A brisk October breeze swept by, and I pulled my jacket a little closer.

Jishnu stared grimly into his coffee cup. Instead of answering my question, he muttered, "You know, Darcy ruined my education. He probably ruined my possibilities of ever getting into an Ivy League college."

"Well, you're still going to a private school." I pointed at his red Regimental jacket. "And you know, as shocking as it may sound, plenty of us public school schlubs do go to good colleges. And guess what—that doesn't just mean the Ivies."

"Sure, yeah, no, of course." Jishnu came out of his reverie. His face relaxed, losing the anger it had been holding for the last few minutes. He smiled now at me a little sheepishly. "Sorry, that was really insensitive of me to say."

"That's okay," I said, not entirely sure it was. "You're just mad about everything that went down after Fitz died, I guess."

"Exactly." Jishnu banged at the metal table, making a few of the other forensicators around us turn their heads. "Exactly. The Darcys were like family, you know? But then, not just lose the only man I'd ever thought of as a father, but to have to switch schools, and have my mom lose her job too."

"They fired your mom from her job?" I asked. "That's outrageous!"

"Well, they made up a bunch of other reasons for it." Jishnu ran his hand through his short hair. "And anyway, her health wasn't super good, so it actually worked out."

I thought about all that Jishnu had told me in the last minutes. "You said the Darcys were like family. So you must know his sister too, Gigi?"

"Cute kid. At least she was cute, when she was a kid. Totally doted on me. Followed me everywhere." Jishnu's face tightened. "But as she grew older, she really became too much like her brother for comfort. Too proud. Too reserved. Too cold."

"I didn't realize you guys had so much history between you." I rubbed my hands together, trying to stay warm. "You're the one with the right to be mad, but to tell you the truth, it was actually Darcy who seemed angrier after the debate."

I thought of how furious he had seemed, and wondered if Darcy was angrier at Jishnu or at me.

Jishnu shrugged, not meeting my eyes. "I try to be the bigger guy, but he always acts like that around me. It's probably the guilt at having ruined my life."

I drank the rest of my tea, not sure how I felt. I couldn't hang with Jishnu's idea that not going to an elite private school was somehow life ruining. On the other hand, Darcy's dad had promised Jishnu the tuition for four years at Netherfield Academy, and then, after he had died, Darcy's mom had gone back on that promise, causing Jishnu to drop out. That really sucked, to put it mildly.

"I'm sorry all that happened to you," I finally said. "It must have been hard."

"It was." Jishnu sighed. "But what doesn't kill us makes us stronger, right?"

I rolled my eyes. "Like not getting to go to a fancy private school."

Jishnu's mouth twisted. "You're determined to keep me honest, aren't you, Leela?"

"I'm not going to play the boo-hoo violin for you just because you're not at an elite private school, if that's what you mean," I agreed. "I do think it's horrible the Darcys went back on their word, but . . ."

"From where you sit, I just sound like I'm being self-indulgent?" Jishnu prompted with that adorable grin of his.

I laughed. "Maybe a little. Just about the private school, though. The other stuff sounds really hard. I'm sorry."

"You're right, you know," Jishnu mused, his face serious again. "Maybe I just use the thing about Netherfield Academy to cover up what really bothers me. Which is losing my extended family just when I needed them most."

I reached out and touched his hand. This time, it was me who didn't let go. "It's incredibly unfair that they cut you out of their family like that. And classist. And mean."

Jishnu squeezed my hand. "Thanks for understanding, Leela. I knew you would."

CHAPTER 16

MADE THE decision at dinner, as soon as I heard I had broken into humorous-interpretation finals for the next day.

"I think I'm quitting speech and taking up debate," I announced.

We were at dinner with the team, minus Jay of course, and I was exhausted and leaning on Tomi's shoulder. We'd made it through the meal without mishap, just the usual high energy of an end-of-competition day. I waited until we were all eating dessert to drop my bombshell.

The first reaction from the team was not what I was expecting.

"Well, that makes sense. I never really thought you were that funny anyway."

At this incredibly rude comment from Lidia, my head popped right up.

"I'm incredibly funny. Everybody says so!" I practically knocked over my tea in my agitation.

"Prove it," Lidia provoked, pointing a fudgy spoon at me. "Prove how funny you are."

Beside her, Kitty giggled uproariously. Then she went back to emptying sugar packets into her mouth and crunching on the grainy contents.

"I've been crushing it in HI this season," I argued.

"Then why are you quitting?" Kitty asked, earning a spoon clink from Lidia.

"Yeah, why would you quit something you're that good at?" Lidia jammed more chocolate cake into her mouth before adding, "Sounds like you might be funny but stupid."

I couldn't help wanting to leap across the table and strangle her. I knew she was just trying to get a rise out of me, but Lidia Rivera always succeeded in pushing my buttons.

"Are you serious, Leela?" Tomi turned to me. "You're really thinking about joining debate? It's not for the reason we discussed before, *is it*?"

At her meaningful look, I remembered I'd told her how Darcy had practically challenged me to try my wits at Lincoln-Douglas debate. I couldn't exactly admit now that I was rising to his bait.

"This isn't about anyone else, it's about me," I assured her. "I'm not growing or learning any more in humorous interpretation. I want to push myself, try something that feels scary."

Then I thought how interesting it had been to hear, even secondhand, the arguments about immigration that Darcy had been making to Jishnu, and continued, more honestly, "I'm kind of itching for the challenge of debate. Developing my own arguments in my own words and all that."

"Or is it that you're itching for a certain Regimental debater?" Lidia smirked as Kitty giggled.

"This has nothing to do with a guy." I said hotly, even as I wondered if it was true. Was my newly discovered passion for LD debate genuine, or did I just want to successfully accomplish what Jishnu had failed to do: humiliate Darcy?

"Sure, Leela. You're very self-actualized." Lidia yawned, showing off chocolate-coated teeth.

"Lidia, cut it out." Tomi sipped at her chamomile. "We're all tired and wired. Not the right time to provoke each other."

"Besides, Leela got very little sleep last night." Even though everyone at the table knew exactly why I hadn't gotten much sleep last night, the way Colin said this made Lidia and Kitty laugh even more, as if he was implying that he had somehow been the reason I'd been up, not Jay's asthma attack.

"What are you laughing at?" Colin spluttered. He reddened a bit, getting some of the implication, if not the entire gist of why the girls were in stitches. "What are they laughing at?"

"Don't worry about it, Colin." Tomi lifted her warm cup to her temple and closed her eyes. "You're too good of a person to get it."

"You shouldn't switch categories, Leela," said Mary from the other end of the table.

"Thanks for your support, Mary!" I singsonged, my voice full of sarcasm.

"I disagree," said Colin. "You always struck me as more of a debater anyway."

"Whatever happened to speech is speech and debate is debate and never the twain shall meet?" asked Tomi, rephrasing the Rudyard Kipling quote.

"For what it's worth, you do like to argue, dear," called Mrs. Bennet from her seat.

"It just seems very sudden," Tomi said dubiously.

"I think it's brave of Leela to challenge herself, put herself out there, try something new." Colin beamed at me.

"I suppose." Tomi bit her lip with worry.

"It's not that big of a deal, Tomes, I just want to try it out," I said. "I can always go back if it doesn't work out."

"You'll hate it! It's so sexist! There are hardly any girls in debate!" Mary interjected. "It's like walking into some old-fashioned boys' club from a century ago! I'd quit myself if I had something else I wanted to do."

"She's right, all the debate categories are quite overrun by boys," Mr. Bennet confirmed. "Although I wouldn't mind seeing some more strong young women give those boys a run for their money."

"Even more reason for me to go into it, then," I said with what I hoped was an attitude of confidence.

"Just know what you're getting into." Mary took a big bite of her dessert. "Do you know what some of my judging comments were from last week? That my skirt was too short! And that I should consider smiling more!"

I considered this. Mary *did* tend to favor the dark-miniskirt-with-dark-tights-and-boots look, and she *did* tend to frown a lot, but it was completely sexist for a judge to remark on either.

"What a jerk!" I said. "They shouldn't let that person judge anymore!"

"That wasn't just one judge, dear!" Mr. Bennet said with a

wry twist of his lips. "I'm afraid just those sorts of comments are given to young women debaters all the time!"

"Really?" Colin puffed up with irritation. "Why didn't we hear about this before?"

"Before Mary, we'd never really had too many debaters on this team," Mrs. Bennet said placidly. "We tended to attract people interested in interpretive categories, me with my regional theater background and all."

"It's not just the judges!" Mary banged her spoon on the dish of ice cream before her. "The guys I've been competing with are total jerks!"

I jumped at this comment. "Jerks—like that Firoze Darcy, right?"

"What?" Mary looked startled. "No, not him. I mean, yeah, he was really good, and kinda grim, and completely destroyed me with his argument, but I'm talking about the dudes that act all relieved when I walk into a room, like they know for sure they'll win just because I'm a girl."

"Or maybe they do that because they know you're bad at it!" Kitty giggled, looking at Lidia for approval.

But even Lidia gave her a dirty look at this point.

"What?" Poor Kitty looked mortified. "I meant it as a joke."

"Well, it wasn't funny," Lidia sniffed, making Kitty deflate even more. "We're talking about institutionalized sexism here! That's no laughing matter, Kitty!"

"I was actually just talking to the Meryton team president, Mariah, about this exact thing," said Tomi, turning people's attention away from Kitty. "A Meryton debater named Sarah King got some kind of an"—Tomi paused—"inappropriate text from a fellow competitor. Telling her he'd throw the round and let her win if she . . . well, did something for him."

"That's outrageous! What was it he asked for?" Lidia's eyes were dancing with curiosity. "And more importantly, did she do it?"

"Lidia!" Mrs. Bennet said. "That is not the point!"

"Why doesn't the league do something about this?" Colin spluttered. "This is harassment! I mean, it's definitely against the rules in the National Forensics Association Official Handbook!"

"The judges don't hear about everything. Or when we do, it's rumors, like this Sarah King issue," Mr. Bennet explained. "She never filed an official complaint!"

"She shouldn't have to, by George!" Beads of sweat were erupting with alarming frequency on Colin's forehead and neck. "Why, in the National Forensics Association Official Handbook, there's an entire subsection outlining clear rules of appropriate conduct between competitors, and admonitions against harassment."

I sighed, not really wanting to hear anything more about the National Forensics Association Official Handbook. Or look at Colin's rapidly multiplying sweat beads.

"Well, I'm in! I'll do it too!" Lidia shot out her tiny chin. "I'm going to try out LD with Leela! Just to make all those sexist judges and competitors stain their shorts."

"Lidia! Where do you pick up such expressions?!" Mrs. Bennet looked ready to faint.

Lidia ignored her and smiled at me. "You've convinced me, Leela!"

I stared at the young girl's determined face, regretting each of my life decisions. I looked around at my teammates. "So you're all okay that I'm doing this?"

"We're doing this!" interjected Lidia.

"We're doing this?" I amended.

"Only if you want to, dear," said Mrs. Bennet with a slurp of her coffee.

"I guess Mrs. Bennet's right, you do like a good argument," Tomi said, grinning.

"*Et tu*, Tomi?" I grabbed my chest, as if I were Caesar and Tomi Brutus, having just stabbed me.

My friend shrugged. "I'm just saying!"

I threw a balled-up napkin at her head, and the conversation disintegrated from there.

CHAPTER 17

WHY DID THAT little brat have to steal my thunder?" I complained to Tomi when we were up in our room after the meal. "I wanted switching to LD to be my thing!"

"Lidia looks up to you—can't you see that?" Tomi laughed. "She's so hardheaded, reminds me of you in a lot of ways!"

"Oh, please, no!" I groaned, flopping over on my bed. "It's been such a weird day already. I mean, all this stuff about what Darcy's really like." I'd only just finished telling Tomi about my informative coffee date.

"You know, Leela, what Jishnu told you about Darcy sounds . . ." Tomi paused, pursing her lips. "Odd, doesn't it?"

"Odd?" I sat up, pushing my hair off my face. "What do you mean?"

"I don't know, the fact that Darcy's father promised to pay Jishnu's tuition at Netherfield for four years." Tomi shrugged. "Do you know how much those schools cost? Where did a professor married to another professor with two kids of his own get that kind of money?"

I frowned. I hadn't thought of that. "Maybe he had family money? Wait, didn't Bingley say something about a trust fund? I mean, Darcy's dad was British, after all."

"You've been watching too many period dramas!" Tomi laughed. "It's not like they're all just landed gentry over there— counts and marquises and earls or something! It's not all like *Downton Abbey.*"

"Ah, but is the plural of marquis really marquises?" I squinted at her. "Also, I'm pretty sure a count is the same thing as an earl."

"You get my point!" Tomi walked into the bathroom and started washing her face with some bright green facial cleanser. "And did you ever wonder why Jishnu would just tell you all this unprovoked? All this long-winded stuff about how awful Darcy and his mom are? Plus that little unnecessary Islamophobia thrown in?"

"He told me to explain why Darcy was so weird when he saw us together in the hallway," I said.

"It couldn't have just been that he was jealous?" Tomi finished rubbing circles of cleanser on her cheeks, forehead, and nose, then rinsed off. As she patted her face dry, she leaned against the doorway of the open bathroom. "You did tell me that Jishnu put his arm around you!"

"That was just a friendly gesture, very casual," I argued, even though I wasn't entirely sure I believed what I was saying. Then I added, "Regardless, Darcy's a total weirdo!"

"From whose perspective, though?" Tomi pressed.

"It's not like Jishnu could have made all that stuff up!" I got up to join Tomi by the bathroom sink. She made room for me as I put toothpaste on my brush. "He told me they were like his extended family. After Darcy's dad died, he felt like they kicked him out of the family!"

"Well, that does sound pretty awful." Tomi stared into the mirror as she tied a silk scarf around her hair, and I brushed my teeth. "But I wonder if the real truth is somewhere in between Darcy being completely awful and Jishnu being completely right."

I finished brushing, then spat and rinsed before saying, "You always want to see the best in people, Tomi. It's why I love you. But I'm not sure that Firoze Darcy deserves your goodness."

"We all deserve the assumption of goodness, Leela." Tomi started brushing her own teeth, mumbling between bubbles, "Even your Mr. Darcy!"

I remembered how Jay had said Darcy was mine in our text exchange earlier in the day and wondered how I'd given my two best friends such a wrong impression. I started washing my own face, but so distractedly that I left a whole eyeful of soap unrinsed. The burning felt like the perfect metaphor for my relationship with Firoze Darcy—something that seems benign, but stings you in the end. I yelped, bending down and splashing more water over my face. In the process, Tomi barely missed spitting her tooth-paste out in my hair.

I came up spluttering, wiping my eyes with a towel. "I can assure you, Tomi, that he's not my Mr. Darcy. Nor will he ever be!"

CHAPTER 18

THERE WAS NO forensics competition the next weekend after the Phillips College competition, which was good, because it was the day of Tomi's SAT retake. Jay and I had arranged to pick her up around noon and, since neither Jay nor I had our licenses yet, have her drive us all over to the local diner for pancakes.

Jay was much better after his asthma attack the previous weekend, having not even missed any school. I wasn't willing to admit it out loud, but Darcy was right. The whole drama with Jay's hospitalization could probably have been prevented by him just remembering to carry his inhaler and other medicines with him.

Since we lived only a few houses away from each other, and a few blocks from Longbourn High School, I walked over to pick up Jay, and then we had a leisurely walk over to the school around noon. It was a glorious October morning, and we made the short walk a bit longer by pausing to do photo shoots in front of every other multicolored tree. When we weren't doing that, Jay picked up random leaves he liked—bright red, orange, yellow—and tucked them into my dark, curly hair.

"A perfect fairy crown for a perfect fairy princess," he said lightly. "Third place at Phillips in HI! Maybe I shouldn't say princess, I should say queen."

"Hardly." I took in a big breath of the crisp air, remembering my fantasy about being a girl in a novel attending an old-fashioned ball. "No matter how we place at any competition, those kinds of stories aren't about us, Jay."

"Who the hecken says so?" Jay jammed a few more leaves into my hair, looking for all the world as if he were arranging flowers in a vase. I put my hand up, trying to feel what he'd done, only to have him laughingly bat my hand away. "Leela," he said firmly. "Don't you know that all the magic is for us and about us? It always was and always will be."

"You don't think we're just, oh, I don't know . . ." I bit my lip, remembering the conversation I'd had with Darcy about *Hamilton* and my recent decision to switch out of HI, despite my successes. ". . . writing ourselves into someone else's story?"

Jay stopped and looked seriously at me. The dappled light filtering through the trees danced across his perfect features. "Leela Bose, tell me this: Why would we have been made so beautiful, so brilliant, and so damn talented if not to become legends?"

I stared at him for a second, feeling something squeezing in my chest. Then I grinned. "Sure enough."

"And don't you forget it." Jay tucked another leaf into my crown. "Even if you are completely bonkers for quitting speech and going over to the dark side. I mean, debate!" Jay gave a little shudder. "Are you up on all your vaccines?"

I ignored his dig. "Bingley certainly thinks you're beautiful, brilliant, and talented."

"I certainly hope so," agreed Jay, unusually serious. "Leela, I really like him. I mean, he was so amazing in the hospital: kind, gentle, thoughtful, the works."

"He's the one, huh?" I asked, hoping for a light, Jay-like answer.

But my friend looked at me, no laughter, only tenderness in his face, and agreed, "He's the one."

I felt a pang of jealousy. Would I ever feel that way about someone? And, more to the point, would someone ever feel that way about me? "I'm really glad for you, Jay."

We walked for a couple of minutes in silence, before I asked, "Remember when we'd watch reruns of that show your mom liked about the New York City high school for performing arts—*Fame?*"

"I'm gonna live forever!" Jay belted out, startling two moms and their kid biking across the street. "I'm gonna learn how to fly—high!"

I joined him for a few bars as he leaped down the sidewalk, singing, "Baby, remember my name!"

After he finally stopped, breathless and laughing from all his fake ballet leaps down the sidewalk, he peered back at me. "You shouldn't be afraid to dance, Leela."

"What makes you think I'm afraid?" I countered, feeling suddenly very exposed as I caught up to him.

"Just like that beautiful brain takes up space by speaking," he said, raising a shrewd eyebrow, "your body deserves to take up room and space too."

"All right, all right, Abuelita. Message received." I didn't want to talk about it anymore, so I squeezed his hand tight and swung it as we walked like we were still little kids.

He squeezed my hand back, forcing me to skip along the sidewalk with him a few steps. "Don't you forget it, we're gonna do great things, Leela Bose. We're gonna make our marks on this world so hard, they ain't never gonna forget us!"

I grinned up at my friend. Jay knew the feeling I had inside me—of always wanting to be more, do more, become more. It was why we had both joined forensics. Why we both loved theater. Why we had both remained friends after so many years. I just needed to figure out how to cut loose those parts of me that didn't serve my dreams.

Unfortunately, my feeling of togetherness was somewhat spoiled as we waited on the bench outside the roundabout of Longbourn High for Tomi. I noticed Jay acting a little fishy. Students were trickling out of the building as their testing rooms finished, and he kept looking around as if waiting to see someone.

"Jay?" I poked him hard in the arm with my finger. "Please tell me you don't have some ulterior motive for being here except to take Tomi out for post-SAT pancakes."

"Ulterior agenda?" Even as he asked the question, he flicked back his hair from his face in a dramatic way. "Whatever can you mean, young Padawan?"

"You fink!" This time I pushed him with both hands. "Are we here perchance because Charles Bingley is taking the SAT at this site? How did you manage that one?"

"Au contraire, I didn't have to manage anything." Jay raised one dark eyebrow at me. "The Fates had already willed it so. Much as I'd like to take credit for his being here, he was already signed up to take it at this location way before he met me. He signed up late, so there were no other seats available closer to where he lives."

I knocked Jay's leg with mine. "So what's the plan, Romeo? You're bailing on me and Tomi?"

"I thought . . ." Jay hesitated, squinting at me. "I thought, if you wouldn't hate it too much, that we could *all* go to the diner together?"

I groaned. "You wouldn't be saying it all hesitant like that if Charles's not-so-charming sister wasn't also taking the SAT in there with him."

"I know she's not your favorite," Jay offered, "but it wasn't her I was thinking of, honestly."

That's when I noticed the car that had just pulled into an empty space nearby. It was a bright blue newer model of one of those electric cars. I stared openmouthed at the futuristic machine for a minute—I wasn't even a car person and I was a little floored by how beautiful it was. And that's when I noticed the driver.

I tried not to change my facial expression as I muttered to Jay out of the side of my mouth. "I take back all that gooey-best-friend stuff. I hate every molecule of your being."

"Now, now, fairy princess, no need to get ugly." Jay had a fixed smile on his face. "He's Bingley's best friend, so of course I had to invite him."

Then he raised his arm and waved. "Hi, Darcy!"

CHAPTER 19

ELLO!" DARCY TURNED off the engine and opened the driver's door. Which was one of those butterfly-type doors, like the time-traveling DeLorean in that old movie *Back to the Future.* "I'm assuming they aren't out yet?"

Darcy walked toward us as I said under my breath, "Oh, that's not ostentatious at all."

"A little show-offy, but you've got to admit, that horse-drawn carriage is mighty purdy," returned Jay. "As is he, I might add."

I wanted to strangle Jay. But Darcy was too close to say anything more now. I noticed that as he approached us, he didn't meet my eyes but, rather, seemed to be looking directly above my face, like he was studying something on my head.

"I like your crown," he said finally, his tone light.

"My what?" I touched my head, remembering the leaves that Jay had tucked in. Embarrassed, I started trying to pull them out, getting them tangled in my curly locks. "I'd forgotten they were there."

"Stop, don't take them out." Darcy approached even closer,

as if he wanted to halt my hands by force. He stopped, jamming his hands into his pockets awkwardly. I remembered that the last time I'd seen him, he'd seemed furious that I was hanging out with Jishnu. "You should keep them in. They . . . they look nice."

Was Darcy making fun of me? Did he actually think I was hideous and was just saying the opposite? The self-conscious humiliation washed over me, and I felt like that little brown ballerina I'd once been, that one who could never become a princess, but must always remain a dirty frog.

I shot Jay a dirty look, but he was just grinning at me like the fool he was, and being of absolutely zero assistance. But I needed help, because the more I was pulling at my hair, the more the leaves were becoming tangled. I was embarrassed at how I must look, and more embarrassed for even caring.

"You didn't take the SAT today? Aren't you a senior?" I asked in a pathetic attempt to distract Darcy from my hair, which was surely getting increasingly frizzy with every tug at it. I felt like a self-fulfilling prophecy, like even if I hadn't been unattractive before, I was going to work hard to make myself so.

"I—sat for it before," Darcy said. "I was happy with my result."

"Lucky for you," Jay said cheerfully, rocking back and forth on his sneakered feet. "I bet you killed it."

I gave Jay a dirty look even as I kept fiddling with my hair. He was *so* going to get it from me when we were alone.

"Here, you're just getting your hair tangled." Darcy reached up and stilled my hands, pushing back some leaves and taking out others that I'd crumbled up in my haste to take them out. "There, I think that works."

"Very nice," said Jay approvingly. "You should consider a career in leaf hairdressing if the whole corporate raider/high-powered lawyer/hedge fund manager/corrupt congressman thing doesn't work out."

"Not really planning on being any of those things," Darcy said, raising a dark eyebrow.

"All right, all right, Che Guevara, don't get your beret in a twist," replied Jay with a grin.

I made a frustrated choking sound, and probably realizing I was about to have an all-out meltdown and absolutely kill him, Jay pulled out his phone and turned the camera view so I could see myself. "Calm down, Leela. You look fine."

I was startled to see my face looking back at me from Jay's phone. I actually looked more than fine. My eyes were glittering, my face was a bit bright with embarrassment, but my hair was curly and, shockingly, not too frizzy. My curls were studded right across the top with beautiful colored leaves in alternating autumnal colors. *It was a perfect woodland fairy crown*, I thought, with a surge of affection for Jay.

"Okay, I guess I can go to the diner like this." I patted my head and Jay put away his phone. "Although I clearly have no choice unless I want my hair to bush out into a frizz halo."

"I like it," Darcy said with surprising sincerity. "It's the kind of thing my sister would do. She was always making us flower crowns out of wildflowers she found on campus."

"Us?" Jay asked.

"I've worn plenty a flower crown in my day." Darcy smiled. "Made my allergies go wild. But it was worth it to make her happy."

The warmth in Darcy's voice as he talked about his sister did funny things to my insides. Feeling like I was in great danger of melting, I purposefully hardened myself, remembering that this was the jerk who thought public school kids were clowns, that I was un-temptation-worthy. This was the weasel who had prevented Jishnu from fulfilling his dreams and destiny.

"I heard you once had kind of a brother too." My tone was even more aggressive than I'd intended.

"A brother?" Darcy wrinkled his brows at me. "No. I . . . I don't have a brother."

"Well, not now that you've forgotten him, abandoned him, made it impossible for him to keep going to your school." I tried to make my voice lighter but felt a righteous anger building in me. Even though Jay was making noises and kind of pulling at my arm, I had no intention of letting Firoze Darcy off the hook. I felt suddenly, incomprehensibly *furious* at him. Like my emotions were the engine of his high-powered automobile and had gone from zero to sixty in five seconds. "What do you say to that, huh?"

Darcy's face was still, and his voice a little strangled. "Who are you talking about, Leela?"

"Jishnu Waddedar!" I announced triumphantly. I felt like a prosecutor entrapping a criminal in the docks. "Do you deny it?"

"Leela," Jay warned. "Come on, leave it."

I ignored Jay. Of course he'd want me to drop the whole thing. He wanted to stay on Darcy's side because Darcy was Bingley's friend. But I had no such compunctions. *Obliterate him*, I thought. *Humiliate him.*

Darcy was staring at me, his expression unreadable. "Deny

what? That we used to be close and we're not anymore? I have no reason to deny it. I'm happy for it."

"Happy for it!" My blood was pounding in my temples now. "How can you say that?"

"He's gotten to you too, then?" Underneath Darcy's fury was such a layer of upset and hurt, it almost took my breath away. "Then nothing I say will matter anyway."

"What are you talking about?" I demanded.

Darcy opened his mouth but didn't say anything else, because just then, the side doors to the school opened and Tomi, Caroline, and Bingley all walked out together.

"Bingley!" Jay leaped up from the bench with some serious relief and waved. The trio turned at his call and headed our way.

Rather than running up to him and giving him a hug, which is what I would have expected Jay to do, he waited for Bingley to reach him.

"How'd it go?" Darcy asked all three test takers. It didn't escape my notice that he'd moved a few steps away and was determinedly not looking in my direction.

"Good, I hope!" answered Tomi, shooting me a look full of questions and curiosity.

I shrugged, not sure what to say. That I'd just provoked Darcy into an almost-fight?

"Terrible," said Ro grimly. "I didn't finish that first math section!"

"I hate taking tests," said Charles with a sad puppy dog face before enfolding Jay in a big embrace.

I tried not to stare but couldn't help notice how warm Jay's cheeks got, and how pleased he looked all smushed up against Bingley's shoulder. Then Ro cleared her throat, and the boys broke apart.

"So, I was promised some authentic Jersey diner pancakes." Bingley gave Jay a shy look, his hands in his jeans pockets.

"Authentic, perhaps," Tomi laughed. "But I hope Jay didn't say anything about them being particularly *good*."

"You kind of slather them in maple syrup to cover up the plastic/cardboard taste." Jay's eyes were fixed on Bingley, who was squinting against the golden October sun. The midday rays were making his light hair glow almost yellow and casting a halo-like effect over his head. I noticed something I'd never seen before on my best friend's face as he watched Bingley—something vulnerable, pure, and real that made me simultaneously really happy and really scared for him.

"Something's come up, I'm going to have to go home," said Darcy abruptly. He was chewing on the inside of his cheek and looked grim. He should feel bad. He deserved a good helping of shame and humiliation after serving me such a big slice.

"What? No pancakes?" Bingley's face was crestfallen.

"I'm afraid I can't." Darcy was studying his keys like they opened the truths of the universe.

Ro gave Darcy a thoughtful look, a small smile playing on her lips. "I guess even fine eyes aren't enough of a temptation?"

Darcy shot her a withering glance. "Are you going to the restaurant, Caroline? Or do you want a ride home?"

"*Perfect*, I'll take a ride home. That was the plan, right?" Ro was still smiling and shot me a slightly malevolent look from under her eyelashes. She yawned ostentatiously, stretching so she arched her chest out in Darcy's direction. "I'm glad we're just going home. I'm tired after that long test anyway."

"We could take a rideshare," her brother began, until she grabbed his arm in a playful-not-really-playful way.

"Come on, Charles, I think Mother needs your help with that thing at home," she said meaningfully. "That thing that only you can do *perfectly*."

"Bingley?" Jay asked, the smile tight on his face.

Bingley looked from his sister to Jay and back again. "I'm so sorry," he said.

Jay scowled at me, to which I gave a slight shrug. It's not like it was my fault Bingley caved in so easily to his friend and sister. I mean, like, grow a spine, rich boy. Still, something inside me twisted with guilt.

With some perfunctory goodbyes, the trio from Netherfield headed to Darcy's car.

"I'll see you next week at our tournament, right?" As Darcy opened the car door, Bingley looked back at Jay, appearing for all the world like a slightly confused golden retriever.

As much as Jay had been scowling just a moment before, he seemed to melt. "You're sure you can't come to pancakes?"

Bingley glanced back at the car, in which Darcy and his sister were already sitting.

"It was a long test," the blond boy said hesitantly. "And my parents—" Bingley cut himself off before finishing his sentence.

Tomi raised her eyebrows at me, and I could tell she was wondering the same thing. Was Bingley not out to his parents? Had his sister threatened to reveal he was gay? Or was there something else going on?

Without saying anything, I scooched closer to Jay. Close enough to graze his arm with mine. I wanted him to know I was right next to him. But instead of leaning into my support, he kind of swatted at my hand and moved away. I felt my insides twist even more.

"Totally, I understand." Jay laughed unconvincingly. "Congratulations on finishing the test!"

"See you next weekend?" repeated Bingley.

"We'll definitely all be at the Netherfield Academy competition," said Tomi firmly.

"We wouldn't miss it!" I added, my eyes glittering with fury.

"Perfect!" repeated Ro again.

It was she who caught my eye as the car backed up, not Darcy. Locking her gaze with mine, she placed her hand over Darcy's forearm as he drove. She smiled, slow and lazy, as if sending me a secret message that he was hers. But the trick was on her, because I hated Darcy anyway. Let her have him!

Then the car finished backing out of the spot and pulled away.

Only when they were gone did Jay whirl on me. "Leela Bose, you complete jerk, I'm never going to speak to you again!"

"What did I do?" I protested, even though I clearly knew.

"What did she do?" Tomi echoed.

"Only picked a fight with Darcy for absolutely no reason and ruined everything!" shouted Jay. "You are the most selfish person I've ever met!"

As he stomped off down the sidewalk, I snorted in indignation.

"Well?" asked Tomi as we headed toward her car. "Did you do it?"

"Pick a fight with Darcy?" I asked hotly. Then I paused. "Well, maybe. Yeah. But for no reason, no!"

"You sure about that, sis?" Tomi asked. "What possible reason could you have to pick a fight with a guy you don't even like as a person?"

I unfortunately didn't have a good answer to that.

CHAPTER 20

WAS DREADING the Netherfield competition. Not only was it at Darcy and the Bingleys' school, but it was the first time both Lidia and I were going to try LD. Unlike Lidia, it wasn't the sexism in debate or the lack of female representation that inspired me. I kind of just wanted to face off with Darcy and show him, once and for all, that he wasn't the boss of me. I wanted to show myself I wasn't afraid. The fact that Darcy wouldn't be competing today, since he and his teammates would help run their home competition, was a little bit of a calculated decision. I wanted to humiliate him, yes. But the chances of my doing so were only improved by getting some practice first.

"Will the Regimental team be there today?" I'd asked Mr. Bennet that morning as we boarded our school bus in the freezing Longbourn High parking lot.

He consulted his list. "I believe so, Leela." He looked up, his light eyes twinkling behind his bifocals. "Why? Is there someone on that team you want to see?"

I'd mumbled some kind of answer, ignoring Kitty's and Lidia's giggles as I walked past them down the school bus aisle.

"You can't keep him all to yourself today, Leela," Kitty had admonished.

"I have no idea who you're talking about," I said lightly as I put my bag down in the seat across from Jay. He gave me a scowl. We hadn't spoken all week since our fight outside Longbourn the past weekend.

"Jishnu Waddedar, of course!" Lidia had yelled, leaning back over the green vinyl bus seat. "We want to hang out with him too!"

"I'm not stopping you!" I countered.

I hadn't seen Jishnu since our coffee date at Phillips College, although I'd had a couple of friendly text exchanges with him in the last couple of weeks. The texts had been fine, but nothing close to that spark I felt when we were face-to-face. I couldn't wait to see him again.

"Hey," I said to Jay once the bus was moving.

"Hey what?" he snapped, crossing his arms over his chest.

"Are you two seriously still not made up yet?" asked Tomi from the seat behind me.

"No. She's ruined my every chance at happiness," sniffed Jay. "And now all ten of my unborn children will be parentless."

"I'm sorry, Jay. Bingley will be there today, won't he?" I asked.

"It's his school," said Jay shortly. The upset was coming off him in waves.

"Seriously, I'm so sorry. I was being selfish last weekend," I said. "I was so riled up about what Jishnu had told me about

Darcy that I just went for the jugular. I'm seriously sorry." I knelt in the bus aisle in front of Jay. "Forgive me?"

Jay gave me a considering look. "Today better go perfectly for me and Bingley. And if it does, I'll *maybe*, just *possibly* consider forgiving you."

"How can I control that?" I protested.

But Jay, who was always able to hold a grudge longer than anyone, just raised his eyebrow. "Not my problem, babe. You should have thought of that before you ruined my pancake date by picking a dumb fight with Darcy! Bingley hasn't texted or responded to any of mine all week!"

I said nothing, wondering if Jay's anger at me wasn't at least a little bit laced with anxiety about what Bingley had been about to say about his parents.

It was less than a thirty-minute drive to Netherfield Academy, but it might as well have been on the other side of the planet. I felt deflated by the tension between my best friend and me. At least Jay and I were talking, but he obviously wasn't ready to forgive and forget anytime soon.

Then I stopped worrying about all that because we pulled up to Netherfield Academy. By the looks of it, we might as well have been pulling up to Cinderella's castle.

"What in the actual Marie Antoinette!" I exclaimed, and Jay even laughed.

I leaned my forehead against the window, taking in the fluttering blue-and-gold banners at their front gates proclaiming their school values: Unity! Community! Integrity!

"Bougie-ty!" Tomi added, causing the rest of us to snort with laughter.

The campus was located on multiple acres of rolling hills, with a tall wrought-iron fence all around it. As our bus approached the front gate, the driver pushed a call button, said something into the box, and only then did the gates swing open with a smooth, automatic motion.

"To keep the proletariat out," said Jay as we rumbled through.

"Hate to tell them, but we're in now!" Mary mumbled from beneath her hoodie.

"The forensics tournament was just a Trojan horse," Tomi said, speaking into her hand like it was a microphone and she a reporter. "The fall of late capitalism came with the public school students being allowed into the hallowed grounds of the elite institution. First came speech and debate, then came *the revolution*!" She said these last words with great dramatic flair.

At first low and under my breath, then louder as Tomi, Mary, Kitty, and Lidia joined me, I started singing "Do You Hear the People Sing?" from *Les Misérables*. When Colin came in with his deep baritone, the rest of us collapsed with laughter. I noticed, however, that Jay didn't join the singing at all.

Unlike our public Longbourn High School, which was one huge, squat building of questionable architecture surrounded by even more questionable landscaping, Netherfield Academy was like a mini college campus. The winding road from the front gate to the parking lots led us past multiple buildings made of shining glass, a greenhouse, and what looked like an outdoor amphitheater surrounded by a garden and a wooden glen. It looked like something straight out of *A Midsummer Night's Dream*, and I wondered with envy what it would be like to act or watch a play in such a space that looked like it could be hosting the fairy queen's revels at any moment. Along the campus drive were stone walkways, farm-rustic fences, and artistically placed outcroppings of natural rocks that had obviously been designed as "conversation areas" for students. It was, I hated to admit, breathtaking.

"Aren't you glad you dressed to impress?" Tomi asked me.

"My brains are beautiful enough," I said haughtily, before laughing. "Yeah, super glad. Thanks again for the beautiful sweater, sis."

Over my protests earlier in the week, Tomi had convinced me to abandon my well-worn competition suit, the one I wore to pretty much every weekend meet. Now that I saw how fancy Netherfield was, I was quite glad not to be dressed in my old, slightly stained outfit. Today, I was wearing simple black slacks, a crisp white button-down that I'd bought at the mall, and a beautiful shimmery blazer-style cardigan of silver-white wool that Tomi had knitted for me as a birthday present a couple of months ago. I'd paired the whole outfit with some freshwater-pearl earrings of Ma's—that I'd promised on my life not to lose. Instead of dousing my curly hair in product and pulling it into a bun, as I usually did for competitions, I'd actually let my locks do their natural, ringlet-y thing. I was worried, of course, about looking like a giant mop by the end of the day, but I'd promised Tomi to at least try to embrace my curly-girl self this one time. I wasn't dancing yet, but these were small steps.

As we all trooped off our yellow school bus in the parking lot, the first thing we saw was a sign for valet parking to the right, at the entrance to the senior parking lot.

"They have valet parking?" Kitty shrieked, pointing to the sign.

"For the students?" Lidia was even louder.

Mrs. Bennet flapped her hands in irritation, shushing them even as she fussed at us all to button up our coats. "Girls! Honestly! Please do not act like this is the first time you've seen a valet parking sign!"

"At a school? It is definitely the first time I've seen a valet parking sign at a school!" Lidia said as Mrs. Bennet forcibly pulled the girl's coat more tightly around her.

"Well, you don't need to advertise it!" Mrs. Bennet looked furtively around the rapidly filling parking lot, where other yellow buses filled with other teams were arriving. "The private school coaches will think that we're country bumpkins!"

"They will think no such thing, my dear," soothed Mr. Bennet.

"If you think about it, having valet parking in a student parking lot is quite logical." Colin stepped off the bus, straightening his tie. Since he was the last person off, the door closed with a pneumatic whoosh behind him. "If you look at how seniors with parking privileges park at Longbourn, you'll note that hardly any of them park appropriately—there's a subset of drivers who are

consistently over the line, crooked, taking up two spaces, and pre-
venting safe parking by others!"

"Excuse me?" Tomi, the only other senior present, asked.

"Present company, of course, excluded!" Colin said with a ridiculous bow that made Kitty and Lidia descend into giggles. "I'm
just observing that the administration at Netherfield Academy has
undoubtedly concluded it's more space efficient to have professionals
handle their parking situation. Something that we at Longbourn
could very well use, if we could, of course, afford it."

"Valet parking—the next educational priority right after
up-to-date textbooks, functional science lab equipment, building
maintenance," I said.

"Not to mention teacher salaries, better ventilation, an edible
lunch program," Jay added. "But right after that, valet parking is
obviously at the top of the list!"

All right, all right. If Jay was trading quips with me, we
might be on the path to repairing our friendship. I gave him a
tentative smile, but he turned away from me with a frown. Like
he'd forgotten he was mad at me for a second but just now re-
remembered. I felt my heart sink once again.

"Come along now, students," blustered Mrs. Bennet as we
walked together against the November wind toward the main
Netherfield Academy upper school building.

The building was one of those glass affairs I'd seen on our
drive in. Now that I was closer, I could appreciate its beauty. It
was a state-award-winning green building—I knew that because
of the tasteful placard outside that said so. Even if I hadn't seen
the sign, though, I would have guessed it by the solar panels on

the artistically slanted roof, the natural stone water catchment features designed into the sides of the building, and the way that the entry lobby had an entire wall of drooping greenery growing up its multistoried face.

"Welcome to Netherfield!" someone called out.

CHAPTER 21

I T WAS Ro Bingley, who was seated at an elegant entrance desk, helping registered teams get their materials. She looked as perfect as ever, her blonde hair hanging around her pert face, a pair of giant pearl earrings in her ears that matched her ginormous pearl necklace. I touched my tiny freshwater-pearl earrings, and wondered if girls like Ro had jewelry boxes full of such precious things—they, who knew they were swan princesses by right.

Ro greeted Mr. and Mrs. Bennet briefly but professionally before handing them a judges' packet. As our coaches moved aside, flipping through their packet of papers and chatting with the other coaches in the lobby, Ro Bingley turned her eyes to us.

"Oh, look, it's the whole darn Longbourn gang!" She said it like we were old-timey bank robbers or the meddling kids from *Scooby-Doo* or something.

"Indeed." I was trying to keep my cool and not stare at the high, wood-beamed ceiling of the lobby, the open staircase sweeping to the right, the fancy furniture, the huge, expensive-looking paintings on the wall.

"Hi, Ro!" Jay said, his voice dripping with saccharine.

"Oh, hey, Jason!" Ro gushed even more fakely. "How *are* you?"

"It's Jay," Tomi corrected her before Jay could even say a word. "You know that, Ro."

"Oops, my bad!" Ro drawled.

"Is your brother here?" asked Jay. I noticed his foot was kind of twisting where he stood. "He said to text him when I arrived."

Ro narrowed her eyes a little. "You might want to ask Darcy where my brother is," she said mysteriously, before pointing at Lidia and Kitty, who were bouncing up and down on a very plush, very fancy-looking sofa in the back of the lobby. "Hey, can you get your teammates to stop that?"

I realized that Lidia and Kitty were putting on a show of sorts for some red-coated Regimental guys, who were crowded around the sofa, laughingly urging them to bounce higher. I recognized Carter and Denny but didn't see Jishnu among the group.

"Mary!" I whispered urgently. "Go tell those ding-dongs not to break the sofa already!"

I probably should have done the job myself, because instead of quietly getting Lidia and Kitty to stop, which was what I'd intended Mary to do, she gleefully called out in ringing tones that echoed across the lobby, "Lidia! Kitty! Stop that, you complete cretins! It's not like we can afford to replace it if you break it!"

"You're such a wet blanket, Mary!" screeched Kitty as Lidia actually stuck out her tongue in our direction. I wished the elegant slate floor would open up and swallow me right then and there.

As if that wasn't bad enough, Colin chose that moment to

point at the green, plant-covered lobby wall and bark out in a way-too-loud voice, "Are those hydroponic?"

The lobby was crowded with competing forensicators now, who all turned around to stare at Colin.

"Hydro-what-ic?" Ro looked both baffled and shocked, like Colin had asked her something pornographic.

"It's very exciting if Netherfield is doing hydroponic farming, or should I say horticulture. Actually, I guess I could say hydro-culture," chuckled Colin, and I knew he was about to launch into one of his interminable lectures. "You skip the soil and go straight to the actual growing in some type of nutrient-rich liquid. Are you using fish excrement for this system?"

"Fish excrement?" Ro looked horrified, and the other students helping her at the desk started to laugh.

The girls were like clones of Ro, even though one had brown hair and the other black. They were both thin, clear skinned, even featured, white, and had their hair hanging iron straight from a middle part. I touched my own curly locks, wondering if Netherfield had a policy against accepting people with anything but bone-straight hair.

"Colin . . ." Tomi was saying gently, "I'm not sure that Ro knows the nutrient used in the plants."

But Colin acted as if she hadn't even spoken, barreling on, "If not fish excrement, maybe it's duck manure?"

The girls next to Ro Bingley were howling with laughter now.

I thought I was going to absolutely die of mortification when a deep, familiar voice called out, "It's actually a chemical nutrient solution, with the roots supported physically by perlite."

It was Darcy. He was standing in the lobby next to the wall of green looking as dapper as ever. I felt like punching him in his perfect nose.

"Perlite!" Colin was saying, touching one of the hanging fronds with something approaching awe. "I was going to guess gravel."

Darcy nodded at the rest of us in a general way. "Welcome to Netherfield Academy. I hope you have a good contest day."

"Have you seen Bingley?" Jay asked eagerly. "Ro said to ask you where he was."

"She did?" Darcy blinked a couple of times, before finally saying, "He's out running some last-minute errands."

"Errands?" Jay repeated.

"Getting some allergy meals for judges," said Darcy briefly. "That sort of thing."

"Oh, okay," Jay said, pulling out his phone from his pocket. "I'll just text him I'm here."

As Jay walked away, I turned on Darcy. "It's interesting that Bingley's not here, even though he said he would be. I wonder who could have sent him on those errands? Not the president of his team, maybe?"

Darcy raised an eyebrow. "What exactly are you accusing me of, Leela? Making up people's gluten and nut allergies?"

I bit my lip. "I'm not accusing you of anything."

"That didn't seem to be the case last weekend outside your high school. You seemed to be accusing me of a lot of things." Darcy fidgeted with his cuffs under his blazer. "Do you always believe the long-winded sob stories of near strangers?"

"Only when they're consistent with what I know of someone's character," I hissed, suddenly conscious of the fact that our conversation was attracting the attention of those around us.

"And you never change your opinion about people once it's set, I imagine?" Darcy's eyes flashed suddenly as he looked up at me. I realized they weren't entirely brown but had shots of hazel and gold running through them.

"Oh, no. My good opinion, once lost, is lost forever." I wasn't even sure I believed them, but the words tumbled from my mouth as if written by another.

"Well, that is a failing of character indeed," said Darcy, his face once again implacable.

I resisted the impulse to kick the guy.

"Every character has a tendency to some particular evil, don't you agree?" I asked, again feeling as if the words were coming from a space and time beyond me. I spread my arms, indicating the ostentatious richness of the Netherfield Academy lobby. "Something that even the best education can't overcome?"

"I really can't laugh at that." And with that incomprehensible proclamation, Darcy turned sharply on his heel and walked away.

CHAPTER 22

A S IF THE encounter with Darcy wasn't enough to throw me off my game, the next thing I realized was that Jishnu wasn't even attending the Netherfield Academy forensics meet.

"I think he felt like he might be unwelcome here," said Carter, one of the Regimental boys Kitty and Lidia had gotten a PhD in flirtation with.

We were all still in the fancy lobby, hanging out before our first rounds of competition began.

"But he didn't mention anything to me." I stared at my cell phone, as if it would give me an answer. "He could have said he wasn't planning on coming."

"He might have felt bad about disappointing you?" suggested Carter.

"Why would Jishnu feel unwelcome here?" Kitty had stopped bouncing on the lobby sofa but was still kind of sprawled over it next to Lidia.

"Because he used to go here and had to leave." Denny, the

other Regimental dude, nodded in my direction. "He told you about that, right?"

Lidia sat up, her eyes getting round like shining saucers. "Are you telling me that Jishnu used to go here before he went to Regimental? Netherfield Academy?" She spread her arms, indicating the splendor all around us.

Carter scratched his pale, pimply nose. "I don't know a lot about why he left. He's very private about it."

"I think something went down between him and the administration. Why else would he come to a military academy?" laughed Denny, pulling at his uniform collar. "We all screwed up in some way in our other schools."

"Not me," said Carter. "I'm at Regimental because my dad went there too. I'm going to apply to the naval academy, like him. We're a military family all the way."

"Spill it, Leela," demanded Lidia, now standing up to confront me. "What did Jishnu do to get him kicked out of this gorgeous place?"

"He didn't do anything! He had to leave because he couldn't afford it." I hesitated, not sure if I should say any more. "It was actually Darcy's family that was helping him pay tuition, and they stopped."

Denny screwed up his beefy face in a quizzical expression. "Jishnu told you that?"

I nodded significantly. "And more."

"That Darcy's kind of a jerk, huh?" Kitty looked in the direction that he'd just left the lobby. The environmentally sound lights overhead glinted softly off her braces.

"Rich people can afford to give offense wherever they go," I said simply.

"Weird, though, that Jishnu would have to leave school for that," Lidia mused. "Don't these schools help you pay once you're in? And how is he affording Regimental? That's not public either, right?"

"I don't know," said Carter with a smile. "Regimental's not free, that's for sure. But I think there's a lot of scholarships, that sort of thing."

Denny patted my arm with his big hand, saying in a low voice, "He said to tell you sorry that he couldn't be here."

I nodded. "Thanks. Tell him I missed him."

The rest of my day went sort of downhill from there. I actually felt prepared for the November-December debate topic: *Resolved—Universities requiring standardized testing for admission is an elitist practice.* I did feel like standardized testing was elitist. These were tests that had been designed with a certain sort of privileged student in mind, and it was shown that working-class students, students of color, and students who were first generation applying to college all did worse on these tests on the average. I mean, who had the time or money or know-how to spend on SAT or ACT prep books, classes, or tutors? Who had the money to take these tests again if they didn't like their original scores?

When I found out I was assigned the affirmative side for my first ever Lincoln-Douglas debate round, I initially felt a surge of confidence. I had a well-developed affirmative argument I had researched and really believed in. Even though I knew none of the Netherfield team would be debating today, there was something about arguing against elitism and privilege while standing in these environmentally sound, architecturally pristine spaces that really appealed to me. There was no way I could lose.

My assigned room was in the super-fancy all-glass science annex of the upper school. I walked down a set of wide-planked wooden stairs with metal handrails, by some café-style tables and an all-glass-enclosed computer lab. I had to admit, the resources of Netherfield Academy were a little overwhelming. On my way to my debate room, I passed science labs that were equipped like colleges, mathematics rooms with floor-to-ceiling whiteboards covered in equations, and even a "maker space" with half-constructed robots all over the benches as well as what looked like a bunch of 3D printers along one wall. I felt a pang of nerdy longing inside me. What I wouldn't give to be able to learn in a place like this!

When I got to my assigned room and opened the door, I realized that the judge, who was a coach from a different team, and my opponent were already chatting. They were in the middle of laughing over something in such a familiar way, it was obvious they somehow knew each other already.

"Well, hello there, young lady," said the judge, not unkindly. "Are you in the right room? This is Lincoln-Douglas debate."

He was younger than I'd thought when I first walked in, kind of a hip, beardy guy in his mid-twenties probably. He looked a bit like he would live in Brooklyn if he didn't teach in New Jersey, and that maybe he enjoyed drinking artisanal beers in his free time.

"Yes, I know. I'm here to argue the affirmative," I said, putting down my bag on the free table across from my opponent, a suit-wearing kid who, despite his tiny, unfashionable glasses, had an air of the corporate raider about him. I took out my laptop and noticed that my opponent kind of sneered at all the feminist stickers I had on it—from a uterus with a raised fist to Frida Kahlo's eyebrows to an image of Ruth Bader Ginsburg. "I'm Leela Bose."

"Bose! Like the speakers!" said the judge, looking up from his judging ballots with my name spelled on them. He pronounced my last name with a hard *s*, almost *z*-like sound. "Love those noise-cancellation headphones of yours. Any chance you can get me a family discount?"

I laughed. It was a comment I was used to hearing. "No relation, sadly."

My opponent, the corporate raider kid whose name was Arthur, chuckled. "Well, obviously. Bose is a German company."

I looked up sharply from organizing my notes but kept my voice sweet. "So how do you know I'm not German?'"

"Well." Arthur flailed his hands in my general direction. "I'm making an assumption based on your appearance."

I felt myself bristle but tried to keep the hostility out of my voice. "Amar Bose, the guy who founded the speaker company, was Bengali. I think his mom was European, but the last name, it's Indian, Bengali. Like mine."

"That's not true. Bose is a German company," the judge said firmly. He stretched out his legs before him, his arms folded around his head. "I mean, that country knows its electronics. I told you, I love those noise-cancellation headphones."

"A lifesaver on planes, am I right?" said annoying Arthur. I wondered how a kid in high school could afford such expensive things.

"Germany could know their electronics," I said, feeling my irritation grow. "But Bose Corporation was founded by Amar Bose, an Indian-American Bengali guy from MIT."

"Why don't you look it up after the round," said Arthur with a condescending smile.

The nerve! Why were they assuming I wouldn't know when Bose was literally my last name and the guy literally shared my ethnicity?

"Why don't *you* look it up right now?" I snapped.

The judge exchanged bemused looks with my opponent, and I wasn't sure, but I thought I caught him actually rolling his eyes at Arthur.

"If you're done having your little temper tantrum about a German speaker company, it's time to begin," said the judge. And that's when I knew everything was going south. I was starting to understand what Mary had been talking about regarding the sexism of debate. It felt like the judge and Arthur were on one team, and I on another.

It wasn't a great way to begin my first ever debate round. Still, I thought I argued my points well. "Tests like the SAT and ACT, in which wealthy white students tend to score better, maintain the social hierarchy by guaranteeing children of privilege access to better educations," I said, gripping the smooth wood lectern so tightly my fingers later ached.

I went on for my allotted six minutes as the affirmative speaker, talking about the cost of tutoring and test prep, the ability to afford to take a test more than once. I spoke quickly, but unlike most debaters, I didn't rely on fast-spat-out facts. Colin and

Tomi had drilled me on the rules of LD debate, so I knew how to support my case with certain criteria. I knew not to look at my opponent when we spoke. I was as well prepared as I possibly could be. I took notes on the other debater's points. I presented cogent and well-thought-out counterarguments. Yet it felt like trying to race up quicksand. Even a strong runner, well trained and at the peak of their athletic prowess, can't run very fast if the ground is giving way right under their feet.

Every time I said something, the judge scribbled on his ballot furiously. Meanwhile, when Arthur spoke, either cross-examining me or presenting his own arguments, the same judge nodded and smiled, hardly noting down anything.

Afterward, I was sure I'd lost the round. And the experience felt more humiliating than I'd realized it would. The beautiful ergonomic chairs, the European-looking wall clock, even the fancy mathematical equations still on the floor-to-ceiling white-board from some weekday math class seemed to be mocking me. I couldn't help feeling crushed, even as I said, "Thank you for judging," and walked out of the room.

CHAPTER 23

COLIN WAS WAITING outside in the hallway for me.

"What are you doing here?" I asked, unsettled. I looked around. "Where's Tomi? She told me she'd come by after my first round."

"I told her I'd come by and see you. She's always running around so much."

I was impressed with Colin's thoughtfulness as we walked over to one of the high café-style tables I'd seen as I walked into the science building.

"I wanted to come and see how your first debate went." He awkwardly perched up on one of the stools at the table, wobbling a bit as he did so.

"I'm not sure." I told him about the judge's behavior, the weird conversation before the round. This wasn't like at big tournaments, where they told LD debaters at the end of each round who won, in order to more fairly match debaters of similar win-loss records, I wouldn't get any feedback until the end of the day.

Colin frowned. "I should tell you to try to stay away from

extraneous chitchat with your judges before the round. But I really think the way he behaved was unprofessional. I will have to refer to the National Forensics Association Handbook, but I believe the rules for judging and impartiality are rather clear."

I really didn't want to hear anything more about the National Forensics Association Handbook but had no way of saying that. So I just nodded, feeling deflated. "Okay, thanks."

"It might have been a new judge, I'll find out," Colin assured me, adjusting his glasses on his face. "But in the meantime, take heart! You get to argue the negative now!"

But the negative was the point of view I was dreading. I'd done my research; I'd made a ton of notes. But did I really *believe* what I was saying? Could I argue that universities using standardized tests was *not* an elitist practice?

I nodded, forcing myself to smile at him as he waved me goodbye. "All right, here goes nothing!"

I was nervous, but Colin was right; my second round of LD felt far less awful. There was no weird banter before the round, and so I could focus on the actual experience of the debate itself. Which felt, surprisingly, kinda cool.

"Standardized testing in college entrance is no more elitist than college itself," I argued, willing my voice to be steady and my hands not to shake.

Even though I was arguing the negative position, I built my argument on ideas I believed in, that everyone who wanted to improve their mind should be given a chance to do so. I used the writings of a Brazilian thinker called Paulo Freire who wrote about education as liberation to argue that it wasn't necessarily the standardized test itself that was the problem, but rather the equal time and means to prepare for it.

I licked my lips, not even needing to look down at my notes as I went on. "My opponent has argued that eliminating standardized testing is a means to achieve educational equality. I would argue it is hardly that, if that same marginalized student who has managed to gain entrance to an elite college because they didn't have to take a biased standardized test, then cannot actually afford to attend the college in question."

I didn't want to admit it, even to myself, but Darcy had been at least partially right. It was nice not to be acting out someone else's words, but speaking my own thoughts, feelings, and sentences. I still had to rely on my theater skills—projection, eye contact, putting conviction in my voice—but it felt really different to be discussing things I actually cared about, like education and equal opportunities available to all. I was starting to see why debaters liked it.

I looked straight at the judge, willing him to understand my argument. "Getting into college is not a mark of educational equity—being able to afford attending college is that mark."

The judge nodded, noting something down, and I felt my heart soar. For a weird, brief moment, it reminded me of arguing with Darcy in the lobby that first night of the Phillips College competition. I felt electric and alive. A little part of me wanted to sing the theme song from *Fame*.

Looking at my time, I barreled on, "For education to be a real opportunity for all, what we need is free and equitable access to not only preparatory classes for standardized tests; we need free and equitable access to higher education, period. Debt forgiveness, free community college, need-blind admissions—these are the real doorways to liberatory education."

As I said these words, I felt myself humming with energy, my brain on fire. Even though my natural inclination was to agree with the affirmative argument, that standardized testing should be eliminated in college applications, arguing the opposite viewpoint actually allowed me to explore far more exciting ideas.

I thought about Jishnu, and how he'd had to drop out of an excellent educational institution like Netherfield, all because he didn't come from a rich family and was dependent on the Darcys' whimsical charity. I thought about how different Longbourn's facilities, books, equipment, and probably teachers were from what I'd seen in just a couple of hours at Netherfield. How could someone like me—no matter how smart and ambitious I was— ever compete with what someone like Firoze Darcy had handed to them on a silver platter?

My third round of debate, in which I was back to arguing the affirmative, started out well. The room was hot, and the judge, an elderly woman, didn't want to open the windows or turn down the heat. So I took off my sweater and laid it on the chair behind me.

As the round went on, I realized there was an undercurrent in the room I couldn't place my finger on. My opponent kept furtively looking over at me and smirking. Finally, I realized he was staring straight at my chest. What was going on here? I felt like stopping the debate and screaming at him to keep his eyes to himself, but I couldn't. I just had to keep going. Did the judge not see what was going on?

I paused, frowning, realizing he'd made me lose my train of thought. I coughed, shook my head, and fumbled with my computer for a second. I felt the heat rise to my face as I knew I was losing grip on the argument I'd just been making. I felt even worse when I saw the judge frown, shake her head, and mark something down on her ballot.

It wasn't until the round itself was over and I was leaving the room that I realized what all his smirking had been about. Because that was when my opponent kind of squeezed by me unnecessarily closely through the doorway, muttering, "Nice bra."

As he said the words, he was so close I could smell the protein bar he'd had before the round on his breath. I felt repulsed, but also frozen in my tracks. By the time my brain turned back on and I remembered to keep walking, my opponent was already halfway down the hall, swinging his leather debate briefcase. I watched him as he high-fived some teammate who'd been waiting for him.

I looked down and realized that my light pink bra was slightly visible through my white shirt. The shirt wasn't even that see-through, but somehow, there was something about the way he'd been smirking, the way he'd said "nice bra" that made my skin crawl. It made me feel like I'd been naked back there during the entirety of the debate round.

I put my backpack down on the floor and threw my sweater back on. I was reeling. How could I have been so stupid as to wear anything but a white bra this morning? Why hadn't I looked at myself in the mirror without my sweater on? I don't know how, but with that one little comment, this guy had made me feel small, and unprofessional, and dirty. I felt slammed back into my always-inadequate body.

It's not that guys hadn't been jerks to me before in school or on the road, but this felt different, worse somehow, because it was so quiet. Guys screaming lewd things at you from a construction site felt awful, yes. But this? This felt like those same guys had come into the privacy of my mind and heart and done the same thing. I felt a hot rush of shame flow through me as I stood there in the Netherfield Academy hallway like some kind of statue, not knowing what to say or do.

CHAPTER 24

L UNCH BROUGHT WITH it no sense of relief. I entered the fancy Netherfield cafeteria in a grim mood, only to be confronted by the unbelievable sights of a sushi bar and a charcuterie station.

And then things went from bad to worse. "Are you finding everything you need?" said a deep voice at my elbow.

It was Darcy, of course. Always showing up like a bad penny just when I was feeling at my lowest.

"Gosh, the pâté you have is so substandard," I replied unnecessarily harshly. "And no sashimi? Only rolls? What kind of a cheap joint is this?"

Darcy's polite smile faded. "Are you all right? Did you have an okay morning? You switched to LD this tournament, right?"

"How did you know that?" I picked up a tray, putting some precut veggies and hummus on it almost without looking.

"I was in charge of most of the scheduling today," Darcy explained, walking alongside me with his hands behind his back like a solicitous waiter. "I am the president of the team."

I threw one of those way-overpriced flavored fizzy waters on my tray with unnecessary violence. "This morning only confirmed my initial suspicions that you debaters are complete goons."

"Some definitely can be." Darcy tilted his head at me as I slammed some sushi rolls on my tray as well. "What do you think of this month's new topic?"

"I actually like it," I admitted almost against my will. Mindlessly, I grabbed a beautiful raspberry confection of a dessert from the display case. "I thought I wouldn't enjoy arguing both positions, but I actually did. In fact, I liked the neg a lot more than I thought I would."

"What did you argue?" Darcy scooched a bit closer to me to let a gaggle of loudly talking competitors from the Meryton team push by us toward the cashiers.

"That it's not just standardized testing that inequitable, it's the price of higher education altogether." I put my hand on my hip and stared at him, daring him to contradict me.

"That makes a lot of sense." Darcy's handsome face was relaxed and attentive, and he had a little smile playing on his lips. I felt something flip nauseatingly in my stomach. Probably an anticipatory reaction to bad sushi.

I turned back to my full tray. Without saying anything, I started slamming all the dishes I'd picked up onto the display shelves.

Darcy reacted with concern. "Wait, don't you want that? That raspberry trifle is delicious!"

"It's too expensive." I felt a sense of fury I couldn't control.

"Sushi, fizzy water, prosciutto wrapped around melon balls! I mean, do you people even get how elitist all this is?"

"You've got to eat something!" Darcy argued. "I mean, I've got some extra judges' lunches in the back if you didn't bring—"

"I don't need your charity!" I hissed, putting just the little tray of six sushi rolls back on my tray, along with a plain water, which was still overpriced. "And I don't need your pity!"

Darcy nodded, and I expected that we were done talking, but like the weirdo he obviously was, he followed me silently toward the cashier. When I noticed him making a little negative head motion to the lady behind the register, I whirled on him, practically impaling him with my (probably) ethically sourced bamboo cafeteria tray.

"Don't you even *dare* pay for me," I snapped. "I told you I didn't need your charity!"

"The thought never crossed my mind!" Darcy protested.

"Give me a break, I saw that little look you just gave her," I returned.

"Cross my heart!" Darcy made an X over his chest. His face was utterly serious. "And hope to die, stick a needle in my thigh."

I stared at him. "Eye."

"What?" He raised his dark eyebrows at me.

"Stick a needle in my eye, not *thigh*," I explained, feeling irritated. "How did you never learn that? Have you been saying 'stick a needle in my thigh' this whole time?"

"Well, 'eye' does make more sense, I guess," Darcy mused. "Although it does sound terribly painful."

It occurred to me that this might be the closest Firoze Darcy would ever come to telling a joke. Was this jerk actually trying to make me feel better? "You are such a weirdo."

I was being unreasonably snippy, I knew. Darcy was trying to be nice, I could see, but it was totally a case of too little too late. I didn't know why he got me so hot under the collar. If Tomi or Jay had asked me why I was laying into Firoze Darcy so much, I would tell them it was because of what he'd done to Jishnu. But the truth was, this whole time we'd been arguing, I hadn't thought of Jishnu once.

As I finished paying way too much for my rolls and water, I picked up my tray and turned toward Darcy. "I'm going to go find my team now. You don't have to follow me."

Darcy gave me a slight bow with his head. "As you wish," he said simply.

I turned sharply. "*The Princess Bride?*"

"I watched it after that one time you mentioned it. It's very good. Anyway, have fun storming the castle!" he said as he sauntered away.

He watched it after that one time I mentioned it? I walked in kind of a daze to the table with the rest of my team. What did it mean when a guy you hated watched a movie you had passingly talked about? Why had he done that? It couldn't be something so mundane as him *liking* me, could it? No, no way. It was undoubtedly some kind of long-game mind-control thing that Darcy was playing at. That had to be it.

Well, he'd see how manipulatable I was when I finally got to debate him. I dug into my sushi, imagining how heady it would feel to crush the unflappable Mr. Darcy in debate. A few rolls later, I sighed, rubbing my aching neck. Even my anticipatory joy at beating Darcy couldn't make up for how soul-crushingly crappy at least two of today's rounds had been.

The rest of lunch continued to be strange. Jay was still not really talking to me but glued to his phone, and Tomi was busy being presidential, checking in on how our other teammates' rounds had gone. Mary was crying again, and I honestly felt like joining her. I couldn't talk about the weird bra thing to anyone without feeling like a complete fool, so I kept it to myself as I miserably ate my sushi.

I was just staring at the empty sushi carton, still feeling hungry, when the cashier lady came by our table.

"You forgot this, miss," she said, dropping the raspberry desert in front of me.

"No, I didn't pay for this," I protested.

"But that sweet boy Firoze did," she explained as she walked away, smiling. "Said it was yours, and that I was not to accept any returns. He bought me one too!" She pointed to her cash register, to show where she had an identical raspberry trifle waiting for her.

"Thank you!" I stared at the dish of raspberries, meringue, cake, and cream like it was some kind of bomb about to go off.

It was lucky that no one else at the table was paying enough attention to hear the woman mention "that sweet boy Firoze" with so much affection. So it was just me facing down my dessert, feeling the emotions churning in my stomach.

"Are you going to eat that or can I have it?" Mary asked suddenly, eyeing the pretty dish.

At first, I was tempted to give the blasted thing to Mary. Then to maybe just throw it to the floor in a dramatic sign of protest. But unfortunately, my stomach rumbled. And I realized that a girl cannot live on spite and symbolic gestures alone.

"I'm going to eat it." I picked up my spoon as if in slow motion and dug into the creamy confection. I lifted the bite to my mouth equally slowly, sighing as I did. "It's kind of amazing."

"I'm going to go get one," said Mary, rising from the table.

"Me too!" said Lidia as she and Kitty joined Mary.

I finished my raspberry dessert in a kind of Zen rapture, before getting up from the table to bus my tray. Tomi was in a deep huddle with Colin and the Bennets, and Jay was sutured to his phone—probably texting Bingley, I guessed.

I was just about to leave the cafeteria and head to the ladies' room when I realized someone was following me.

"Wait up, Leela!"

CHAPTER 25

I TURNED AROUND and saw that it was Colin, huffing and puffing as he ran after me. He looked like he was sweating inside his too-tight olive-green suit.

As soon as I saw him, I got a bad feeling. Clearly, the bad vibes of the Netherfield competition weren't done with me yet. I thought with a lurch about how attentive Colin had been to me lately, supporting my switch to LD and showing up after my first round. I remembered how Jay had once teased me at the Hartford High competition about Colin having a crush on me.

"What's up, Colin?" I tugged at my own shirt collar, glad for the coverage, if not the warmth, of Tomi's sweater over it.

"Can we talk?" He was licking at his dry lips. Someone really ought to tell him about ChapStick.

"I guess." Better to get this over with sooner than later. But also better to do this away from prying ears. I indicated a nice-looking bench right outside the cafeteria doorway.

"I think I know what you want to say to me," I said as Colin stood awkwardly over the bench, fidgeting.

"You do?" Colin looked relieved. "I'm so glad, I wasn't sure how to bring it up. This isn't easy for me." He let out a big breath and suddenly plunged down to one knee.

"Don't do that!" I wanted to leap up, but Colin was too close. He was both kneeling and clasping his hands together before him, as if begging me for something. His round face was all lit up with emotion.

"Leela, let me assure you, I have too much respect for you not to make my request plain," Colin said in a rushed, unnatural way. "I wanted to state clearly my reasons for wanting to obtain a girlfriend."

"Obtain a girlfriend"? This guy really needed to work on his delivery. Did he think girlfriends were electronic goods to be picked up at a box store?

"I don't think you need to state your reasons," I said in what I hoped was an "I'm letting you down lightly" sort of voice. "I think I know."

"No, I've been practicing, let me do this." Colin said enthusiastically. "My reasons for wanting to have a girlfriend, are, firstly, that I've turned eighteen now, and although I've had a few crushes, I feel like a serious girlfriend is perhaps the next step in my maturation as a teenager."

"You've been practicing?" I burbled, an uncontrollable giggle escaping my throat.

"Second." Colin was still on one knee, counting on his fingers. "I am convinced that having a girlfriend will add very greatly indeed to my happiness."

"Um, Colin?" I felt near hysterical, but the speech competitor in me couldn't help asking a question. "You've seriously planned this speech out and memorized it?"

Colin looked both surprised and pleased. "Well, obviously, I've been thinking about this for a while, but I wanted to say it to you. So you could tell me if it had as spontaneous and nonstudied an air as possible."

Um, what? I had absolutely no idea what to make of that last statement. Had Colin lost his mind? Or was his attraction to me just so strong he couldn't help himself? Was I one of those she-creatures from a fantasy story with the extra-powerful pheromones or something?

"And thirdly, which maybe I should have mentioned earlier," Colin said in a rush, "it was the strictest recommendation of my elocution coach, the world-renowned Professor Catherine de Bourgh."

"Your elocution coach?" I choked out.

"I was at her offices on the Rosings College campus last week, and in between instructing me on how to roll my *r*'s with an appropriate timbre, she said to me, 'Colin, my boy, what are you doing with your spare time? You can't simply be involved in extracurricular activities; to be a well-rounded applicant for college, a teenager must date! Choose a girlfriend whose behavior you respect, not someone brought up too high, not someone too experienced or too pretty, but someone decent-looking with a good, solid character and, of course, clear diction.'" Colin paused self-consciously. "Maybe I shouldn't have mentioned the thing about being too pretty. Let me assure you, Leela, no matter what anyone else says, I think the object of my affections is very attractive."

"Thank you?!" I was sure I had passed into a surreal fugue state. Had there been psychedelic drugs in my sushi? Or was this the Bad Place? Was my head even attached to my body anymore?

Colin went on, "And now nothing remains but for me to reassure you in the most animated language of the violence of my affection . . ."

"Colin, stop," I protested. "What you're talking about is completely impossible."

"What?" Colin looked shocked. "Is it my speech? Is it the thing about not being traditionally pretty? Is it my breath?" Much to my chagrin, Colin did that thing where he breathed into his hand and inhaled. "Please don't think that a lack of experience or dating history is a problem for me," Colin went on in what I assumed he thought was an uplifting way.

"Colin, you're a sweet guy," I tried again. Where was a miracle when you needed one? Like the hallway floor opening up and zooming me to the ninth circle of hell or whatever? Surely nothing Dante had imagined was worse torture than this. "But let me repeat, nothing is going to happen between us!"

Colin frowned, sitting back on his heels. I felt horrible. Obviously, I'd devastated him. "What did you say?"

I leaned forward, taking his slightly clammy hand in mine in what I hoped was a sisterly way. "I know it's hard to hear, because I really do like you, Colin. But I could never *like* like you."

Colin blinked at me. Was he going to cry? He licked his dry lips yet again. "Why are you saying this? I think you might have misunderstood my point."

Oh, bollocks, he was clearly not going to take this well. I

leaped up finally from the bench, forcibly pushing Colin to make room. The poor boy fell backward onto his not-inconsiderable butt. I realized with sudden horror that we had attracted a bit of a crowd, who were watching us from the entrance to the cafeteria.

"Colin, we're never going to date," I said in a bit too loud a voice. The day's stresses were making me feel like I was made of glass, brittle and about to break. "I like you. I really do. But romantically, you would never make me happy and I'm convinced I'm the last person who could make you happy. And were your elocution coach, Professor de Burgh, to meet me, I'm sure she would agree!"

Colin slowly got up off the floor, his expression bewildered. "I think we might be in the midst of a serious misunderstanding. I wasn't asking you to be my girlfriend, Leela."

A flash of cold horror went through me. "You weren't? Then what were you doing there on the floor?" I asked accusingly.

"I was begging for your help as I press my suit with . . . someone else," Colin mumbled, his ears now bright red and his face excessively sweaty.

I wasn't sure whether to believe him. Was this just one of those manly face-saving things that dudes did? Well, even if it was, it probably didn't make sense to do anything but agree. Let the poor chap down gently, as it were.

"Sorry for the misunderstanding," I said in as gracious a way as possible. I really should have my pheromones tested. Maybe scientists could use them in some way for humanity's good?

Colin muttered, in uncharacteristically poor diction, "I'm

sorry, I thought . . . but obviously I was mistaken. I will trouble you no further."

As Colin finally walked off, I heard a tittering from the crowd around us.

"Nothing to see here, folks! We were just practicing for a dramatic duo performance!" I said, completely sure no one would believe the lie.

The tittering grew louder. I pushed back my hair and picked up my bag, only realizing, with utter horror, that the Netherfield team was a part of the people who had been watching our embarrassing scene. Which made the titterer, of course, none other than Ro Bingley.

That meant, naturally, that the person next to her was Firoze Darcy. He met my eyes gravely just as I felt my cheeks blooming with embarrassment. With a choking, ungraceful squeak, I picked up my bag and ran down the hallway.

CHAPTER 26

THE REST OF the Netherfield competition was tense, to say the least. For obvious reasons, I spent most of the day avoiding Colin.

Since this was a school competition in our local league, there were four rounds of debate only and no semifinal or final rounds. At least it wasn't one of those cutthroat competitions where the losing debater got cut after every round. That would have been humiliating. The timing was such that I actually got to go see the speech finals, so I went to see Tomi's final round in original oratory, which she absolutely smashed. Her speech, which was about being an ambitious woman, was a combination of poetry by greats like Anzaldúa and Audre Lorde, and her own prose. When she used Anzaldúa's metaphor to talk about her own body being a borderland, it straight up brought tears to the eyes of everyone in the room. I'd never been more proud of her. She seemed so quiet and steady in person, but when she was performing, Tomi transformed into someone else. Not someone else exactly, a more perfect version of herself. I guess that's what speech and debate did for all of us.

Unfortunately, Colin was there in the audience too, so it made for some awkward trying-to-avoid-eye-contact moments. I felt alternately furious at him for his ridiculous public display of affection, and furious at myself for not having seen it coming. For his part, he pretended like I wasn't even in the room, which suited me just fine.

Since Tomi was the first person to go in her round, I was able to sneak out after her performance to go see Jay's final round in dramatic interpretation. He was doing a piece from *The Piano Lesson* which I'd seen him perform so many times before, I could almost recite it with him. But I wasn't alone in the room watching Jay. Even though Bingley was nowhere to be seen, Darcy was incomprehensibly there, sitting in the back, watching Jay so intensely it was like he was one of the judges. What was he doing here? And why did he look so darned grim?

I tried to ignore him and concentrate on Jay's amazing performance. When Jay said the line about everyone having stones in their way, and that we should walk over or around them, but not carry them with us, I choked up a little.

"All you got to do is set them down by the side of the road. You ain't got to carry them with you," said Jay in his clear voice, his face pained and expressive.

I wondered about what burdens in my life I should set down. I felt like the unvarnished racism I'd experienced in my early years had messed with my internal instrumental system somehow— making it hard for me to distinguish what was reality and what was deep-rooted self-hating insecurity. What was it that Tomi had said? That I rushed to judgment about people too fast? Was that because of that childhood stone I had yet to figure out how to put down?

At the end of the round, I walked tentatively up to Jay, wanting to congratulate him, wanting to give him a hug, but not sure if he was ready yet to forgive and forget.

"You were great," I said softly, very conscious of Darcy still standing like some kind of gloomy crow in the back of the room.

"Thanks," Jay said shortly, and I could tell he was still holding on to his anger like one of those stones he'd just been talking about.

"Were you able to get in touch with Bingley?" I crossed my fingers that he had.

Jay shook his head, looking daggers at me. "He hasn't even answered a single one of my texts today. So thanks a ton for that."

My stomach tensed up. Jay obviously blamed me for whatever was going wrong between him and Bingley. And I, in turn, blamed Darcy. If only he hadn't treated Jishnu the way he had. If only he hadn't provoked me into that fight outside Longbourn last week. If only he hadn't said that thing about me not being beautiful enough to tempt him the first time we'd met. If only I'd never met the infuriating guy, my best friend would still be talking to me.

I shot my eyes back accusingly to where Darcy had been standing, ready to confront him, ready to ask him why he had been able to come to Jay's final if Bingley hadn't. Unfortunately, by the time I turned around, he was gone.

There was no sign of Bingley at the end of competition day awards ceremony either, which was seriously fishy.

"He's ghosting me," breathed Jay as he returned to his seat after collecting his second-place DI trophy. "He's actually ghosting me."

He looked so upset, I reached over and squeezed his arm, not caring if he was still mad at me, not caring that this was the first awards ceremony in over a year in which my name hadn't been called. "I'm sure there's a logical explanation. I'm sure Bingley's mislaid his phone, or he's been super busy today with running the tournament, or something."

Yet none of this explained why we'd seen Ro, Darcy, and a bunch of their other teammates all day. Was Bingley really too busy to even attend the awards ceremony?

"I was blaming Darcy, but this must be something real." Jay was biting his lip, as if pushing back tears. "He's just not interested in me and is too nice of a guy to say so directly."

"I can't believe that." I put on an encouraging voice. "I think you'll get back in touch and then he'll be back in love with you sooner than you think!"

Jay gave me a withering look, full of so much loathing I almost took a step backward to get away from its force. "Shut up, Leela. You know what? Just shut up and leave me alone!"

I felt like bursting into tears, but they dried up as soon as I saw him—the root of all my problems: Darcy. Jay might be convinced this had nothing to do with him, but I wasn't so sure. Bingley was a sweet guy but way too dependent on his friend's good opinion. I knew that Darcy had somehow convinced his best friend to drop mine. This was all on him. I just knew it.

As I stared back at him across the auditorium rows, Darcy

caught my eye and gave a little mocking bow before sauntering off. Just that little gesture got my blood pressure boiling. Oh, I hated that guy so much. And I was going to figure out a way to make him pay for all the pain he'd caused me and mine.

But first, I'd have to deal with all the people who hated me on my own team.

CHAPTER 27

THE TRIP BACK home to Longbourn was stressful, as the first thing I saw was Colin sitting in a defeated heap in the very first row of the bus.

"Colin, I . . ." I tried to say, but he just turned his head away from me.

"I should go make sure he's okay," Tomi had said to me before sliding into the seat next to him. "He is my vice president, after all."

I didn't feel like dealing with Jay, and so I found myself a seat somewhere near the middle of the still-cold bus, near where Mary was slouched, head fully inside her coat hood. So it was her I turned to when Mr. Bennet walked up the bus aisle as he always did post-competition, handing out our ballots—the evaluations we each received from the judges. The coach hesitated a second before handing me my ballots—he'd obviously already looked at them.

"Leela, I don't want you to take these comments to heart. Especially those by the first- or the third-round judge," he said gravely.

"What did they say?" I felt my heart beating in frightened anticipation.

"Smile more!" Mary was shouting in the seat next to me. "They told me *again* to smile more!"

I quickly looked over the ballots that Mr. Bennet had handed me. There were comments and suggestions regarding my arguments, my use of time, the way I'd supported my assertions with certain values or not. But then, at the bottom, were some additional comments.

> **ROUND 1: AFFIRMATIVE**—Be sure not to appear quite so aggressive either before or during the round. You might consider toning down the shrillness too.

> **ROUND 3: AFFIRMATIVE**—Your inappropriate and immodest clothing choices distracted from your performance and were, in this judge's opinion, utterly unprofessional. Reconsider your style of dress prior to your next competition.

I stared at the ballots, feeling like I'd been slapped.

"What do they say?" Mary grabbed them out of my hand, then quickly skimmed the papers. Her mouth fell open. "Immodest clothing? Were you wearing something different than you're wearing now? You should protest this—that judge is confusing you with someone else!"

I shook my head, rubbing my now-throbbing temples. "No, she's right."

"What?" Tomi turned around from her seat in the front of the bus. "Someone told you the sweater I knit for you was inappropriate tournament wear?"

"I took off the sweater," I explained to basically the whole bus, as my entire team seemed to be listening now. "And I was wearing a white blouse under."

"So what?" Lidia demanded. "This is complete sexist bogusness!"

"No, it's my fault." I felt so embarrassed to have to admit this in front of the coaches, but there was no choice now. "I guess . . . I guess I didn't realize you could see my bra a little through the shirt. Under the lights of the room or whatever."

I choked up a little as I said this, the emotion of having been leered at by my opponent all flooding back to me. I felt so foolish, so cheap. The entire bus was quiet for a moment, and I felt them all judging me. How could I have been so stupid? How could I have been so naive? I felt like curling in on myself, taking up even less space, going on a quest to begin erasing my body again.

"I think I've realized LD maybe just isn't for me. I made a mistake. I'm going back to what I know, what I'm good at." I shut my eyes as the hot tears threatened to flood down my face. I opened them only when I felt someone's warm arm wrapping around my shoulder.

"Fork 'em!" Jay announced loudly, squeezing me tight to him. "Fork 'em, Leela! It was obviously an accident, and what bloody business is it of theirs anyway?"

"But LD, it's just too much . . ." I mumbled into his arm, feeling grateful he'd decided to forgive me, at least for now. "I think I'll just go back to speech categories."

"Don't let the haters have the last word!" Jay shook me a little. "Are you kidding me right now with this quitting stuff? Is this the same girl who is so hungry and ambitious to be the best version of herself, she's practically bursting out of her skin?"

"Leela Bose!" a different voice called out from the front of the bus. It was Mrs. Bennet. "If you are going to let one terrible ballot derail you like this, why, you're not the argumentative forensicator I thought you were."

"Two ballots!" I called to her in the rumbling dark.

"Even still!" Mrs. Bennet shouted back.

"I just feel so ridiculous for not realizing," I said, choking up again. "I mean, my opponent was staring at me the entire time, and I couldn't figure it out."

"That's harassment!" announced Lidia, who'd barreled down the aisle of the moving bus to squeeze in next to Mary.

"Sit down, miss!" called the bus driver.

Lidia made a little sound of protest, then went on, "It's all a part of the sexist clothing industrial complex—I mean, don't show your bra or your bra strap, don't wear your skirt too short, don't show your belly, don't be distracting to boys."

I had the strong feeling Lidia may have been reprimanded for doing one or all of those things in school. She sounded like she was speaking from experience.

"How about instead of telling girls what to wear, we tell boys to stop being so damn distractible?" Mary piped up.

"Exactly," Tomi shouted back from her seat. "This is ridiculous, Leela. I don't care if you were JUST wearing your bra in competition!"

"Well, to be honest, I wouldn't tell any of my competitors to just wear a bra . . ." Mrs. Bennet began.

"I believe she's simply making a point, Mrs. B!" Colin called out. I was glad to hear he sounded like his usual self.

"Now gimme those ballots, girl," Jay demanded, grabbing them from my hand.

"Give 'em back!" I tried to reach them, but Jay's arm was too long. "Jay, don't. I want to read those more carefully!"

He jumped up from the seat, earning himself a reprimand from the driver.

"Everyone's got to sit down while the bus is in motion!" he called.

"Sir, I'm terribly sorry!" Jay yelled formally, before sitting down again. He had the ballots up in one arm while the other was holding me off. "But this is a mission of justice."

And then, with a dramatic gesture, Jay ripped up my ballots, scattering them over me like rain. There rose a cheer from my teammates.

"Fork 'em!" called Jay again.

"Spoon 'em too!" yelled Tomi.

"Knife 'em!" suggested Kitty, to many cheers from everyone else.

"You're going to have to keep it down, kids!" yelled the frustrated bus driver.

"Team!" the shrill voice of Mrs. Bennet called out, and we all quieted down.

The rest of the ride home, I rested my head on Jay's shoulder. "Thanks, my brother," I said softly. All around us, our teammates had finally calmed down, and the rumbling of the bus driving down the highway was rocking us to sleep.

"Who knew you were such an exhibitionist?" he muttered. "Showing off your leopard-print bra . . ."

"It is pink!" I punched him in the arm.

"You're a complete freak. No wonder that Jishnu kid is so into you," he went on, as if I hadn't even spoken. "He obviously likes it freaky."

"That is so wrong!" I laughed. "You have a sick imagination, dude."

"You're all right, Leela," said Jay softly.

"You too, Leopard Print," I murmured into his shoulder, glad to have my friend and brother back.

CHAPTER 28

CAN'T WE SKIP going to Milli Mashi's for Thanksgiving this year?" I begged Ma. It was the Sunday before Thanksgiving, the day after the Netherfield competition, and I wasn't feeling up to a big social scene.

Baba looked like he was willing to give me some support. "Shothhi," he murmured over his morning mug of tea, "that unfortunate turkey Milli makes every year . . ."

He let the sentence hang in the air as Ma whirled around from the stove to shake a spatula at him. "Don't say it!"

Baba shrugged sadly at me, clearly unwilling to continue a losing battle. He slipped his glasses up to his forehead so he could go back to reading the Bengali newspaper on his phone. I didn't blame him for backing off. I knew that, like me, he wasn't a fan of Milli Mashi's annual Bengali turkey day. Despite all her efforts to Indian-ify the turkey by marinating it in cumin, coriander, garlic, ginger, and onions, it was honestly always disgusting. The sides and appetizers, on the other hand—from sweet potato chips to Brussels sprout chochchori—were outstanding. But he and I both knew that getting Ma to agree to a different Thanksgiving plan was all but impossible.

"Come on, Ma, can't we just do a small Thanksgiving with our family for once?" I traced the lines of the elaborate breakfast table place mat that we had brought from Kolkata on our last trip.

It wasn't just the turkey that was putting me off from going, but the thought of the big dance party that Milli Mashi's kids, Riya and Arko, always organized in the basement for us teenagers. When we were younger, we'd played video games, watched dumb TV shows, and played Monopoly. Now that everyone was so into dancing, I always had to make up some excuse not to join in—chatting with someone on the sofa, or, when that failed, helping the aunties upstairs with the food. But I just couldn't stomach an entire evening of pretending I didn't like to dance, and it was too awkward to always turn away when my girlfriends tried to pull me up onto the floor with them. I thought about what Jay had said, about me giving my body permission to take up space, but it was a lot easier said than done.

"Our community is our family in this country! Milli was my first friend in America. We had our children together, learned to make our way so far from home together." Ma took the Indian French toast off the stove, scooping slices of the bread, coated in egg, chili, tomato, and onion, from the frying pan directly onto three plates. Her face softened a little as she admitted, "I'll grant you the turkey she makes is not the best, but how about I bring that artichoke dip you like so much? The one that our neighbor Mrs. Shaffer taught me to make when you were little?"

And so I found myself getting dressed up in Indian clothes

on Thursday afternoon. By then, the sting of everything that had happened at the Netherfield competition had somewhat worn off, and I was actually looking forward to a chance to catch up with the Bengali community friends I'd known forever.

As I walked down the stairs into Milli Mashi's old-fashioned paneled basement, I realized how comforting it was to enter a house whose decor hadn't changed in decades. The house was the same, the food was the same, even the families there were all the same. I sighed. All this familiarity was probably exactly what I needed after all the recent drama of forensics competitions. Little did I know, I'd see one familiar speech and debate face that evening.

"Jishnu!" I exclaimed as he walked down the carpeted basement stairs. Like most of the other guys, he was dressed in Western, not Indian, clothes. Unlike most of the other guys, who were in button-downs and nice sweaters picked out, undoubtedly, by their moms, Jishnu was in his familiar Regimental track sweatshirt. But that didn't mean he didn't look as cute as ever.

"Leela!" Jishnu exclaimed, pausing halfway down the stairs. "What are you doing here?"

"I'm here for Thanksgiving every year." My stomach was doing something gymnastic and pleasant at the sight of him. "What are *you* doing here? I thought you hung out with the Jersey City Bengali crew."

"Naw. This year, I'm here." Jishnu shrugged.

"I can see that," I laughed, adjusting my silk orna over my shoulders.

But if I was hoping for any more conversation, I was going to be waiting a long time, because Jishnu rapidly disappeared into the garage, where some boys were secretly siphoning off Alok Mesho's whiskey collection.

It was a full half hour before Jishnu walked back into the basement from the garage, in a noticeably better, and louder, mood. Like he had in the coffee shop at the Phillips College competition, he zoomed around, saying hi to pretty much every other girl in the room but me. I thought he was going to at least acknowledge me, but then he gave not me but Milli Mashi's daughter, Riya, a giant, kind of too-long hug. The girl, who was dressed in an extremely bright wedding-fancy lehenga for her mom's Thanksgiving shindig, gave a high-pitched giggle, her light brown skin turning pink with pleasure. Some of the guys playing Xbox near them let out an "ooooh."

I tried to catch his attention, but Jishnu kept refusing to meet my eyes. In fact, he was behaving as if he didn't even notice my presence or, if he did notice it, as if he had never met me before in his life. I felt the same sense of shame and humiliation I had when I'd overheard Darcy's cruel comment about me not being beautiful. And yet, Jishnu was making me feel that way without saying a single word.

Then Riya's brother, Arko, turned down the lights and turned up the music. Some people moved the sofa and gaming station aside to make a dance floor, and almost everybody cut loose. I found myself a corner of the sofa to watch the dancing from, hoping no one would notice I wasn't dancing. Jishnu, certainly, didn't seem to miss me. He danced first with Riya, then with my friend Mitali, then with a gaggle of other girls. But he never spared a single glance in my direction. I felt the stone I was carrying weighing heavy on me.

Finally, Jishnu made his way over to me, edging me away from the sofa and toward the paneled wall of the basement. As if he could only be seen talking to me when no one else would notice.

"So?" I finally shouted over the music.

"You're mad." Jishnu gave me what I suppose he intended as an endearing grin. He leaned close, cornering me by leaning against the wall I was backed up against. I could smell the alcohol on his breath, see the glint of his toothy smile. I shivered. All of a sudden, he seemed a lot less like the funny and charming guy I'd met in forensics and a lot more like a big bad wolf I would meet in the woods.

"Why would I be mad?" I shrugged, smiling kind of blankly. I wanted nothing more than to get out of this conversation, out of this dark basement, and back to familiar spaces of light.

"Don't be like that," Jishnu said, an aggressive edge to his voice.

As we were talking, I noticed Riya looking over at us repeatedly. And then something occurred to me. "Are you dating her?" I nodded toward Riya, who was in a circle dancing her heart out with a few other girls, shaking their ornas and lehenga skirts.

"No, but our dads were friends, and—" he began, but I cut him off.

"You don't owe me any explanations," I said, putting my hand up to his face.

Jishnu made a frustrated noise and looked over his shoulder. He repositioned himself so that my back was to the wall and his was blocking out our view from the rest of the room. "You're different," he muttered, caressing my cheek with his finger. "Not like her."

I pushed away his hand. My skin burned unpleasantly where he'd been touching it. My heart was thumping in my chest as I ground out, "Are you kidding me right now?"

The music changed again to a song that had a deep bass beat, and all of a sudden I felt like it was the same rhythm as the headache beating now in my head.

"What about you and me?" Jishnu looked like he was about to yell at me, but couldn't because of all the people around us.

I lowered my voice, even though I felt like screaming. "There is no you and me. You couldn't even say hello to me properly when you arrived."

Jishnu's expression changed again. He gave me that crooked grin that made my stomach flop. He reached out to tuck a strand of hair behind my ear. "You're so jealous you're not even dancing."

I pushed him aside, finally ducking under his arm when he didn't really move. "I think Milli Mashi is calling us for dessert," I said loudly, causing a virtual stampede to the stairs.

"I made the pumpkin pie," said Riya proudly, winding her arm through Jishnu's.

"Yum," I said, refusing to meet Jishnu's eyes. "I can't wait to try it."

The evening ended without me talking to Jishnu again, despite him trying several times to corner me and, when that failed, text me.

Each time he tried, I just looked down at my phone and ostentatiously didn't reply. Until he finally just stopped trying.

It was only when we were all crowding into the front hallway, stuffed to the gills with turkey and chochchori and rashogollas and pie, that he finally succeeded in cornering me again. Jishnu lowered his voice, leaning toward me with the most ridiculously fake hangdog expression on his face. "Don't be this way, Leela. I can't be the same way I am at forensics meets when I'm here!"

"Sure, no, of course not," I said, rubbing my temples. "Why would I expect consistency from my friends?"

"For sure. I knew you'd be cool about it!" Jishnu was either too clueless or still too drunk to understand my sarcasm. "Then I won't say goodbye, but as they say in French class, au revoir!"

As he walked out of Milli Mashi's house with his mother into the cold night, waving and calling his goodbyes to his buddies, I mumbled my response to his retreating back.

"Yes, go! Go! I would not want you back again!"

CHAPTER 29

As if Jishnu wasn't enough of a Thanksgiving surprise, the next Saturday morning, Tomi randomly dropped by my house.

"Come on in, Tomi, come in," Baba boomed from the front door.

"Thanks, Uncle," Tomi said as she removed her shoes in the entrance hall.

Ma ran forward to give Tomi a big hug. "You want some tea, sweetheart?"

"No, thank you, Auntie," Tomi said, biting her lip. "I mean, actually, no, I mean, yes, I'd love some actually."

I gave her a sharp look. Tomi being unsure of herself meant the sky was probably falling.

"You sure you're all right?" I asked when we were alone, my parents having gone out to run some errands.

"Fine, why?" said Tomi, taking a sip from her mug of tea.

"No reason at all." I changed the subject, and told her in detail about my very special Bengali Thanksgiving surprise.

"You know, I don't mean to be that person," Tomi said slowly.

"But I thought there was something off about that Jishnu kid the very first time I met him. And that whole story about how he got swindled out of his tuition to Netherfield. I don't know, Leela."

I sighed. "You can say 'I told you so,' I give you permission."

"Nah, I'll take a pass." Tomi laughed. "But he's very, very shady indeed."

We lapsed again into an awkward silence.

She was looking so uncharacteristically fidgety, it was making me uncomfortable.

"Tomi, was there something you came over here to tell me?" I finally asked.

"Um . . . has Jay heard from Bingley yet, do you know?" she said, not meeting my eye. Her knee was shaking like a million miles a minute.

"I don't think so." I let out a whoosh of air from my mouth. "I can't help but think it's Darcy's fault."

Tomi frowned. "I don't know. Did you hear Ro that day outside Longbourn? Kept saying that word *perfect* as if it was a threat to her brother."

"I do remember." I took a sip of my tea. "You mean it's more than her just being a terrible, manipulative person?"

"Well, probably that too," Tomi laughed. "In this regard, *you* are more than free to say 'I told you so.'"

"I did tell you so," I said without missing a beat. "Ro Bingley is the worst."

"Way to take the high road, sis," snorted Tomi.

"But what's this about the *perfect* thing?" I cradled my tea, studying Tomi's wide-eyed face.

"I don't know, just trying to put it together with something she told me that day in the hotel lobby, when we were walking aimlessly around together?" Tomi peered into her tea.

"Oh, I remember that day—you were taking a turn about the room, I believe," I said in as hoity-toity a manner as I could muster.

"Indeed," laughed Tomi. "But during that walk, she said something I didn't really pay attention to at the time, about how her parents were accepting of her brother being gay, but just wanted anyone he dated to be absolutely perfect."

"No pressure there," I scoffed. "But seriously, Tomes, I don't think you need to stretch that far to find our villain. I think Darcy must have planted some bug in Bingley's ear to make him dump Jay like this."

"Remember what I said about not forming judgments too quickly," said Tomi. "Are you sure you're reading his character right?"

I was about to shoot off a retort, but I realized that I hadn't recently been reading too many people's characters right. Case in point was Jishnu—I'd thought he was such a great guy, mostly because he was familiar, funny, and, if I was being honest with myself, Bengali. But as it turned out, being Bengali didn't stop someone from being a complete jerk too.

"I don't know why that guy Darcy just brings out the absolute worst in me," I said honestly.

"Oh? Do you not know why?" Tomi said the words with a tiny smile on her face. She brought her tea mug to her lips and took a leisurely sip.

"Don't even," I said firmly. "It's not what you're thinking at all. I'm not pulling his pigtails because I like him or something."

"I would never say that. That kind of thinking is extremely sexist." Tomi still had that little annoying smile playing at her lips.

"You know what I mean." I grinned. "Now, as lovely as this conversation is, Tomi, you never told me why you stopped by here today in the first place."

"Um, to see you?" Tomi looked all uncomfortable again, and her knee started moving so fast, I was afraid it would fly off.

"Okay, great. But you usually text or call or something first. I mean, we are supposed to be getting together tomorrow anyway with Jay, right?" I pried. "Why did you come over today? Was there something you wanted to talk about without Jay there?"

"Kind of." Tomi was looking like she wanted to fling down her mug and run from the room. "It's about Colin, actually."

I rubbed my hand across my forehead. I should have guessed. He was her vice president, and they were friends. She was probably here to scold me about how I'd been too harsh when I'd let him down or something. No wonder she was being so weird.

"Is he still mad at me too?" I asked with a sigh. "I just can't, Tomi, with the way he made a scene at Netherfield. It was horrifying."

Tomi put up a hand to stop me. "I know. It sounds like it was very embarrassing. He's very sincere. Heart on his sleeve, the whole thing."

"Yeah, for sure. A properly nice guy." I squinted at my friend. "Tomi, why don't you just spit it out?"

"What?" Tomi looked alarmed.

"Whatever it is you and Colin talked about after the Netherfield meet." I poked her kitchen chair with my foot. "Out with it already."

Tomi studied the clock over my kitchen microwave for a minute, then the ice maker on the fridge. Then an invisible, but apparently fascinating, speck on my kitchen counter. Finally, she started twisting her mug around and around in her hands. "The thing is, Leela . . ."

"Yes?" I prompted. What in the world had gotten into my normally self-confident BFF?

"Colin and I are kind of, well, dating," Tomi said in a giant rush.

I almost fell off my stool. "What?"

That was *not* what I'd been expecting.

"I am more than well aware he didn't make himself clear, but when he approached you in the hallway outside the Netherfield cafeteria, he was trying to get your advice about asking *me* out." Tomi looked both completely embarrassed and completely happy.

"He was?" I rewound the events of that day, as much as I could remember them. Oh my gosh, had Colin ever mentioned me by name when he was going on and on about his reasons for "obtaining" a girlfriend? I guess he hadn't! And he had said he was trying to get my advice about someone else. I just had chosen not to believe him.

"Oh, Tomi, I'm such a jerk!" I put my head in my hands. "I totally thought he was asking *me* out!"

"I know, he told me," Tomi confessed. "*Not* that you were a jerk! That you didn't understand, I mean. That's why this feels so awkward."

Ugh, yet another case of Leela misinterprets a situation. Then another thought occurred to me. "Wait a minute, when you talked about being interested in someone that night at the Phillips College conference, were you talking about him?"

Looking far less like the cool and collected president of our team, and far more like an embarrassed schoolgirl, Tomi nodded. "I've liked him for a long time."

I couldn't help but smile, seeing the happiness on her face. "Really?"

Tomi grinned, her face relaxing for the first time since she'd come over. "Yeah. He's sweet. He's sincere. He's always thoughtful about others."

"But"—I softened my voice, wishing I could erase all the terrible things I must have said about Colin to Tomi over the years—"you really like him."

She nodded, giving me a look that was half-defiance, half-bashfulness. "I know you must think I'm ridiculous."

"No!" I protested. "Not if you really like him. You're right. He is sweet and sincere. He's always checking up on his teammates. He's a good guy. Very, uh, unique."

"Unique is right." Tomi laughed ruefully. "But that's what I like about him. He's not embarrassed to say what he feels, to be who he is."

I nodded, feeling like my entire worldview might need to be readjusted.

"Is this going to be weird for you, Leela?" Tomi touched my arm. "I came over because, honestly, I was worried that it might be weird for you."

"Don't be silly," I protested, forcing a cheery expression onto my features. "I was kind of a fool at the Netherfield meet. I wish I'd just let him speak rather than jump to conclusions about what he was saying."

Tomi gave me meaningful raised-eyebrow look. "Oh, really?"

"Stop! Just because I was deeply wrong about Colin, and Jishnu, and even Lidia, it doesn't mean I'm wrong about Darcy!"

"Okay, sis, you keep believing that," Tomi shot back.

"Colin's lucky to have you, you know," I said sincerely. "I hope he knows how lucky."

Tomi looked me straight in the eyes. "This isn't weird for you, though? I don't want this to be weird for you."

"It's not weird; I'm totally psyched for you," I said, only kind of lying.

I got up and gave her a huge hug. "You deserve all the happiness in the world," I added, not lying at all.

CHAPTER 30

CHALK UP my agreeing to go down to Professor Catherine de Bourgh's elocution workshop that Saturday in December to guilt. It was guilt at how I'd blown off Colin all along, guilt at how I'd treated him that day at Netherfield, guilt that he and Tomi would have to live with my nonsensical assumptions between them. So I immediately agreed when Tomi invited me to join her and Colin for Professor de Bourgh's special invitation-only high school weekend diction lessons.

The drive was pleasant enough. Rosings College, where Colin's elocution teacher taught, was about an hour south of where we lived, which made it about forty-five minutes north from Pemberley University—a distance whose relevance would become shortly obvious. We drove down together in Colin's very sensible sedan, inherited from his older sister, who was at college. It was just the three of us, as the rest of the team had turned down Tomi's invitation, much to her chagrin.

"Colin has been going to her for years now," she'd explained at our last forensics meeting after school.

"More the reason not to go," Mary had mumbled under her breath.

I couldn't help but agree, at least privately. Colin spoke like he had a serious spike up his . . . well, unmentionable region. But far be it from me to draw attention to such a failing. Plus, I saw my role as bolstering Tomi's new relationship.

"We can't go. We're going shopping," announced Kitty, with a look at Lidia.

Lidia looked up from her phone with a serious expression. I wondered who was texting her. "Um, what? Yeah, absolutely, shopping."

"Well, I'm delighted to go improve my diction," I'd announced, with a pointed look at Jay. "It'll help my forensics, but also just in general, in life."

Tomi looked pleased. I was beginning to realize my friend was really, stupidly in love. She looked at Colin in such an adoring way, and he then back at her, that I actually felt a twinge of wistfulness. Which was super odd, because this was, after all, the painfully annoying *Colin Kang*! But I guess he had some good qualities I'd never seen until Tomi pointed them out.

"I can't go," Jay had said firmly. "It's my tiya Alma's wedding."

"This weekend?" I asked.

"Yeah." Jay looked so sad. "Not that I have a date to take or anything."

That kind of deflated me. Jay's and my friendship was pretty much back to old form, but he was devastated at Bingley still giving him the cold shoulder. That was part of the reason why I'd been counting on going to the workshop together. It was time

I'd hoped to cheer Jay up, maybe figure out between us what Darcy had done to drive them apart. Now I'd be the kabab-me-haddi, the third wheel to Colin and Tomi's lovebird pair, if no one else decided to go.

And of course, since no one else did, that's exactly what happened.

"Is the temperature okay back there?" Tomi asked from the passenger's seat.

"Fine, thanks," I chirped. I couldn't help but feel like a kid in the back riding with her mom and dad.

Tomi only reinforced the feeling when she pulled out a small tin she'd brought with her. "Want a blueberry scone? Just baked them this morning."

"Sis, you are too much." I gratefully took one of the scones. It was still warm. And bloody delicious. "This is amazing."

"You want me to feed you one, Colin?" Tomi asked, and I almost gagged on my scone.

"I fear its deliciousness would interfere with my driving." I noticed that Colin didn't even look over at her as he said this, but kept his eyes fixed on the road, both hands on the wheel like we were taught in driver's ed. "Tomi, my dear, would you look at the directions again on that phone app?"

"I could just put the phone where you can see it," Tomi suggested, starting to slip the phone into Colin's dashboard charger.

"My dear!" Colin exclaimed. "No, please don't! I take safe driving very seriously and don't believe in any visual distractions!"

"Of course, don't worry, I got it," said Tomi smoothly. "You keep going straight here until exit forty-two."

"Thank you, my dear," Colin replied, still not moving his eyes off the road. "I cannot tell you how much it relieves me to have you help navigate our way."

"I'm happy to do it," Tomi replied in her calm way. "I won't take out my knitting in that case either."

"I do appreciate that." Colin smiled. "You're very considerate, my dear."

I tried not to laugh. They'd only been dating for a week or two and already they were like an old married couple. Maybe they really were meant for each other. I finished off my scone with a lick of my fingers.

"You see, dear Leela," Colin said suddenly. "I could not be more lucky, or more happy."

There was a brief, awkward silence, and I was spared having to reply to Colin's comment by the fortuitous appearance of exit forty-two.

In about ten minutes, we drove through the gates of Rosings College, which was a small liberal arts–type school. Even though it was freezing outside, there were plenty of students out and about, although no one was sitting on the cold-looking iron benches.

"It's apparently reading period," said Tomi. "So everyone's studying for finals."

"Which is also why Professor Catherine de Bourgh had the time to generously bestow her wisdom upon us this Saturday afternoon," announced Colin. "She is extremely busy with her students usually, and so we are very lucky she is offering this opportunity. I really cannot imagine why, my dear Tomi, our other teammates did not make use of this once-in-a-lifetime chance."

Tomi snuck me a little look, and I smiled. "It's their loss for sure," she said placidly.

We drove to the theater building, which was where Professor de Bourgh had her office. As he held open the car door for me, Colin gave me a critical look. "Don't be nervous, Leela. Your Jersey accent is not something you can acquit yourself of at a moment's notice."

"My Jersey accent?" I repeated. Did I have an accent?

"Professor de Bourgh is a paragon of kindness itself. She will not think lesser of you because you speak as you do," Colin continued. "She is acutely sensitive to differences in upbringing, geography, and class that affect our diction. She has a deep appreciation for such differences, and will not think ill of you due to your particularities in speech and enunciation."

Even Tomi, as in love with Colin as she was, rolled her eyes a little at this speech behind Colin's back. I gave him a little, tight grin. "Thanks, Colin, I appreciate your thoughtfulness."

"You will both be entranced by her, I am convinced of this," Colin continued as we headed up the stone steps to the theater building. "And today will transform you both in ways that you never would have believed. I find I am quite a different person now than I ever was due to her beneficent tutelage."

"So are we paying her for this?" I asked offhandedly.

"Leela!" Colin stopped halfway into opening the building door. "We do not speak of such crude things with Professor de Bourgh. I pay her for my lessons, yes, but today is an act of supreme generosity on her part."

"And an effort, maybe, to attract more private students?" suggested Tomi mildly.

"Perhaps, my dear," Colin sounded a little miffed. "But I'm sure that Professor de Bourgh had no such pecuniary thoughts in mind when she offered me and a few friends a private workshop session."

Tomi and I exchanged a look, and I wondered how she could tolerate dating a guy with such obvious, well, flaws? Although I guess everybody had flaws; wasn't being in love supposed to be about only seeing the other person in a positive light?

Still, Tomi seemed so into him. But maybe happily ever after wasn't exactly how all the books made it out to be.

CHAPTER 31

DIDN'T HAVE time for any more such philosophical consid-
erations, because that was when Colin led us into the Rosings
College theater. As we walked down the aisle toward the stage,
I saw a tall elderly woman in the middle of the single spotlight,
staring not at us, but up, stage left.

"Shhh!" Colin put out a hand, halting us halfway up the aisle.
"She speaks!"

Professor Catherine de Bourgh was of a formidable height,
made even more formidable due to the heels on her dance shoes.
She was thin and bony with improbably bright red hair she wore
in a high bun twisted with a silk scarf. She was dressed as if from
another era, with shawls and bangles and fringy things draping
off her skeletal arms. Each finger had at least two rings on it, and
her eyes were lined with way too much kohl—and I'm saying this
as an Indian girl who has a deep personal relationship with her
eyeliner.

The professor cleared her throat, moving her hands in an
ethereal, strange way, like she was doing a ballet move with

invisible creatures. I thought, after all that, she would recite some Shakespeare at least, but as it turns out she just cleared her throat and said, absurdly: "Red leather, yellow leather. Red leather, yellow leather."

It felt, I have to say, seriously surreal. "Is she okay?" I whispered to Colin.

"Shhh!" he said again, quietly, reverently. "This is a part of her process."

After repeating the "red leather, yellow leather" line a few times, Professor de Bourgh became even more obscure. "Imagine an imaginary menagerie manager imagining managing an imaginary menagerie!" she announced.

"Wow," whispered Tomi. Having been friends with her for years, I could hear the sarcasm embedded in that one simple word, but apparently Colin couldn't.

"Indeed," he said reverently. "These are the stepping-stones to better diction. The good professor shows us the path, but it is up to us to walk it!"

Finally, Professor de Bourgh seemed to break out of her trance. "Come, young thespians! Come forward!" she beckoned with a spidery gesture.

I almost lost it at her use of the word *thespians*, but out of respect to Tomi and her burgeoning, if incomprehensible, relationship, I stopped myself from actually giggling out loud. That didn't mean, of course, that I managed to prevent myself from letting out a little snort.

Colin gave me a sideways glance and said in a low voice, "It is normal to feel nervous when approaching such greatness. Do not worry, Leela, Professor de Bourgh will appreciate your appropriate levels of awe."

Not giggling after that pretty much took all my self-control. As did fighting the instinct to curtsy when we were introduced to Professor de Bourgh.

"Greetings!" she intoned in an ominous voice. "Friends of young Colin, you are wise to seek entry into a better world, a brighter future, through the power of ar-tic-u-lation and perfect dic-tion."

She emphasized the first syllable of the word *diction* so much, even Tomi couldn't resist letting out a little muted laugh. I felt the mirth bubbling up inside me like a shook-up bottle of some sort of obnoxious fizzy drink.

Colin introduced us to Professor de Bourgh, seriously and ceremoniously. Then he pointed to a figure I hadn't noticed before who was sitting quietly in the darkened first row. "And this is the honorable Miss Anne de Bourgh, an attendee of the exclusive St. Magdalene's Academy."

"You state speech and debate competitors may be unfamiliar with my daughter, as she is unable to compete in your for-en-sics competitions," enunciated Professor de Bourgh. "Indeed, had St. Magdalene's been less exclusive, or larger, they would have a team, to be sure. And were that the case, Anne would be the shining forensics star, mark my words!"

I couldn't really mark those words, because Anne looked like a tiny lump of a girl, snuffly and sad-faced. Even her "hello" to us was at such a reduced volume, it was almost impossible to hear her. This was the daughter of the great actress?

"Up on the stage, young thespians, up on the stage!" commanded Professor de Bourgh, and as we three scrambled up, the spotlight split, illuminating each of us in our own personal halo of eye-dazzling light.

"Thank you, Mrs. Jenkinson!" called the professor in imperious tones. She waved at the invisible person controlling the lighting.

Professor de Bourgh may have looked a little flaky, but she was no joke. She first led us through several more bizarre diction exercises, including, "Upon a slitted sheet she'll sit," which sounded so almost-dirty I let out a whooping laugh.

"Diction is no laughing matter!" scolded Colin, aghast.

"I'm sorry!" I said, fixing my features into an expression of repentance. "I choked on something!"

The next diction exercise was a bit less scandalous, but no less complicated: "Round the rugged rocks the ragged rascal ran."

"Round!" Professor de Bourgh commanded, rolling her *r* off her tongue with a dramatic sound.

"Round!" Colin repeated, almost exactly imitating her accent.

"Round!" said Tomi clearly, but without the same flair.

"Almost, dear, almost!" singsonged the professor. She pulled out a small hand mirror from one of her shawls and handed it to Tomi. "Examine your epiglottis! Position your tongue at the posterior of your teeth!"

She demonstrated, rather comically I thought, how to place her tongue up behind her front teeth.

As Tomi dutifully held the mirror to her mouth, trying to imitate Professor de Bourgh's rolling *r*, it was my turn.

"Round!" I said, in my best imitation of the professor's trilling sound.

Her eyes opened wide in shock. "Oh dear!" She tsk-tsked, shaking her head sadly like I'd just had some life-threatening medical results. "Lots of work to be done with this one, young Colin! You were right to bring her to me!"

As Colin and Tomi got to move on, actually working on some Shakespearean sonnets together, I kept having to say the damn thing about the ragged rascal running around the rugged rocks. I had to say it so many times my mouth started to cramp and my tongue started to get fatigued.

"Louder!" Professor de Bourgh kept shouting at me. "Louder, girl!"

I was practically bellowing the phrase "Round the rugged rocks the ragged rascal ran" when the doors to the auditorium swung open, letting in two visitors. With Mrs. Jenkinson's spotlight dazzling my eyes, I could only see them in dark outline. Like everyone else, I shielded my eyes to see who they were.

"Ah! There they are! My nephew of the blood and my nephew of the heart!" announced the professor dramatically. "What took you so long, my dears? The drive up from Pemberley could not have been so crowded!"

Pemberley? I thought in shock. She couldn't have just said Pemberley?

And yet, of course she had, because who else should be standing in the front row before us but Firoze Darcy.

CHAPTER 32

AM CONFIDENT I told you boys to be here at ten o'clock! I cannot emphasize how very particular I am about punctuality!" scolded Professor de Bourgh. She flapped her arms, making her bangles rattle to emphasize her disapproval. "Well? Explain yourselves!"

The two boys—Darcy and a giant, football-player-sized dude whose red hair echoed the shade of Catherine de Bourgh's bottled color—stepped up onto the stage. They both kissed her on the cheek simultaneously, briefly making an old-actress sandwich between them. Despite her scolding, the old actress in question looked inordinately pleased.

"We're terribly sorry, Aunt Catherine!" said Darcy. I remembered suddenly how he had once said that he and Colin's elocution teacher were family friends, and deeply regretted not remembering that prior to agreeing to come today. But how could I have guessed that Firoze Darcy, of all people, would find attending an elocution workshop an exciting way to spend a free Saturday?

"We stopped by your favorite patisserie to bring some

sustenance!" Darcy opened a fancy pink-and-gold box he'd been holding under his arm, showing off row after row of beautiful macarons.

"Ah! From Didier's shop on Pemberley's high street! How I do miss the enchantments of civilized life!" crooned the old woman, plucking a raspberry macaron from the box and taking a delicate bite.

"Do you forgive us, Auntie?" said the red-haired giant, showing off some open-faced sandwiches, undoubtedly also bought from the same shop.

"How can I not forgive such charmant gentlemen?" said the professor. She glanced at the three of us behind her, and introduced us formally to Darcy and her red-haired nephew, whose name was William Colonel.

"We have been working hard! Perhaps it is time for a bit of a repast, n'est-ce pas?" The ancient actress waved at an old picnic blanket—perhaps part of some stage set—that was upstage. "I believe an indoor picnic is in order! You young people set it up! I will be back after I powder my nose!" And with a rushing of bangles and fringe, Professor Catherine de Bourgh whisked herself out of the theater.

There was a small noise from the front row, and we all turned to look, realizing that Miss Anne de Bourgh was still sitting there. Had she been there this entire time?

"Anne, would you like a sandwich?" Colin solicitously grabbed some snacks to offer Professor de Bourgh's daughter, who looked like a small lump in the front row. She murmured her thanks, barely audible, nearly a human manifestation of a sandwich herself.

Since Tomi followed Colin down to talk with Anne de Bourgh, that left me on the now fully lit stage (thanks to the invisible Mrs. Jenkinson) with Darcy and his friend. The boys spread out the picnic blanket and I brought over the boxes of snacks. I was steeling myself for the inevitable awkwardness of having to speak to Firoze Darcy again when something unexpected happened. William Colonel, that red-haired, freckle-faced, giant nephew of Professor de Bourgh, ended up being a completely nice guy.

"Hey! Leela Bose, how awesome to finally meet you!" Will clapped his hands together as if he'd been relishing the treat for ages. He was sprawled out on the blanket and patted the spot next to him for me to sit. "I've heard so much about you from my buddy Darcy here!"

"You have?" I returned his way-too-enthusiastic handshake, smiling at him despite myself. "Believe none of it! I'm sure he's told you all lies!"

"Lies?" exclaimed Will with dramatic outrage. "Not at all! I can see with my own eyes that every word he told me is the absolute truth!"

I felt my face heating up as I understood the compliment. "Well, I'm sure he was exaggerating, whatever he said."

"No way, dude!" Will reminded me of a giant, friendly leprechaun. "Darcy here hardly gives out compliments, so when he does, you better believe they're sincere!"

All this time, Darcy himself had said nothing, but just stared down at us with quiet interest. Finally, he sat down on a far corner of the blanket himself, folding his limbs under him with such ease it did something to my equilibrium.

I hid my confusion by taking a bite of one of the delicious sand-wiches the boys had brought from the French bakery. Chewing and swallowing the bite of mozzarella and olive tapenade, I turned to Will. "Should I tell you the impression your buddy Darcy here has made on my public-private school forensics league?"

"Oh, yes, do!" Will wiggled his fingers in the air before lac-ing them under his chin, pantomiming such rapt attention that I laughed. "Pray tell what my friend here is like when away from the idyllic campuses of Pemberley and Netherfield!"

"You see, the first time I met him," I said in a conspiratorial voice, "I was at a public school forensics meet." I looked at Will curiously.

"Speech and debate, yes, I'm aware," he said. "Pray continue."

Nodding, I did. "And, it just so happened, during lunchtime, to, erm, release my competition-day tensions, I happened to be per-forming a musical number whilst standing on a cafeteria table."

"Well, very rightly so." Will nodded, his cherubic face beam-ing sincerity. "As one does."

"Indeed." I was trying my best to keep my composure. "And yet, your friend found my performance a bit, how shall I say this, undignified."

"For shame, Darcy!" Will tsk-tsked. "Aunt Catherine would be deeply disappointed to hear that you weren't welcoming of the muse of musical theater."

I looked over at Darcy, echoing Will's outraged expression. "A muse best invoked from the top of a cafeteria table."

"In my defense," Darcy said in such a friendly way it abso-lutely startled me, "it wasn't the standing on the table itself I found problematic, but the fact that you were singing *at me*."

"Were you, then?" Will swiveled his face around to look at me. "This is a detail you did not include in your first description! Please go on! I'm afraid I must hear the entire story before I can pronounce judgment."

I laughed despite myself. "I believe it was the line about his perfume smelling like his daddy's got money that irked him the most." Even as these words escaped my mouth, it hit me that Darcy's father had died. Was *that* why he'd reacted so badly?

Neither of the boys said anything about this, though. Instead, Will out-and-out guffawed, pounding Darcy on the back with a meaty hand. "She's got you there, bud. Your perfume does smell very expensive."

Darcy swatted Will's hand off him good-naturedly. "Then maybe you should stop smelling me."

"But I can't resist." Will mockingly took in a big whiff of Darcy's hair. "'Cause you smell so darn good."

"Bug off!" Darcy pushed Will, sending the giant boy rolling off him with a dramatic exclamation.

"And then," I rushed on, "your friend here said something about public school kids lacking class and ran off!"

"What? He did not!" exclaimed Will, straightening up again. "Mr. Netherfield Academy made disparaging remarks about public school education? For shame!"

"It pains me to say it, but he did do exactly that!" I assured the redhead.

"I didn't say that part about lacking class, did I?" Darcy had the grace to look embarrassed.

"Something like it." Hoping that his feelings weren't hurt by the comment about his dad, I gave him a little smile.

To my surprise, Darcy smiled back. "It was very wrong of me, I'll admit it. But here's the explanation, if not really an excuse: I'm not very good with people I don't know."

"Not good with people he doesn't know!" I exclaimed, turning to Will. "Should we press him further? Why should someone like Darcy—well traveled, well educated, multilingual, skilled at covering screens and embroidering cushions—not be good with people he doesn't know?"

"Yeah, Darcy, what about your skills in embroidering cushions?" Will sat up, pointing a thick finger in his friend's face. "Have you been holding out on me?"

"Sadly, my expert skills in cushion embroidery don't help with meeting new people." Darcy spread out his hands, shrugging sadly.

"And whose fault is that?" I asked, arching an eyebrow. "As you recently heard, I'm sure, I'm not very good at rolling my *r*'s, but I would imagine that's because I haven't practiced enough."

"You're right! Not going to argue with you there!" Darcy agreed immediately. "You're not very good at rolling your *r*'s."

"Excuse me!" I threw a macaron at his head. "I meant that you should consider practicing meeting new people! Just like I should practice my diction exercises!"

Darcy deftly caught the sweet out of the air and popped it into his mouth. "Ah! Is *that* what you meant?"

There came the clippety-clop of heels upon the stage, and we all looked up.

"What are you three chatting about in such animated tones?" demanded Professor de Bourgh. She was holding a big walking stick, which she bashed forcefully on the floor. "I must have my share!"

And then we were joined by Colin and a very curious-appearing Tomi again, and began an afternoon of more ridiculous diction exercises and scene work.

I didn't have more chances to talk to Darcy, although I did notice that he kept looking over at me. It made me want to pull a little-kid move—shout "What?" at him and make a face—but I restrained myself.

Finally it was the end of the workshop. I shrugged on my coat, eager to get out of there, only to hear Colin begin to ask Professor de Bourgh a long-winded question about the correct way to expectorate consonants. I felt desperate. I had to leave. Working alongside Darcy all afternoon had been, at best, confusing. And Tomi, occupied as she was with Colin, was hardly as much help as she could have been. Only Will, with his boundless good cheer and energy, had kept me going.

Tomi, bless her, finally noticed my distress, because she leaned over to me, whispering, "Go on, I'll text you when we're heading toward the parking lot. Go walk around outside if you want."

I nodded gratefully and, after thanking Professor de Bourgh once again, made a beeline for the door of the theater. If I'd expected it to be Darcy who chased me out, I was wrong. It was, to my surprise, Will.

"Wait up!" he called cheerfully, bounding up the aisle. I looked over his shoulder but didn't notice where Darcy had gone.

"With pleasure!" I said, bowing and offering Will my arm.

With a very elegant curtsy, given his size, Will linked his elbow through mine, and we skipped out of the theater, like we were off to see the Wizard.

It was cold outside the building, but a refreshing change from the stuffy, complicated world of Professor Catherine de Bourgh's elocution workshop.

"Do all those diction exercises sound dirty after a while or is it just me?" I mused.

Will exploded in his characteristic laughter. "It's not just you! The one about the mother pheasant plucker! I almost lost it at that one!"

"You did lose it!" I batted at his arm playfully.

Will looked at me, his face suddenly suffused with affection. "You know, if I didn't have a girlfriend . . ." he began. "And of course, also a boyfriend . . ."

"Bup, bup!" I made a noise to stop him, feeling both flattered and, somehow, sisterly. "Stop. Don't say anything you'll regret. Or that I'll have to cry about into my diary for months.

"You don't keep a diary." Will narrowed his eyes at me. "Do you?"

"I'll never tell!" I declared dramatically.

Will sighed, shaking his head. "Anyway, you're right. I'm a blabbermouth. I should be more like Darcy, speak only when my words will register a hit."

"What do you mean?" I frowned, wondering if this had something to do with Darcy's relationship with Jishnu.

Will pulled out some chewing gum and stuck it in his mouth,

chewing thoughtfully. Thank goodness I wasn't interested in him, I thought. That openmouthed chewing would have definitely been a deal breaker.

"You know, he saved his buddy Bingley recently from a really bad situation," said Will in between chews. "That's the kind of a friend he is, you know? Willing to stick his neck out for his peeps."

"What kind of a bad situation?" I asked curiously.

"I'm not sure, but all I know is that it was something romantic. It was really bad, and Bingley was totally miserable." Will paused, chewing some more. "So Darcy hopped in and fixed it."

I felt my heart plummet. He was talking about Bingley dating Jay. I was sure of it. But describing that situation as one that made Bingley miserable was such a complete lie. Darcy hopping in and fixing it must be when he stepped in and told Bingley to ghost Jay and not respond to him anymore!

"He fixed it, huh?" I rubbed my temple, feeling dizzy with fury.

"Hey, you okay?" Will leaned down toward me.

"Headache!" I blurted out. "It's been a long day. I probably just need to go home."

"Well, let me get Colin and Tomi for you," said Will kindly, bounding back into the theater building.

I watched his wide form disappear inside, wondering how in the world I was going to keep this horrible news from Jay. And how in the world I wasn't going to kill Firoze Darcy the next chance I got.

CHAPTER 33

THE OPPORTUNITY CAME quicker than I'd thought. I was at home the next Sunday morning when I heard a ring at the door.

"Can you get it, shona?" Ma called from the study. She and my father had just begun a home-exercise regimen and were in the middle of a workout. "Probably a delivery!"

"Be careful, look first!" called Baba urgently.

"Sure!" I called back. "Don't worry, I'll be careful!"

But it wasn't the delivery guy my mother was expecting. Or the ax murderer my father was fearing. It was, instead, Firoze Darcy. Standing on my stoop. Outside my house. Studying my mother's sunrise doormat, or maybe his own shoes.

"You?" I was completely floored. "What are you doing here?"

He looked up at me without really meeting my eyes. "Would you like to take a walk?"

"A walk?" I repeated. I was wearing sweats and my hair was pulled into a ponytail. But that didn't really matter. For whatever reason, the universe had given me the opportunity to find out exactly what Darcy had been thinking when he broke up Jay and Bingley, and I was going to take it.

"Fine, just give me a second." Not knowing what else to do, and not wanting to invite him into my small, comfortable but totally un-fancy home, I shut the door in his face and bounded up to my parents in the study.

"It's Jay," I lied. "He wants to talk to me about something. I'm going to take a walk with him."

"Oh, good, you two made up!" Ma beamed, barely out of breath from her exertions. She was wearing her old 1980s work-out clothes—including a scrunchie in her hair. I was glad I'd left Darcy literally cooling his heels outside. My parents weren't exactly in a position to make the best impression right now. "I was worried when I didn't see him over here as often lately," Ma continued.

"You're taking a walk? In this weather?" Baba's face was sweaty from the low-impact jumping jacks the lady on the screen was still doing. He looked miserable, like he'd much rather be playing cricket.

"Fresh air is healthy for young people!" Ma reassured him, her scrunchied ponytail bobbing. "Just take a hat, Leela! And your phone, please!"

"I'll be back before you're done working out!" I called as I darted back down the stairs. I was pulling on my coat and shoes when I opened the door again, wondering if seeing Darcy there had been some sort of bizarre hallucination.

It wasn't. There he was, waiting patiently in front of my door. He gave me a tight-lipped smile. "Shall we?"

"Sure." I pulled out my hat from my pocket, a homemade pom-pommed affair from Tomi, and jammed it on my head. As opposed to me, in my sneakers, sweatpants, poofy coat, and hat, Darcy was looking immensely cool and chic in a blue peacoat and close-fitting knit cap. We started walking in the direction of the high school at a brisk pace, neither of us speaking for a few moments.

"How did you find out where I lived?" I finally asked.

"I asked Colin." Darcy's breath was frosty in the air.

"You have his number?" I was astounded.

"He insisted I take it." Darcy looked over at me with a wry smile.

"I can imagine." I kept walking, staring straight ahead. "But it must have taken a long time to come up here from Pemberley's campus."

"I listen to a lot of books on tape." He blew on his glove-less hands.

There elapsed a few minutes during which all I could hear was our matched footsteps on the sidewalk, and my own breathing. What in the world had come over Darcy? Why had he sought me out? What did he want?

We walked in silence, block after block, until we reached the elementary school next door to Longbourn High. There, we wandered, as if by agreement, toward the cold and empty elementary school playground. I sat down on an old rubber-seated swing, twisting one way and the other, waiting for Darcy to say something.

Finally, he stopped pacing around the swing set and turned to me, his eyes glittering with some unknown emotion.

"I've struggled for too long, but I can't stop it." Darcy's light brown cheeks were pink, but I couldn't tell if it was from the cold.

"Struggled? What do you mean?" I turned this way and that on my creaky, freezing swing.

"No matter how hard I try, they won't be repressed. These feelings." Darcy beat at his chest like he was showing me their location. "I've fought against myself, my own better judgment, but I've lost."

I stopped twisting. "What are you talking about?"

"Leela, you must allow me to tell you how ardently I admire you . . . I . . . I . . . think, no, *know*." Darcy paused to look down at me. "I'm in love with you."

"What?" My surprise came out of my mouth with a harsh exhale, taking shape like a ghost in the cold air. But then something else floated into me on the in breath. It was expanding, filling me up with something warm and very much alive.

If only he'd just stopped when he was ahead.

"I know it's ridiculous!" Darcy continued on, a train come off his well-laid tracks. He plunked down now on the swing next to mine. "You and me! I mean—the differences in our upbringings! The company you keep! Your teammates' embarrassing behavior!"

"What about my teammates' behavior?" I pushed my legs hard on the ground, swinging away from him.

"Come on! Mrs. Bennet dithering around, wailing about her nerves! Kitty and Lidia flirting with anything that moves! Your bizarre public conversation about dating with Colin the other week!" Darcy kicked his legs, now swinging too. Only he was off-kilter to me, going up just when I was coming down. "Even you must admit your team is a bit sloppy!"

"I don't have to admit anything!" I yelled into the cold air. "Except maybe that you're too uptight to forgive normal human fallibility? But maybe what really bothers you is the fact that we're from a public school and not some fancy private academy with its own hydroponic wall!"

"I . . . didn't mean that," Darcy protested. "I mean to say—"

"Or maybe that we're just not beautiful enough to tempt you," I shouted, not even knowing I was going to say the words until I did.

Darcy stopped swinging and sat stock-still. "What did you say?"

Instead of answering him, I planted my feet on the ground and jumped up from my swing. "I have no idea why you chose to come all the way here on a Sunday morning to insult me, but I'm not sure—ill brought up as I am, ugly lump that I am—what I'm supposed to say here. Am I to express gratitude or obligation? Am I supposed to thank you? Well, I can't do any of those things."

"I . . . please, let me explain what I meant . . . what you overheard." Darcy's words seemed stuck coming out of his mouth.

"I'm speaking," I said, putting up a hand. I stamped my feet to keep them warm, not sure how I was still standing. "I have never wanted your good opinion, and you've granted it to me now fairly unwillingly."

Not sure what to say next, and wanting to bring some blood flow back into my now-numb thighs, I resolutely turned around and started fast-walking out of the park.

"Wait!" Darcy jumped off his swing, running after me. "Wait!"

"What?" I snapped, my breath making icy knives in the air. I faced him down at the edge of the frozen playground. "Am I supposed to fall down with gratitude that you fancy yourself—how did you put it—*in love* with me despite your best intentions? Despite our deep differences in, what, stature and upbringing? Despite me being so hideously ugly?"

"I didn't mean that at all . . ." Darcy began, his voice halting. His face was screwed up with humiliation, but that was only as it should be.

"I mean, are you one of those self-hating brown guys who's only attracted to white girls?" I blurted out. I could feel tears of humiliation and fury choking me. "Or is it colorism—that I'm dark? Bingley thought I was beautiful enough, but I still wasn't good enough for you, huh?"

"Let me explain, please," Darcy said in such a voice of alarm and upset, I would have normally paused to listen. But I was too angry to stop now.

I stomped my foot on the icy ground. "But even if I hadn't overheard that nasty description of me, even if you hadn't phrased your 'declaration'"—I made air quotes—"in such a rude and offensive way, do you think anything could convince me to have feelings for someone who has ruined the happiness of my best friend? Someone who's like a brother to me?"

With furious energy, I spun the cold, metallic merry-go-round before me, watching its faded colors swirling by.

When he said nothing, I pressed on. "Do you deny it?"

"Wait." Darcy shook his head, like he was clearing it of cobwebs. "What are you blaming me for now?"

"Separating Jay and Bingley, you awful homophobe!" I shouted.

Darcy sounded choked up now too. "Is that really what you think of me? Is that really how you think I'd treat a friend?"

"Yes!" I marched out of the playground, trying to measure my steps so it didn't seem like I was actually running away from him. I turned around to yell, "Will told me you fixed a difficult romantic situation for Bingley—obviously that was when you broke them up!"

"Wait!" he called again, jogging a little to keep up. "Did Will tell you I broke Jay and Bingley up?"

I thought back to my brief conversation with Will Colonel, the one that had resulted in a pounding migraine. "If not in so many words, the implication was clearly there."

"'Not in so many words,'" Darcy spat out. "I see. And you don't admit that maybe you jump to understand people before you have all the facts? That maybe you're not the best judge of character?"

His words stung, finding their mark. I resented the heck out of him for his perceptiveness.

"It's not only because of that, though, that I hate you." I spun around, spitting these words at him through the air.

This time, it was he who looked as if he'd been slapped across the face. "Hate?" he repeated.

"I got to see behind the curtain of your personality weeks ago now, when I heard what you did to Jishnu Waddedar. What excuses do you have for that? What explanations can you give for that cruelty?" I hurled the accusation at him like a spear as I ran across the street. He hurried to keep up with me as the light changed, almost getting run over by a Volvo.

We were walking so fast now up the sidewalk, my legs burned from the effort of keeping up the pace. I thought of my parents, cozily exercising, Ma berating Baba to do one more push-up, for his health. I wanted to get back to them now, and away from this horrible conversation with Darcy, as fast as I could.

"You seem to take a lot of interest in that guy's concerns." Darcy's face was redder now that it had been, and I knew it wasn't from the cold.

"How can I not? How can anyone who knows how he's suffered not feel for him?" I didn't know why I was arguing at this point on Jishnu's behalf, Jishnu who had turned out to be such a disappointment, such a creep. I turned my eyes back to the road. Just a couple of blocks now, and I'd be home.

"Suffered!" Darcy repeated, his voice dripping with disdain. "What exactly has that guy suffered?"

"Being kicked out of Netherfield, having the education that was promised to him snatched away!" I stopped walking and shouted this at him. I didn't know why, but I was practically crying now. I had a feeling it wasn't really about Jishnu's lost education at all. "And more importantly, getting kicked out of the family he'd loved like it was his own!"

Darcy's face looked like he'd been dropped from the sky. "Well, if this is what you choose to believe, that I've done all that, then my faults are heavy indeed! But maybe you could have overlooked all this had your pride not been hurt by the way I chose to tell you about my feelings, what you think you overheard me say about your attractiveness. Did you want me to, what, flatter you with lies and performances and pretty words? Is that who you are, Leela? An actor at heart? A fake? I thought we were both believers in honesty—I thought that's why you switched to LD!"

"There's a difference between being artificial and being kind!" I yelled. "Or is it cruelty that you're actually in love with? Are you such a debater you're more interested in using your voice to win every bloody argument than using it to be truthful and real?"

He looked so shocked at this that I pressed on. "From the moment I met you, your manners convinced me of your arrogance, your conceit, your selfish disdain for the feelings of others. I understand why you're such a champion debater, because you don't care about what you say, you just care about being right, about being able to lord your ultimate rightness over other people."

"Enough." Darcy's voice was soft but firm. He was staring at the sidewalk like he wanted to murder it. "You've said enough, Leela. I understand your feelings perfectly and now am just ashamed of what my own have been. I'm so sorry for taking up so much of your time, and bothering you and your family on a Sunday."

With these words, he turned on his heel and walked toward his car. Which was only one driveway over. In my distraction of fighting with him, I'd not noticed that I'd finally arrived outside my own house.

I'd been longing to rush inside, but now I dillydallied outside, not wanting to go in and face my parents. Firoze Darcy had driven all the way here to tell me that he had feelings for me—was *in love* with me? He had accused me of pride, but it was his pride, his confidence in his superiority and rightness that had ruined it all. He didn't want to express his feelings to me; he wanted to win me. And ultimately, that was the difference between a speech competitor and a debater.

So occupied was I with these thoughts that I barely registered when he pulled out of the driveway and drove away.

CHAPTER 34

AVOIDED MA and Baba as long as I could that day, declaring that I had a lot of homework. I didn't answer any texts from my friends, or engage with anyone on social media, or really look at my phone at all until the evening.

That was when I saw the email from Darcy. I didn't have to ask how he'd gotten my personal email address. Colin was obviously to answer for that too.

Dear Leela, it began.

I took a big breath. Did I want to read this? Darcy's face floated before my mind's eye. I could, feasibly, just trash and block his email. Never have anything to do with the jerk again. But there was something deep inside me that wouldn't let me make that decision. I wanted to hear what he had to say. In fact, I was realizing I needed to hear what he had to say. I couldn't entirely articulate why, but I did.

Don't be alarmed on receiving this email. In fact, I write it with the trust you will delete it as soon as you read it.

I don't write to renew any declarations of feelings that were so disgusting to you earlier today. Rather, to clarify some opinions you had of my character. I don't know why it matters, but indulge me in this.

He wrote the way he spoke. Formal, measured, as if from another stick-up-the-arse era. I could practically hear his uptight voice through his words even as I read them.

"Oh, I'll indulge you all right," I muttered angrily to myself.

You accused me of two offenses very different in nature. The first was the separation of Jay and Bingley. Let me ask you this—if they really cared for each other that much, could anything I said have kept them apart?

"What?" I muttered out loud. "Is he kidding me here? They only just met, were starting to get to know each other. This isn't some happily ever after story, my dude. This is high school; of course something you said could have kept them apart."

If you choose to think it was me who kept Jay and Bingley apart, if you really think I would stand in the way of my best friend's happiness, then there is nothing I can say that will change your mind. Fine, blame me.

"I will!" I was practically growling at my computer screen. "I will blame you, you jerk!"

Your next accusation was about Jishnu Waddedar, who, you're right, grew up at Pemberley with me, almost like a brother.

"And this is how you treat your brothers?" I mumbled. "First, you destroy Jishnu's happiness, then Bingley's?"

My father did help Jishnu with the part of his Netherfield tuition that his scholarship didn't cover. It was less about Jishnu himself and more about my family's gratitude to his mother, Sharmila. But it wasn't because of my father's death that Jishnu left Netherfield. That was entirely of his own doing.

I leaned forward now, practically shoving my nose into my computer. What excuse was Darcy going to cook up to explain Jishnu leaving Netherfield?

This is the part that I'm going to have to trust that you don't repeat to anyone, as it makes someone I care very much about vulnerable to the world. My sister, Gigi, was only a seventh grader when Jishnu started in on her—his attentions changing from concerned older brother figure to something else. Gigi was too young to know better, and our mother and I were too distracted by my father's newly diagnosed cancer. Gigi needed someone to lean on, and Jishnu was there when I couldn't be.

Wait, what was he saying? I felt my opinions shift 180 degrees. I'd been going along, hating Darcy, but now I felt my heart leap to my throat and a sensation of revulsion dance across my skin. I, like every other girl in the world, could guess where this story was going. And I didn't like it one bit. I remembered back to that one "accidental" touch by that uncle backstage at a performance. The way that one grandpa in India squeezed me a bit too long when I was little. I thought about that slimy debate kid who had stared at my chest, muttering "Nice bra" like it was some kind of come-on.

When Jishnu started sending her pictures and asking her to send them back, it was innocent enough. A selfie with the dog, that kind of thing. But then, he got more explicit, asking her to send things and do things that she wasn't ready to do. When he asked her to let him into the house one night when we were all at the hospital, she did.

I almost couldn't breathe as I read on. I could see the scene unfolding even as Darcy painted it. And I knew, deep inside, that Jishnu was perfectly capable of what Darcy was saying, and more.

I don't know why my mother decided to drop me home when she did. I guess she didn't feel comfortable about leaving Gigi alone so late by herself . . . Anyway, it was me who walked in on him trying to take advantage of her. He was kissing her, and she was crying, and I lost my mind. I threw him off her, and out of the house.

"Oh, Jishnu, you total asshole!" I wanted to throw the computer across the room and wash my brain out with soap. "She was in the seventh grade! How could you?"

You have to understand, Leela, at this time, my father was dying; my mother was beside herself with worry. I couldn't add to their burden. I did the only thing I knew how to do. I wrote to my dean at school, explaining what Jishnu had done. He was kicked out immediately for assaulting a middle schooler and for sexting.

"No wonder you hate him so much," I said, as if Darcy had transported himself through his email into my room. "I'm impressed you didn't kill him."

My mother, who never got the full story until after my father died, still did the decent thing out of the respect she had for Jishnu's mother. She helped him get into Regimental, and even helped his mom with the deposit. Since then, our family has had little to no dealings with Jishnu Waddedar or his family.

I tell you all this because, despite everything we said to each other today, I trust you, Leela, to be particularly careful with this information about my little sister. She is the most precious thing in the world to me, and I would not share this information with anyone but you.

I sat back, feeling like someone had sucked all the air out of my lungs.

All of winter break, I kept going over and over the details in my mind—a vulnerable tween whose dad is literally in the hospital dying, a distracted mom and older brother, a brother-like figure paying a little girl the attention she craves. It was sick. It was horrific. And yet, how did I know, in my very bones, that it was true?

I hated Darcy. He was snotty, and arrogant, and always thought he was right. But he wouldn't lie about such a thing, not when it came to his sister. He wouldn't lie about such a thing, not when I knew his feelings for me.

But then, what about Jishnu? I thought about that wolfish leer that he had given me in Milli Mashi's basement, when he thought no one else was looking. How he'd flirted with other girls, ignoring me, only to corner me and tell me I was different from them. He was a predator all right. He was the wolf waiting in all those fairy tales for unsuspecting girls walking through the woods.

It was a lot to think about. Especially without anyone to speak about it to. I longed to tell at least Tomi, but I felt like I had to keep my promise to Darcy.

My head was spinning.

But even more surprising, so was my heart.

CHAPTER 35

THE FIRST FORENSICS tournament after the break was at Kent High School. Even though I'd considered dropping debate after my not-so-spectacular previous performances, there was something in me now that told me to give it one last chance. And for whatever reason, since Lidia had joined LD, I felt like I had to stay, give her and Mary company somehow in the male-dominated category.

There was a new January-February debate topic: *Resolved—School choice is unjust.* I believed in the affirmative case, as it was fundamentally about the preservation of the public school system. Since I had prepared for much of the break, not feeling a lot like socializing, I knew I had a solid case built up. What I didn't know was how thrown off I'd be by my first opponent.

Darcy.

I got to the room—your standard bleak public high school classroom with wonky desks and multiple decades-old pieces of educational wall decor—and saw him there. His handsome face was grim at the sight of me, and I knew he was thinking of our

240

last encounter, his confessional email. I wanted to say something, but it was time for the round to begin. There was no time to be ourselves. It was time for us to debate.

I was arguing affirmative. I tried to clear my head and keep my voice steady, my attention on my notes and not on all I had learned about Darcy, and Jishnu, and, if I was being honest, myself.

"Already," I argued, "the wealthy pull their children out of public schools and send them to private institutions—like Netherfield or Regimental—but school choice makes the racial and economic disparities between private and public schools that much worse. Now the middle class can, with vouchers, abandon community-based public schools too—and for what purpose?"

Darcy followed up with an initially unimpeachable cross-examination. "Do you believe that parents know what's best for their children? Or that the state knows best?" he asked; then something in his face changed.

He looked away from his notes, like what he said next came from inside him, and not anything he'd prepared. "What about a child with a d . . . disability, who needs special services not available at a public school? What about a kid who's bullied, who needs a smaller class size, a place with a stricter anti-bullying policy? Should that child's parents not have the option to find a safer, more healthy environment for him?"

There was something about Darcy's use of the male pronoun, the way he stammered a little as he argued his point that startled me. With a lurch, I realized he might be talking about himself. I suddenly had a stark memory of something Colin had said, about the way Darcy sometimes switched around words, and paused before he spoke, and my stomach twisted. Was Darcy debating me, or using the debate to tell me something personal and private about himself?

"If there was no school choice, then communities could be invested in making sure that all schools had disability services, or stricter anti-bullying policies," I countered.

"In an ideal world, yes," Darcy said. Because of the rules of the debate, he was looking straight ahead as he spoke, but still, he snuck a quick look at me. "But we don't live in an ideal world; we live in a human world constructed by human foibles within which we all have to do the best we can by others."

My heart squeezed, and I knew he was no longer debating me. He was apologizing to me. He was trying to speak his truth to me.

As the debate went on, I couldn't help but feel that Darcy and I were in motion together—dancing, but with our words. Instead of a hand at his shoulder, I placed a question before him. Instead of a hand at my waist, he placed an answer before me. Steps and pauses, swirls and sways, our words danced about the room and each other. Our arguments twirled like turns around a ballroom; our points and counterpoints dipped and flowed, rising and falling on the music of our voices. My body was still as I stood, gripping the cold wooden lectern before me. But my mind was dancing and pausing, responding and challenging, in an invisible pattern of movement with his. And I realized that we'd always been doing this complicated dance with each other—since the first time we'd argued in the lobby of the hotel at the Phillips

College competition. We'd been parrying with words, moving in formation around each other, coming together only to move apart again. We'd always been dancing partners. I just hadn't realized it until now.

At the end of the round, there was a moment of quiet during which neither of us spoke, neither of us moved. I felt suspended in the moment of our intellectual dance, frozen in time and space mid-twirl.

Only when our judge looked up, smiled, and said "Thank you" was the spell broken.

I had no idea who won. I had no idea who lost. All I knew was that I wanted to keep dancing.

And yet, because of everything I'd said to him that day on the playground, that could never happen. I'd lost my chance forever.

"Nice round," Darcy said in his serious way, but I couldn't find any words to return to him.

He nodded at me, a little sadly, and made his way out of the room.

I watched him as he went, feeling like I'd lost something I could never get back. And yet, even as I walked into the hallway, I could still hear the music we'd been dancing to.

I never wanted it to stop, I realized.

And that realization was enough to break my heart.

CHAPTER 36

THE REST OF the day was standard LD racist and sexist fare. A competitor who winked at me, a judge who said something about "those people" under his breath when I was making the case for diversity in public education. But I was still thinking about my debate with Darcy.

My ballots, which I read on the bus, were as hurtful as ever. *A bit shrill*, said one. *Great argument, but be less combative; you come off as a know-it-all*, wrote another. Only my ballot from my debate with Darcy commented on how well constructed my argument had been, how close the judging was. I had won against him, but I didn't even feel any happiness from that realization. Because the truth was, what I'd really discovered was all that I'd lost.

"More excellent comments on your ballots?" shouted Lidia, leaning out of her seat to look at me.

"Yup," I said, my voice as light as I could make it. "One person suggested I wear a dress instead of a pantsuit, so that's not sexist at all. You?"

"Same, plus a guy I was debating who offered to throw the round if I . . ." She trailed off.

"This is getting absolutely ridiculous," Tomi fumed. She raised her voice so the coaches, all the way up front, could hear her over the hum of the bus engine. "When are we going to do something about this?"

"I'm going to bring it up at the all-state judges' meeting before the Regimental debate competition," called Mr. Bennet from his seat.

"There's a Regimental competition?" I wondered why this was the first time I was hearing about this.

"Not for a few weeks. It's a small competition, purely novice debate, and for ninth and tenth graders only," returned Mrs. Bennet. "This is the first year we're going."

"Mary can't go that weekend, so it's going to be me all on my lonesome!" laughed Lidia. "But I figure a ninth- and tenth-graders-only competition will be easier for me. I want to get the experience so I can really humiliate some of those debate jerks I've been facing."

"Do you think it's a good idea to go alone?" I wondered aloud. Lidia at Regimental by herself, with no other teammates to keep her company, or in check?

"It's a good chance for our Lidia to practice her debate skills in a less competitive environment," Mrs. Bennet called. "It will be a fun girls' day."

That made me feel even more concerned. Mrs. Bennet was definitely the flakier of our two coaches. "Mr. Bennet, you're not going?"

"Mr. Bennet has some tooth surgery scheduled," called back his wife a little too gaily. "Never a good idea to put off a root canal!"

I didn't say anything, but looked out the window into the darkness, biting my lip.

"What's up?" asked Jay in a low voice from his seat across the aisle. "You worried about Lidia going to Regimental by herself?"

"A little bit," I answered, grateful for any normal interactions I could have with Jay. He was still a little cold these days, but I knew his change in his mood had less to do with me and more to do with how much he was missing Bingley. "You know how she is."

"She'll be with Mrs. Bennet," Jay said in only a partially reassuring way.

"Do you think that's going to be of much help?" I answered in a low voice.

"True, that," laughed Jay. "But don't worry about it, Leels. How much trouble could one ninth grader get into at a debate competition?"

"That's exactly what I'm worried about," I muttered to myself. Lidia was too confident to doubt herself, but there were dangerous things out there in the woods.

I let the bus lull me into a stupor for the rest of the ride home. There were too many worries of my own floating around in my head for me to stay worried about Lidia for any longer.

Soon, the motion of the bus and the day's exertions lulled me into a fitful sleep.

CHAPTER 37

THE REGIMENTAL DEBATE competition turned out to be the week of February break, the week my parents had planned to take me on a few local college tours. I was so occupied getting ready for my college visits that I hardly remembered my concern about Lidia attending that meet essentially alone. She'd be fine. She'd matured a lot over the last few months. Or at least so I told myself.

My week was busy. My mother, always enthusiastic, had planned at least two college visits per day. Most of the schools were within a two-hour drive from our house, except for the first weekend, when we were driving up to Boston, but staying with some Bengali family friends for the night. Heaven forbid my parents would ever spend money on a hotel.

The weekend was fun, seeing friends I hadn't seen in a long time and sitting around after our tours, drinking endless cups of tea and eating shingara in their kitchen. On Monday, we returned home, only to have a number of local schools set up all week. One day, it was multiple schools in New York City, then the next, a couple of schools north of us in the Hudson Valley. At first, it was exciting, wondering if I could see myself on the different campuses. I'd play a game with myself, to see if I could find someone who looked anything like me in the crowds of college kids milling around. After a few days, though, the car rides were getting tedious, and each college was starting to blend into the others. And the sight of my parents' faces tightening up at discussions of tuition and financial aid was enough to make my stomach tie itself in some serious knots.

By Friday night, I was exhausted. "What's on the agenda for tomorrow, Ma?" I asked, yawning.

We'd eaten dinner on the road, yet again, so there was no cleaning up, but we were all gathered together around the kitchen table anyway with tea and cookies. My feet were aching from all the campus walking tours, and I noticed Baba was rubbing his neck.

Ma, ever perky, didn't seem tired at all, though. She took an enthusiastic slurp of her tea and looked at the notes section of her phone. "A leisurely day! Only one college on the agenda! I've set us up for a tour of Pemberley."

"Pemberley!" I echoed hollowly. I felt that old desire to attend the university, the one I'd stuffed away, rearing its head. "Isn't that kind of an expensive school?"

"If you get in, they guarantee they will give you enough financial aid!" said Baba enthusiastically. "And it's such a beautiful campus!"

"There's kind of an obnoxious guy I know through the debate circuit who lives on Pemberley's campus. His mom is actually the president, if you'll believe it," I said in a rush.

"You are debating against Dr. Fatima Khan-Darcy's son?" Ma looked up from her phone, her expression amazed.

"You know Darcy's mom?" I almost spilled my decaf tea in my agitation.

"No, of course not. But a Pakistani immigrant woman who's the president of such a well-known university, of course I know her name!" Ma enthused. "That decides it! We *must* tour Pemberley!"

"Ma, I don't want to meet this guy," I explained slowly and firmly. "He's one of those rude debaters I was telling you about—super arrogant, prideful, just awful."

"What are the chances the president of the university and her family take the college tours?" Baba asked. "Did you bump into any other college presidents or their families on our other tours?"

"No," I agreed.

"So it's highly unlikely, isn't it, we will see one solitary boy—no matter how obnoxious—on such a big-big campus?" he concluded, dunking his tea biscuit in his mug.

And with those fateful words, we were heading down to Pemberley early the next morning. Exhausted from the tours of the week, I slept most of the way down the New Jersey Turnpike. It was only when Ma woke me up on the outskirts of the campus that I started to appreciate why Tomi was so set on coming here.

The campus was set on acres of rolling greens that were cut through with woods and picturesque streams. After the crowds on the ugly New Jersey highways, and the local suburban sprawl of strip malls and chain eateries, it was like entering a magical fairyland dedicated to knowledge.

As we parked and headed toward the admissions building, a

bell tower chimed the hour with a beautiful sweeping sound.

"Lovely!" breathed Ma.

The day was cold, but with a golden sun that hinted at a new, brighter season waiting around the bend.

We walked up curved walkways, passing buildings that were old and stately. While everything at Netherfield had been state-of-the-art new and shiny, everything at Pemberley had clearly stood the test of time. Everywhere I looked was an arched stone doorway, or an ivy-covered wall. There were plenty of students passing along the crisscrossing college walk, but an equal number of squirrels and birds populating the plentiful, generous trees. Even though their branches were now empty of leaves, I could imagine how the campus would look in the spring, when everything was dappled and green.

The tour went about like every other college tour had gone, with a student tour guide walking backward, enthusiastically giving us information on this building and that, dorm life, educational opportunities, and campus culture. But this tour was a little different because I knew that this was the place that actual people I had actually met grew up. My parents seemed to feel this too, because during the question and answer, Ma asked, "Can you tell us about your president? Does she have much interaction with you students?"

"I'd love to tell you about Dr. Khan-Darcy!" replied the tour guide, Reyna. "I don't know what college presidents are like on other campuses, but she's really hands-on, involved in our day-to-day lives. She and her kids will have pizza nights for us in their residence every week, and different parties and events all the time.

She's always walking around campus, buying students coffee, asking us how our days are going."

I was surprised. This was a different picture of Darcy's mom than the cold one I'd painted in my head. Only, I remembered, I'd painted that image in my head because of Jishnu's descriptions of her.

Unprompted, Reyna went on, "She's got two really great kids. Her son, Firoze, got in here early decision. You might think it's because his mom's president, but she was really open about not wanting her son to stay on campus. She wanted him to go somewhere else, get a new experience. But he decided to anyway, despite the very president of the university being against it."

"Why?" asked another parent on the tour.

"Well, he has a younger sister who he's really close to, and their dad died a couple years ago," said the tour guide, still walking backward. "And I think he wanted to be around to support her. He's a great kid. But it's also that great of a school. Why would you ever want to leave?"

"Why would you indeed?" murmured Baba as we walked by a beautiful outdoor sculpture garden next to a tranquil pond. "It's heaven."

"It is," I breathed. Despite myself, I adored the campus. I adored the buildings, the grounds, the tranquil charm of it all. I loved how happy everyone seemed, particularly our enthusiastic tour guide, Reyna, who knew so much about Darcy's family.

As the tour circled back to the admissions building, Ma leaned toward me, linking my arm through hers. "The tour guide gave quite a different report of this young man," she said curiously.

"Maybe he's not quite as obnoxious here as he is during a debate match?"

"Maybe," I agreed, purposefully not meeting Ma's curious gaze.

I couldn't stop thinking about what Reyna had said about Darcy and his family, not to mention the warmth in her voice as she talked about them. She was just a random college student, and all that information she'd added about the president and her family were surely not a part of the standard tour. I'd never heard such details at any other campus we'd visited, certainly. And yet, Reyna had included all that without much prompting.

"I'm going to visit the restroom," Baba said once we were about to leave the admissions building.

"I will too." Ma headed down the broad wooden stairs behind him. "Do you want to come?"

"No, I'll wait for you on the outside steps," I said, heading toward the front door.

"Are you sure?" Ma wheedled.

"Ma, I'm sixteen years old, I know when I have to go to the bathroom!" I insisted. Lucky for me, we were speaking in Bengali, because a few other families gave us curious looks.

"Okay, okay!" Ma waved her hand at me benignly as she headed down the stairs. "Just figure out where you want to eat lunch. Maybe we can visit that art gallery and go to the bookstore after."

"Sure!" I agreed, thinking hungrily about that dosa shop we'd seen as we'd driven into the college town. But the moment I stepped out through the glass front doors of the admissions building and into the cool February air, I stopped short. There was a boy walking by the stone steps of the admissions building with three of the most incongruous dogs I'd ever seen put together—a huge, drooly Saint Bernard, a pugnacious pit bull, and a miniature labradoodle that looked like a toy.

"Darcy!" I exclaimed, totally horrified.

CHAPTER 38

L eela!" Darcy yelped, and at the sound of his surprise, all three dogs started barking. "Down! Boys! Leave it! Stop!" Darcy commanded, looking utterly overwhelmed as the three leashes he was holding got immediately tangled, with the labradoodle creating the most ruckus, the Saint Bernard getting excited, and the pit bull cowering behind his legs.

In the melee, the Saint Bernard tried to jump up on me. "Mr. Gardiner! Mrs. Gardiner! Lambton! Down!" Darcy yelled desperately.

"You named your dogs Mr. and Mrs. Gardiner?" I asked, laughing as the giant dog covered me in friendly licks.

"The Gardiners aren't mine!" Darcy assured me over the ruckus. His coat was absolutely *covered* in dog hair. "Only Lambton is! I'm not even their regular dog walker! I just promised my sister I'd do it for her this morning, in a moment of obvious weakness!"

"I didn't think I'd see you!" I shouted over the yelping and barking. I was terrified Darcy might think I was stalking him.

"What are you doing here?" Darcy asked as he desperately tried to disentangle the dogs from one another.

That was it; he obviously thought I was stalking him.

"I'm on a tour of the college with my parents!" I pointed to the admissions building as if my parents would emerge, confirming my story on demand. They didn't.

Finally able to get the dogs somewhat calm, Darcy studied me seriously. His dark eyes shone. "Do you mind waiting here for a minute?"

"Why?" As if aware of my discomfort, Lambton, the Bernard, rubbed his giant head into my leg as I talked. I scratched his soft ears absentmindedly. "We were going to leave. Get some dosas. Go to the museum, maybe the bookstore," I rambled. "It's not like we were going to stay here, on your campus, stalking you or something."

Oh no, why had I mentioned the word *stalking*? Clearly, he would now think I was stalking him if he hadn't assumed so already.

"Just wait here," Darcy reiterated firmly. "I'm just going to go drop these dogs off, I'll be right back!"

In the meantime, my parents were making their way down the steps from the building.

"Who was that boy with all the dogs you were talking to?" Ma asked, her eyes bright with curiosity.

"What boy?" I blurted out, as if I could just pretend the interaction with Darcy didn't happen. I changed tack quickly, feeling far more flustered than necessary. "Oh, that was Firoze Darcy, the president's son."

"I guess we did bump into him after all!" said Baba, watching him go.

255

"He wanted us to wait here for him. He'll be right back." As soon as I said the words, I regretted them. Oh, what had gotten into me; why hadn't I just ignored Darcy and left?

"Oh! Then of course we will!" Ma said cheerily.

"Although I was looking forward to those dosas!" Baba rubbed his stomach as if from hunger.

My parents chitchatted about how much they had enjoyed the tour, and how I should definitely apply to Pemberley early, and how nice it was that I knew the president's son, while I studied my shoes, looked blankly at my phone and, finally, at my own nails.

Darcy came back in probably ten minutes, but it felt like a hundred. He was sans dogs, and looked a little bit like he'd taken a second to run a comb through his hair. Huh.

"Hello! Auntie, Uncle, I'm Firoze Darcy," he said, giving my parents each a polite "Namaste."

"Hello, beta!" My father nodded, using the Hindi word for *son*.

"So nice to meet you, Firoze," Ma said. "I hear you know our Leela from forensics?"

"Yes, that's right. She only recently switched to Lincoln-Douglas debate," said Darcy, all charm and smiles. "And beat me soundly."

"I think it was a pretty close round," I said, meeting Darcy's eyes. "You made some powerful points."

"As did you," he answered, bowing his head a little.

We both paused, not saying anything, remembering the pleasure of matching words and wits. I noticed Ma giving me a quizzical glance.

Darcy jumped into the silence. "I was hoping I might convince you all to join my family and me for lunch."

"No, no! We couldn't impose!" Baba protested.

"No imposition at all!" Darcy insisted. He pointed to the beautiful ivy-covered president's residence, a building that had been on our tour. "My house is just over there. And I took the liberty of telling my mother and sister you were coming. They are very much looking forward to meeting you!"

"If you're sure it's no imposition," Ma said hesitantly, shooting me a surprised look.

"Quite the opposite!" Darcy smiled. "And maybe afterward I can take you over to the museum and bookstore—Leela said you were interested in going there."

"That would be wonderful. Thank you, beta," Baba said, laying a gentle hand on Darcy's shoulder. I couldn't help but notice a longing look that flitted across Darcy's face as he looked at my father.

"It's my pleasure, Uncle. Truly," he said, clearing his throat. "Did you enjoy the tour?"

As my father and Darcy walked together up toward the president's house, Ma leaned toward me. "Is this the obnoxious boy you were telling us about? He's all ease and generosity, no false pride at all!"

"It's quite a change. I can't imagine why he's so different!" I admitted.

"Can't you?" Ma said, her lips quivering with a suppressed smile.

CHAPTER 39

THOUGHT MEETING a college president would feel intimidating, but it didn't. For openers, Lambton was so huge and loving and bumbling, he kind of cut through any tension there might have been by jumping all over us at the door.

"Hey, boy! Hi, Lambton!" I said, kneeling down to receive my licks. Lambton mewled in ecstasy like I was a long-lost friend and not a stranger he had met for the first time all of fifteen minutes ago.

"Welcome! Welcome! I'm sorry about our ill-behaved dog! Please, do ignore him!" Dr. Khan-Darcy looked like any other Desi auntie I'd ever met—if maybe a little better dressed. She was about my father's age, with her long, still mostly black hair in a bun, wearing a small nose ring and a delicate embroidered kurta top under her suit jacket.

"Call me Fatima!" she said to my parents merrily as she took our jackets.

We left our shoes in the little shoe rack by the front door and walked in.

I'd expected the president's residence to be formal and cold, but as soon as we were past the foyer, we entered a family home, decorated with Desi tapestries and art, pillowcases and carpets. The living room was lined with bookshelves stuffed to the brim with books, plants, and a giant piano in the corner. The thick Persian rug under my feet was old but soft, its intricate if faded pattern dancing under our feet.

"That enormous instrument is my sister's," said Darcy with a smile. "She deigns to let me play on it sometimes, but it's hers."

Just as he said this, a girl who looked like the spitting image of Darcy, just in girl form, tripped into the room. "Hello! I'm Jaleela!" she announced.

"Jaleela! Why, you girls have almost the same name!" Ma said, beaming. "Leela—Jaleela!"

"We call her Gigi!" said Darcy's mother affectionately.

I studied the girl's open, friendly face and how she obviously doted on her big brother. Her hazel eyes kept shooting to him, as if for approval. I remembered how Darcy had told me he'd been the one sometimes to care for her when she had her asthma attacks, and how Reyna the tour guide had told us Darcy had decided to go to college here to be close to his sister.

As the adults continued to chat, Gigi turned enthusiastically to me, her high ponytail bobbing. "I'm so excited to meet you, Leela! My brother's been telling me all about you!"

I remembered that Will had said almost the same thing. Why in the world was Darcy talking to all his friends and relatives about me? To hide my confusion, I bent down to give Lambton some scratches. As I hit a sweet spot behind his shoulder, his back leg started moving as if on its own.

"It's all lies!" I said darkly, looking up at the girl. "Don't believe a word he says!"

"Oh, no!" quipped Gigi, her eyes rounding in a sarcastically innocent expression. "You must be mistaken, Leela, because my brother isn't capable of lying! He's too good and pure!"

"Shut up, brat!" Darcy said with a big grin.

"Seriously," Gigi continued, wrapping her arms around Darcy's chest and giving him a squeeze. "This guy won't stop talking about you."

I felt a rush of emotions flow through me at this but tried to keep my face neutral.

"Gigi, quit!" Darcy coughed, pushing his little sister off him. He turned to me, his expression embarrassed. "Sorry, my sister isn't exactly one for subtlety."

Gigi made a face at him. "Do you have any annoying brothers and sisters, Leela?"

"No, I'm an only child. When my parents immigrated here, they weren't sure if they would make it, you know? I think they didn't want to risk having more than one kid to feed!" I laughed, but the words were true enough. "No brothers and sisters for me. Unless you count my forensics team."

"Lucky you." Gigi rolled her eyes. "Can you believe this enormous goon is going to stick around here at Pemberley just to torture me, instead of going off and finding fame and glory elsewhere?"

"No choice. Had to stay to keep you in line, brat." As Darcy looked at his sister with such warmth, and she back at him, something almost painful pricked in my chest. "Plus nowhere else wanted me."

"As if!" Gigi protested. "You didn't even apply anywhere else."

"I stand corrected." Darcy pulled out a dog treat from his pocket and commanded Lambton to shake hands. Instead, the giant animal lay down on the carpet with a groan, turning up his belly to be petted.

"Lambton!" Gigi scolded. "You're hopeless."

"He's a free spirit!" I said defensively, scratching the dog's offered belly. "Don't judge!"

"Takes one to know one!" Darcy said.

"Sorry?" I looked up from the wiggling, moaning dog.

"A free spirit," Darcy clarified, his face easing into a grin.

"I think I have, on many an occasion, shocked your brother," I confessed to Gigi. "The first time he met me I was on a cafeteria table."

"I heard you were singing into a shoe," said Gigi seriously. "Which is far more scandalous."

I laughed. "Indeed. And then there is my ramshackle, completely embarrassing public high school forensics team. A crafter, an actor, a rule-abider, a goth, and two incorrigible dingbat flirts. Not to mention our slightly flaky coaches. And complete lack of funding. Or, to be honest, actual training."

Gigi grinned. "Your team sounds completely wonderful."

I returned the grin. "It is."

Man, despite myself, I really liked this girl.

Lunch was, shockingly enough, no fancy catered affair but takeout from the dosa restaurant eaten in a fancy dining room on a giant mahogany table. Clearly, the Darcys hadn't decorated this room from their personal collection, because all around the walls were the frowning portraits of the all-white, all-male past presidents of the university.

"I bet the founders of your university never imagined a bunch of Desis eating at this table with their hands!" my father laughed, tearing off a bit of his crepe-like dosa to scoop up some of its potato and pea filling.

For a second, I was embarrassed. But then the feeling passed as I noticed Darcy's mom laughing too as she finished off her sambar with relish. "To be honest, Sumit-ji, I have that thought every time I sit down to eat here," she admitted. "But the only other choice is our quite messy kitchen table. So I figured I would risk the disapproval of my formidable predecessors!"

"You remembered we were going to go eat dosas!" I said to Darcy as I popped another delicious bite into my mouth.

"It's our favorite meal too." Gigi took a hearty bite of a fried vadai. "Man, South Indian food is the best."

"Don't let Nani hear you say that," Darcy warned. Then he looked over at me. "Our grandma visits every winter from Lahore. She's an amazing cook—but obviously, no dosas."

After our leisurely lunch, Gigi and Darcy offered to walk us over to the bookstore. To my surprise, their mom spoke up. "You kids go. I think we grown-ups will have some nice tea here."

"That would be lovely," Ma enthused. I noticed Baba had already ensconced himself comfortably on a puffy chair.

"It's been too long since I've enjoyed myself like this," Darcy's mom admitted, smiling at Ma. "I'm so very glad you came."

There was something in her voice that made me want to tear up. Ma must have heard it too, because she grasped the other woman's hand in both her own. "Next time, you will all come to us. You must take time for yourself, behen-ji! You're very busy, I know, but taking time to be with family is always important."

There passed something unspoken between the two moms that squeezed at my heart.

Then suddenly, as we were heading out the door, Gigi remembered that she had to practice her piano.

"You have to practice right now?" I asked, incredulous.

"Yes, absolutely, right now," she replied with a wicked grin.

And so it was just Darcy and me heading out. Which, from the expressions on all our relatives' faces, seemed to have been the plan all along.

CHAPTER 40

SOMETHING UNNAMABLE HAD shifted between Darcy and me. Maybe it was the letter. Maybe it was our parents getting along so well. Maybe it was his sister and me having versions of the same name. Maybe it was me seeing him fumbling his dog-walking job. Or maybe it was what he said next.

"You know, I joined forensics because of my stutter." His hands were jammed in his coat pockets, and he was looking at the sky.

I didn't say anything for a second. Then I stopped on the sidewalk and looked at him. "You told me when we were debating."

"Was it that obvious I was talking about myself?" We were in front of the admissions office again, and he perched on the stone balustrade.

I hopped up beside him, studying his face. "Not obvious, but I tried to listen between the words, if you know what I mean. I'm trying to get better at reading people, listening to what they're saying instead of jumping to conclusions."

Darcy looked back at me, and we were both frozen there for

a minute, our frosty breath hanging in the air between us. Then someone called his name, and he waved absently to some college students we passed on the walk. "It's why I started training at first with Aunt Catherine. It's why I sometimes talk slowly. Change words around, that sort of thing."

It all made sense now, that slow, from-another-era way he spoke. It wasn't arrogance at all, but the way he dealt with his stutter.

We didn't say anything for a few moments more, and then I took a big breath. "Thanks for trusting me enough to tell me. One of my uncles stutters—my favorite mama. He got teased a lot as a kid, he told me."

Darcy nodded, scratching his nose against his coat. "Yeah. I got that too—schoolyard bullying plus some teachers thinking I was too slow to understand things. It was part of the reason my parents sent me to Netherfield. Netherfield had smaller class sizes, a speech therapist on site, and a much stricter policy against bullying."

I thought about my own overcrowded, slightly chaotic public elementary school. I'd been lucky enough to have amazing teachers, but I wondered how many kids hadn't been so lucky. "That makes sense," I finally said. I hopped up, rubbing my hands together against the cold. "I'm glad Netherfield was a good place for you."

He nodded seriously at me. "I hear you, you know, when you talk about the elitism of private schools."

"Look, I just think *all* kids should have the chance to have small classes, go to a school with a speech therapist or any other help they need, have a strict no-bullying policy," I explained.

"I agreed with you when you said so in the debate." Darcy stood up and continued to walk as I joined him. "It's why you deserved the win. But in the moment, my parents were just trying to do the best they could for their kid who was really hurting. And I appreciate them for it."

We made our way down the campus walk for a few more minutes.

"Your email," I began, then paused. There was so much to say, but I had no idea where to begin. "I didn't know," I finally added.

"How could you?" Darcy was walking along the sidewalk, looking straight ahead as he spoke. "Thanks for letting me unburden all that on you."

"Thanks for trusting me," I returned. My own voice sounded funny to my ears. "You didn't have to tell me all of that. But I appreciate it. And I won't tell anyone."

Darcy nodded, looking over at me. His expression made something melt in my chest. "I know you won't. I wouldn't have told you otherwise."

"Is that why Gigi quit forensics?" I asked, wondering if I was being too nosy.

"It was too uncomfortable for her to be around that snake Jishnu," Darcy said, his voice hard. "Sometimes I wonder why I didn't quit too. Every time I see that guy . . ." His voice trailed off.

I smiled reassuringly at him. "You're a good brother. Gigi obviously adores you."

"The feeling's mutual," Darcy said simply. "She's so resilient.

I don't know if I could have dealt with all that, and then our dad dying, like she did."

"I get why you're staying on campus, though." I shrugged the collar of my jacket up against a sudden cold wind. "It seems like the right choice. Congratulations." Then I paused, biting my lip. "Tomi got deferred when she applied early."

Darcy glanced at me with an amused expression. "Leela, you know I don't have anything to do with admissions, right?"

"Right," I agreed. "No, right. I know."

That was when both our phones buzzed in our pockets at the same time. We both laughed, reaching to see who was texting us. What I saw, though, wiped the smile off my face.

"I can't believe it." I finished reading Jay's text and looked up. "That little idiot."

"Lidia," said Darcy, looking up from his phone.

I nodded, my chest clenching with shock. "I was worried she'd do something like this. But I kind of can't believe it." I looked up from my phone. "Who wrote you about it?"

"Ro," admitted Darcy.

I thought of how much glee Ro Bingley must have felt as she texted Darcy the news of Lidia's downfall. I felt the humiliation creep over me like a slow-moving wave. "One of the Longbourn forensics team kicked out of the league for having sex during a tournament, and the entire team on probation. It's just Ro Bingley's lucky day."

"She's not like that," Darcy began.

"Oh, isn't she?" I spat out the words bitterly. "She's probably having a party that me and my team are being publicly humiliated like this. Oh, but Lidia? How could she? Always leaping before she looks, that stupid, stupid girl!"

"Caroline wouldn't crow over someone else's difficulties," said Darcy in a less-than-convincing voice. "And as for Lidia—we don't know all the facts yet; don't jump to conclusions."

"Of course I'll jump to conclusions! So will everyone, and rightly so!" I felt the heat rising to my face. "Lidia is a professional flirt, you said it yourself. She's been throwing herself at these Regimental guys all year. I *knew* she shouldn't have gone to that tournament by herself! If only one of us were there with her!"

"But she wasn't alone; your coach was there, wasn't she?" asked Darcy.

"Yeah, sure, and this just proves how subgrade our public school teachers and coaches are, right?" I knew everything that was happening would just confirm Darcy's bad impression of me and my team. If I hadn't ruined everything with how I'd behaved to him in the playground that day, this was surely the ultimate slamming of the door between us. "That's what you're thinking, right?"

"No, it's not!" Darcy argued. "Please, don't hold that stupid nonsense I said that day against me! And still, it may not all be as it looks!"

"It's useless! Hopeless!" I wanted to shake him. Then I realized something. "You better not be seen with me anymore."

"Wha—What?" Darcy seemed breathless.

"I mean, you were right. We're too different—our upbringings, our schoolings." I waved my hands around. "Private is private and public is public and never the twain shall meet."

"Stop! That isn't what this is about!" Darcy protested.

"I have to get my parents and go back home," I said, blinking away the tears threatening to obscure my vision. "I've got to go talk to my team."

I ran back down the walk toward his house. No matter what the details of this latest disaster involving Lidia, Darcy was ultimately right. Our team was a mess. We were an embarrassment to the league. And how could all that not reflect badly on his impression of me?

CHAPTER 41

Our forensics team meeting on Monday afternoon was a grim affair going over what we knew about Lidia's actions, and how they were going to impact our team's very existence.

"According to Mariah, the president of the Meryton team, Lidia got caught in an empty classroom with one of the Regimental guys." Tomi rubbed her face. She was obviously exhausted, yet she was running the meeting because Mr. and Mrs. Bennet were both out—he recovering from his dental surgery, and she from the shame of Lidia's behavior. The only other missing member of the team was, for obvious reasons, Lidia herself, who'd not just been expelled from the forensics league but suspended from school as well.

"I could absolutely kill her," I ground out. All I could think of was Darcy's shocked face when we got the news. Every time I thought of that, I felt the sharp stab of humiliation again and again.

Colin placed a gentle hand on my shoulder. "She's just a high-spirited kid, Leela."

I gave Tomi a startled look and she shot me back a "see, I told you so" sort of expression. Okay, I'll give her the fact that Colin was a pretty nice, reasonable guy. Plus, since he'd started going out with Tomi, he'd changed his greased-back hairstyle and shaved his mustache. It was definitely a big improvement.

"Whether she's just a kid or not, she's gotten herself kicked out of the league and put our entire team on probation," Jay pointed out. "It's not a joke; it's going to look really bad for those of us who still have to apply to college."

"Don't remind me," Tomi said sadly.

"You were deferred, not rejected from Pemberley!" reassured Colin. "And it might be a blessing in disguise—you can always attend Rosings College with your dear boyfriend and learn under the esteemed Professor Catherine de Bourgh!"

I exchanged a look with Jay. I took all my pleasant thoughts of him back. Colin was just as annoying as ever.

"Well, I for one don't see how Lidia's done something so wrong!" piped up Kitty.

"Kitty, honestly!" scolded Tomi.

"What?" Kitty insisted. "It's like Lidia is always saying, aren't you guys just playing into the sexist double standard where girls are punished for doing the same things that guys get patted on the back for?"

"The guy is going to get in plenty of trouble too, Kitty," Colin assured her. "It was utterly inappropriate on both their parts to hook up during a debate tournament."

"And to be careless enough to get caught by a teacher," muttered Jay.

"I still can't believe it." I shook my head, smothering a groan.

"So who's the guy?" Mary asked finally.

"What guy?" I asked, confused.

"Uh, the guy she was caught with in that classroom. The one who was, according to what I heard, in a serious state of undress," Mary reminded me.

I looked at her practically openmouthed. In all my fury at Lidia's irresponsible behavior, I'd forgotten to ask about which of the Regimental guys she'd been caught with. That's when I saw Tomi and Jay exchanging a knowing look.

"So who was it? Carter? That dude Denny?" I asked them.

Jay shook his head, saying nothing. But his expression told me all I needed to know.

"No. That's not possible. Why didn't you guys tell me this until now?" I felt my heartbeat speed up in my chest. "Are you kidding me?"

Tomi shook her head sadly. "I heard from Mariah but wasn't sure how to tell you."

"It was *Jishnu?*" I screeched. "Lidia was found in a classroom undressed with Jishnu Waddedar?"

"Well, from what I heard it was he who was more undressed," said Colin under his breath.

"Babe, not helping," Tomi admonished.

"Sorry." He grinned, reaching over to kiss her on the cheek. She beamed, and I wanted to hug and smack them both, simultaneously.

"So what's going to happen to our team?" asked Mary. It was a question no one had answers for.

"We're not sure, Mary. We're going to have to wait and see what the league president says," Tomi sighed.

"I don't understand why anything should happen to anyone!" pouted Kitty. "Aren't we supposed to be sex-positive and not slut-shaming and all that?"

"Fooling around in a classroom during a forensics match isn't the revolutionary act you think it is, Kitty," Jay said, but I shook my head.

"Where's Lidia?" I demanded, staring at Kitty.

Tomi gave me a knowing look. I could see her putting the pieces together, even though I hadn't even told her everything I knew about Jishnu. "You don't think . . ." She let her sentence hang in the air.

"I do," I said grimly.

I swallowed hard, wanting to kick myself for not speaking directly to Lidia sooner. I was ashamed that I'd jumped to conclusions, as usual, instead of giving her the benefit of the doubt, as Darcy had asked me to do.

And then who should saunter in the room but the person of the hour: Lidia. Everyone started pummeling her with questions and accusations, except for me and Tomi. We stood up and went to take her hands.

"Shut up, everyone!" I said to my team. And then, turning to the girl who had always gotten on my very last nerve, I asked in as gentle a voice as I could muster, "What happened, Lidia? We've got your back. We're here to listen."

CHAPTER 42

I T WASN'T UNTIL that night that I saw the first of the social media posts. There were so many already up that I don't know how I hadn't seen them before.

All the posts on DebateStories started the same—they began with a page that was a content warning. *CW—Sexism*, the first post read. *CW—Ableism, Toxic Team Environment*, read another. *CW—Misogyny, Eating Disorder,* and so on. It made sense. It was so that someone feeling vulnerable about those specific issues wouldn't stumble across something without forewarning.

The post that drew my eye like a magnet had a CW for Sexual Assault and Grooming. I swiped on the first image and read the post:

> *I'm new to debate but have already noticed how it*
> *allows the worst in people to come out. Maybe it's*
> *because it's a sport that trains students to defend morally*
> *horrible positions and rewards them for it. Maybe it's*
> *because it just attracts jerks, I don't know. Over the*

last few weeks, my two women teammates and I have
received more sexist remarks on our ballots and during
our debates than we've probably gotten in our lifetimes.
I've also gotten a number of proposals—if I send nudes,
my competitor will throw the round. If I meet him
in X place, my competitor will throw the round. It's
humiliating and infuriating and unacceptable. But
no matter how many times I bring it up to my team
or my coaches, no one seems to do anything about
it. Even though everyone agrees that it's a problem
they're all aware of. My team president even said that
another team's female debaters were getting the same
harassment—to send nudes to fellow debaters. Yet no
one does anything. So I decided to take matters into my
own hands and record a meeting with a pretty well-
known debater. Listen to this grossness at your own
peril.

"Lidia," I breathed to myself. "Oh, Lidia. If only I'd told you before what he was like."

The recording she'd posted alongside her words started with a lot of heavy breathing, and a lot of fabric noises, like the device was in someone's pocket. Then, Lidia's distinctive, high-pitched voice: "So why did you want me to come in here with you?"

Jishnu's growl: "You know why."

Some noises like Lidia was moving. "No, seriously. You weren't shy about being clear about what you wanted in your texts."

"You didn't send me the nudes I asked for," Jishnu said accusingly. "But I guess you can make up for it now."

I felt sick, and sickened, and scared, even though I knew that the recording was from the past, and Lidia was all right. Still, to hear what she had gone through made me ill.

"Did you mean what you said?" Lidia asked.

More movement noises.

"Where are you going?" Jishnu demanded. It sounded like there was a lot of moving around now. "Come here!"

"Hey, slow down!" I heard the fear in Lidia's voice, and it made my own heart freeze.

What made me the most upset was that Lidia felt so unbacked up by her team, so alone, that she thought she had to conduct some kind of sting operation. It made me ashamed that she felt like no one would trust her word if she didn't have concrete proof. But then I remembered how often sexual assault survivors aren't believed, even in court with plenty of evidence. It was part of the seriously screwed-up way our society, and legal system, worked.

"Seriously, did you mean what you said? About what you'd do if I met you here today?" Lidia's voice was starting to become shrill with strain. I had to take in a big breath. This was terrible, and seriously dangerous.

"That if you had sex with me, I'd fix it in the judges' room so that you won all your rounds?" Jishnu sounded angry, impatient. "Yeah, course I meant it, baby! It's my school, I can do whatever I want! Now come here, and let me do whatever I want!"

"Well, that doesn't sound like a good deal to me after all,"

Lidia said. I could hear the relief in her voice. She'd gotten what she was after. A recorded confession.

"Wait, no way, where are you going?" More movement noises.

Then the sound of a door opening, and a new voice. The teacher who caught them. "What's going on here?"

Then came the sound of the recording cutting out.

But it didn't matter; she had his words recorded there for all posterity.

And as we forensicators knew, better than anyone, words were all-powerful.

CHAPTER 43

IT WAS DÁRCY, you know," Lidia said to me as we walked into Purvis High School for a forensics competition one mild March morning. It was one of those cool mornings that held a hint of sun, like the promise of spring right around the corner.

Our team was reinstated to the league, and instead of Lidia, it was Jishnu who had to quit in shame. I'd heard a rumor he'd been expelled from Regimental too.

"What was Darcy?" I stopped in my tracks in the doorway, making at least two guys bump into me, dropping their backpacks.

"Watch it!" yelled the first. What the second yelled I will not repeat here for the sake of delicacy.

Then, realizing who we were, the two debaters started whispering among themselves. I gave them a serious glare and they scuttled away.

"Darcy," Lidia said again after we'd extricated ourselves from the entrance hallway kerfuffle. "He was the one who reached out to me, told me to post my story if I wanted on DebateStories."

"How did he know?" I was flabbergasted.

"About DebateStories? Oh, apparently his little sister was the one who started it, with his help, I think," Lidia explained as we walked toward the cafeteria where breakfast was being served. "That turd Jishnu harassed her too when she was little, and then again, when she started debating as a ninth grader. She apparently quit debate altogether because of it."

I put my stuff down on the cafeteria table next to our teammates, my head spinning with this news. I was reminded of the similar table at Hartford High, the one I'd been standing on the day I first met Darcy.

It was early still; Purvis wasn't too far from Longbourn and we'd arrived well before all the other teams from farther away.

"The architecture of this school is simply dreadful!" said Mrs. Bennet, fussing with the scarf around her neck. "So drafty! Like an attic!"

"You'll warm up soon enough, my dear," soothed Mr. Bennet.

If it wasn't for the furtive glances other teams and coaches were giving ours, you'd have thought nothing had happened. But something had happened, something big and important. Gigi and Lidia had opened a door for competitors to start talking about harassment, sexism, and abuse in forensics. Although not everyone was happy about it, some serious truths had been let out to breathe in the open air. And there was no putting truth back in its cage once it was free.

I had just returned to the table from getting some tea and a dry-looking bagel when the cafeteria doors burst open. Well, they were already propped open, but there burst through the open doorway such a bundle of energy and emotion that it was as if the doors themselves were blown in.

"Where is Miss Leela Bose?" demanded an imperious, and familiar, voice. The voice was accompanied by a clattering of bangles and a swish of shawls.

My entire team swiveled around to look at the speaker. "Professor de Bourgh!" exclaimed Colin, getting up from his seat.

"No! Do not rise, I beg you!" intoned Catherine de Bourgh, raising a thin, ringed hand in Colin's direction. "I am here to see that young person!" She pointed now at me.

"Me?" I stood up hesitantly from my seat, not at all sure what was happening.

"Did you forget to thank her after you attended her workshop?" hissed Mrs. Bennet, her face twisted with worry. After the incident with Lidia, it was clear her nerves couldn't handle any more drama with her team.

"I don't think so." I cast my eyes toward Tomi, who shrugged, looking just as confused as me.

"Come with me, Miss Bose, do not waste my time, I beg you!" Professor de Bourgh snapped her fingers. "I have not driven all the way up from Rosings to this poorly heated excuse for a public high school to stand about in the draft."

"She came all the way up from Rosings College?" whispered Mr. Bennet under his breath. "What can she want to talk to you about?"

"Hurry up!" urged Colin.

And so I did. There wasn't a ton of time until my first round, and as I'd decided to drop LD debate and take the lessons I'd learned there into a brand-new category, I was nervous about it.

I didn't need this bejeweled and bangled weirdo of an elocution teacher derailing me, or making me late.

I met Professor de Bourgh in the corner of the cafeteria where she stood. Today, in addition to her usual shawls and capes and jewels, she was wearing a rather precarious-looking turban on top of her bottle-red-haired head.

Before I had a chance to say anything about the turban or anything else, she announced, "You can be at no loss, Miss Bose, to understand the reason for my journey to this suburban outpost of northern New Jersey. Your own heart, your own conscience, must tell you why I've come."

I looked at her with true astonishment. "You're mistaken, Professor. I have no guess as to why you've honored us by coming here."

"Walk with me into the hallway, Miss Bose!" Professor de Bourgh snapped, with so much enunciation to her consonants, she sprayed me with spittle.

I wiped my face with the back of my hand, then followed her silently into the hall. I could feel the curious stares of all the teams and coaches in the cafeteria behind us.

"Miss Bose!" the elocution coach began again, once we were in the Purvis High hallway. Her turban wobbled as if expressing her agitation. "You ought to know that I am not to be trifled with! However insincere you may choose to be, you shall not find *me* so."

"I'm all attention." I kept my eye on the turban, wondering if it was going to leap off her head and attack me.

"A report of a most alarming nature reached me at my idyllic college haven a few days ago!" The woman bit off her words. "I was told that you, Miss Bose, were dating my nephew-of-the-heart Firoze Darcy. Though I knew it must be a scandalous falsehood, though I would not injure him so much as to suppose the truth of it possible, I resolved immediately to find you wherever you may be, as to discover the truth, if any, in this narrative."

"If you believed it impossible, I wonder why you took the trouble of coming so far." I felt my cheeks warm and palms sweating, but tried to keep my outward appearance of calm. Still, my heart was beating hard beneath my new Tomi-gifted sweater. "Why did you do such a thing—and on a Saturday morning of all times?"

"I came to insist upon having this ridiculous spate of—how do you say it?—*fake news* immediately contradicted!" announced Catherine de Bourgh in such ringing tones I knew everyone in the cafeteria could hear. I was only grateful that the Netherfield team hadn't arrived to the competition yet. "Since your ragamuffin team seems to specialize in scandalous behavior and debasing the English language, I knew you must be the author of this false narrative!"

"Won't you coming all the way here confirm rather than deny this story?" I asked.

"Surely you are the author of this salacious rumor?" The woman stopped pacing back and forth in front of me to point a long-nailed finger in my face. "Do you deny it?"

I sighed. This was like some demented episode of one of those courtroom dramas. What exactly was she accusing me of? "Categorically. I didn't make up any rumor about myself and your 'nephew of the heart.'"

Professor de Bourgh looked visibly relieved. She put her hand on her beaded breast and took a big breath. "This is not to be borne, Miss Bose. I insist on knowing. Has he, my nephew, declared his affections to you?"

Now that was something I couldn't deny. Nor, I realized, did I want to. "Well, you yourself have said it was impossible, fake news!"

"It ought to be so, it must be so, while he remembers who is, where he was educated, what future lies ahead of him!" Professor de Bourgh was back to pacing agitatedly around. "But *your* tricks and allurements may have ensnared his senses, and made him forget what he owes his extended family, his own destiny! You may have beguiled him!"

If I hadn't been so irritated, I might have felt complimented. She was painting me out to be quite the femme fatale. "If I had, as you say, beguiled Darcy, I would surely be the last person to confess it?"

"Do you know who I am, Miss Bose?" My words angered Professor de Bourgh so profoundly I really thought her turban would come flying off. "I am a fully tenured professor of theater, a legend on and off the Great White Way. As well as, I might add, a significant number of regional and community theaters! I have not been accustomed to such language as this. After his father died, I took the young man under my wing! I am entitled to know all his dearest concerns!"

"That may be so, but you're not entitled to know mine!" I was done with this absurd conversation. "And behaving like this is hardly likely to make me want to confess my deepest secrets to you."

"Let me make myself abundantly clear. The romance to

which you have the presumption to aspire will never take place!" Catherine de Bourgh really looked as if her head were about to spin backward or something. "Darcy is engaged to *my daughter* and has been since birth!"

"Engaged since birth to that sandwich!" I couldn't help blurting out. "Now I've heard everything! And they give South Asians a bad rap for arranging marriages!"

"Obstinate, headstrong girl! I am ashamed of you! Referring to your superior of birth as a sandwich; what is this new level of trickery?" Professor de Bourgh was all spittle and confusion now. Her voice was so loud and clear, though, I was sure everyone inside the cafeteria could hear her every word. "But I will not be distracted by your plebian, public school nonsense! A sandwich indeed! No! My daughter and Darcy are descended from noble academic stock! They are meant for each other!"

"Then I wish them happy," I said, suddenly feeling very tired.

The woman seemed to deflate a little, her anger waning. "Tell me, once and for all, are you involved romantically with him?"

Was I? I'd certainly never kissed Darcy, or even held his hand. By all normal measures, there was only one answer I could make. "No," I said wearily.

Now Catherine de Bourgh smiled, happier than when I'd pronounced my *r*'s correctly in her elocution workshop. "Then will you promise me never to engage in any relationship of a romantic nature with my nephew Darcy?"

"I will do no such thing," I insisted. "And now, I really have to go and rejoin my team. It will be time soon for my first round and

I haven't been able to eat any of my breakfast." I turned to go back to the cafeteria, feeling almost dizzy from the bizarre encounter.

"Not so hasty, if you please!" Like a talon, Professor de Bourgh's bony hand grabbed my shoulder and turned me back toward her. "Breakfast! You speak of breakfast and sandwiches when I would speak of matters of real import! My girl, you come from a school and a team of no repute. Your style of speech is pathetic, with very little grace and little hope of improvement. I know your teammate was involved in an infamous scandal and your great friend was rejected from Pemberley! I also know that one such as you will have little hopes of attending such an august institution."

"Actually, I'm applying there early action," I blurted out for unclear reasons.

"Heaven and earth!" yelled Professor de Bourgh, as if she were performing in a play. "Are the shades of Pemberley to be thus polluted?"

"Polluted?" I spat back. "Just because Tomi got deferred, just because Lidia was brave enough to report a serial sexual harasser, just because my team is from a public school, do you think we're somehow less than, inferior? How dare you? You've insulted me and mine in every way possible, and I'm going back to my team."

"You have no regard, then, for the honor, the credit, the future career of my nephew! You would pull him down to your base level and your unclear consonants!" I was walking away now, but Professor de Bourgh was swish-swashing her way behind me. "You will disgrace him in the eyes of all who know him!"

We were back inside the cafeteria by now, but I was so furious I turned on her, shouting, "If I want to date Firoze Darcy, I will date Firoze Darcy, and nothing you can possibly say can dissuade me!"

"I am most seriously displeased!" The cafeteria quieted down to a pin-drop silence as Professor de Bourgh screeched, "Do not imagine, Miss Bose, that your scheming, grabbing ambition will ever be gratified! I do not invite you back to my elocution workshops! I condemn you to a lifetime of unclear pronunciation! I take no leave of you or your coaches! You deserve no such attention!"

And with a swirl of her not-inconsiderable capes and scarves, she was gone.

After a moment's shocked silence, the cafeteria erupted into riotous applause. I saw Jay stomping his feet and Lidia standing on the table, letting out sharp whistles through the fingers in her mouth.

And so I did the only thing I could do: I gracefully tucked one leg behind the other and took bow after bow before my adoring audience.

But that was when I noticed that Jay wasn't alone at our cafeteria table, but had Bingley beside him, clapping for me too. They were touching shoulders and looked like they had actually made up.

Which meant the Netherfield team was here. I looked up and locked eyes with Darcy in the far corner of the room. Ro was beside him, looking miffed and huffy—and whether she was more bothered by her brother reuniting with Jay or what I'd just said about dating Darcy, I couldn't be sure. But it didn't matter to me anymore what that girl thought or did, because I could see the look on Darcy's face. I saw him, not through the haze of my own insecurities or the shield of my own prejudices. I could see his true face before me, and it felt like it had when we were debating. It felt like we were dancing.

Without understanding why I did it, I nodded to Darcy and gestured to him with a deep, regal adaab.

CHAPTER 44

THEN I DIDN'T have time to worry about how Darcy had taken my declaration that I would date him if I wanted to. I didn't have time to worry about how the rest of the forensics league had taken my very public fight with Professor de Bourgh. I didn't have time to engage with the misogynist haters, who doubted that Lidia had been in the right and Jishnu in the wrong, or those who knew that Lidia was right but who resented her for bringing the truth to light. I didn't owe anyone anything, including my mental and emotional energy.

It was my first time writing and performing an original oratory, or "OO" piece, a ten-minute factual speech in my own words, aimed to persuade my audience of a point I was arguing. Tomi had talked me into trying her favorite category. It used the part of debate I had enjoyed the most—arguing with my own words—but allowed me to engage in a less combative and more honest way with my audience. The title of my original oratory was "Little Red Debating Hood," and despite it being the first time I'd given that speech, the first time I'd competed in that category, I made it through to finals that day.

Emptying myself of everything but the words I had to say, I stood before the packed room during my final round, and began.

"I'm on my way to grandmother's house, to grandmother's house, to grandmother's house." My voice was high-pitched as I skipped a few steps, like a child.

I turned and faced my audience. The final was standing room only, and I knew they were mostly there to hear me. Word had gotten out on what my OO topic was about, and of course, after all the drama with Lidia and the DebateStories Instagram handle, everyone wanted to come and see me perform. It didn't make me nervous, though, even when I caught Darcy's gaze on me.

I swept my gaze from Darcy across the room, meeting the eyes of many of my own teammates: those who hadn't broken into finals, and those who had made sure they could go late in their own final rounds so they could attend mine. There was Lidia, front and center, shooting me a fierce look of support. Although she wasn't physically there, I could feel Gigi's presence too, her words on the Instagram story crowding into my mind. Both girls had given me permission to speak, as had so many other girls and women who had come before me.

"So what is it about Little Red Riding Hood?" I asked the audience. We all knew the story, I explained, that classic cautionary tale warning little girls not to walk alone through the woods, not to be curious or adventurous, but to stay on the path and keep their heads down lest they be targeted, seduced, and ultimately eaten by Big Bad Wolves.

"Female debaters, like little ol' Red, are taught the same thing—to be polite, not shrill, calm, not loud, to dress conservatively—'not too much cleavage lest your competitor be distracted!'" I said, using a brittle judges' voice. We were taught these lessons, I explained, through little remarks made by judges and fellow debaters; we were taught these lessons by the little comments at the bottoms of our judging ballots.

"And as we're skipping through our arguments," I went on, "trying to keep the basket of our points and counterpoints warm, we're also supposed to get used to the dark forest of our mostly male fellow debaters speaking over us, belittling us, and sending us suggestive texts asking if we'll send a nude, or meet someone in a hotel room/hallway/abandoned classroom in exchange for the guy throwing the round for us. But if we're caught, hey, it'll be *us* most likely to be punished. The wolf will claim it was mutual, it was our idea; he has such a good record, why would he ever want to throw the round?"

I could feel the vibrations in the room change—sharpening as if everyone leaned forward in their chair at the same time, so much the better to see and hear me with. I felt myself settling into my groove.

"Sexism in debate is everywhere, in the trees, in the shadows, lurking in the doorway of Grandma's house." That one got a laugh.

I came out of my Red Riding Hood posture and straightened up, like a debater making a point behind an invisible lectern. "Women's participation in top-level debate tournaments has decreased over the last years, and the ratio of men to women participating in debate at a national level is four to one. Which I guess we are meant to understand that . . ." And here I paused, miming like I was throwing down the lectern, smashing it to pieces. I raised my voice, finishing the sentence: "There are wolves everywhere."

I saw Lidia's eyes filling with righteous fury, and Tomi's eyes bright now with unshed tears. Colin was holding on to her hand. Kitty and Mary were huddled together on either side of Lidia, and there was Jay like a beacon, nodding at me, urging me forward. Beside him, stuck like glue, was Bingley, shy still but beaming goodness at me. I almost couldn't bear to look at my coaches, who were in the front row, proud and worried too, like the parent figures they were. And there, there like a steady ship in turbulent waters, was Darcy, his brows drawn furiously over his face, leaning toward me as if to lend me strength and courage.

I took a big breath. "But what if we're not the victims in this story?"

I pantomimed playing soccer across the front of the room. "In a commencement speech to Barnard College in 2018, two-time Olympic gold medalist and soccer goddess Abby Wambach told the story of Little Red Riding Hood, and told the audience of, in her words, '619 badass women graduates,' this."

I stopped playing soccer and picked up my invisible ball, looking out at the audience with it still balanced under my arm.

"That although she too had been taught to stay on the path, keep her head down, do her job, and be grateful for what she had, she could also demand what she deserved. Be that pay equity, or respect, or in the case of speech and debate, freedom from harassment. And she told those 619 badass women graduates what I'm going to tell all of you now. What if we women aren't Red Hiding Hood?" I paused as people laughed, realizing my play on words. "I mean, what if we women aren't Red Riding Hood. What if we never were? What if, instead, we were always the wolf?"

The audience broke into wild applause at this. It made me feel fierce, and righteous, and strong.

"In a statement to the press, leaders of our National Forensics Association said they 'take seriously any allegation of intimidation, racism, harassment, or bullying at our competitions.' But they also said this: 'We believe that speech and debate can empower students to speak out against these injustices.'"

I looked out thoughtfully at the audience, making my voice louder and louder with each repetition of the sentence, until I was basically yelling. "We believe that speech and debate can empower students to speak out against these injustices. We believe that speech and debate can empower students to speak out against these injustices.

"Well," I said, clearing my throat and straightening a make-believe tie. "Today I am using that empowerment and that voice that forensics competitions have given me to speak out about what lies in the shadows of wooden paths. I speak not just for myself, but for my fellow forensicators, fellow debaters, fellow human beings who are tired of keeping our heads down beneath our red,

Handmaid's Tale–like hoods. Because we are not little girls afraid of what lurks in the woods."

I breathed out, taking a moment for all this to sink in. I paced back and forth a little, adopting a more professorial tone.

"In the 1920s, the last wolf pack in Yellowstone was killed off by the US government in an attempt to, and I quote, 'tame the wilderness.' That decision had devastating and cascading effects. Animals like deer and elk, whose populations would have been culled by wolves, grew. They stripped bare trees, changed the course of rivers, and altered the whole park ecosystem. But when the wolves were reintroduced, they regulated these out-of-control animal populations, and the trees strengthened and stabilized the riverbanks, and the entire ecosystem was saved by that which was once seen as its biggest threat."

I had struggled so much with this ending. I had rewritten and performed it over and over again in my bedroom until I got it right.

I waited a beat or two, looking out at the audience. "We women are the wolves, not alone, but supporting each other's stories and voices in a pack. We are the wolves, pushing our ecosystems, our clubs and communities, to be better. We are the wolves. We are, like it or not, culling out that which would ultimately destroy all of us with our teeth, our truths, our voices raised strong and together."

There was silence when I finished, and then an almost audible exhalation, like everyone had released a collectively held breath. Then came the applause, steady and strong. At first it was my team and my friends who stood up, and then it was everyone.

I knew it wasn't me they were applauding but all of us, the wolf pack, the strength of women who weren't willing to be afraid anymore.

I gave a little bow and sat down, no longer embarrassed at the attention. Lidia gave me a tight squeeze, and I whispered in her ear, "Was that okay, wolf captain?"

"Yes!" she whispered back, her voice thick with emotion. "Yes!"

CHAPTER 45

AFTER MY ROUND was over, everyone wanted to talk to me. My own teammates, but also gossipmongers from other teams who wanted to know how much of what I'd talked about was about Lidia, how much about Mary, how much about myself. But there was only one person I wanted to speak with. I had Jay and Bingley run interference for me so I could get past everyone and grab Darcy by the sleeve.

"Come on!" I urged, dragging him outside into the parking lot.

The temperamental March morning had turned rainy, and we were in serious danger of both getting drenched the moment we stepped outside. "Maybe I didn't think this entirely through," I admitted, my coat held out over my head.

"Let's go sit in my car," Darcy urged, and we ran, laughing, toward his fancy fuel-efficient space carriage.

As he started the car to give us a little warmth, I settled into the passenger's seat and turned toward him. "So it was you who helped your sister start DebateStories."

Darcy looked over at me, his hands still on the steering wheel. "I know you know this, but your speech was amazing."

"Why don't you want to take credit?" I rubbed my cold, wet hands, holding them in front of the heating vents to dry them.

"The part about Little Red Riding Hood, the wolf, Yellowstone, it was all inspired," Darcy went on. "I can't believe you wrote that. I mean, I can. It was so powerful."

"I realized there were parts of both speech and debate I liked—the performance part and the speaking your own truth part," I admitted. "Original oratory allowed me to do both."

"Listen, Leela." Darcy turned toward me abruptly from his seat. His face and voice were tight as his words tumbled out of his mouth. "Don't play with me. Are your feelings the same as they were that day we talked in the playground? Mine haven't changed, but I don't want to bring it up again if it's painful to you." He took a deep breath, steadying himself. "Tell me, do I have any reason to hope?"

I looked at the fancy control panel in front of me, more like a computer than a car. I felt suddenly very shy. I thought back to the playground and all I had said in anger. I thought back to how Darcy and I had been speaking words at each other, but neither was really listening. Back then, we had been like swings set at opposite rhythms, always trying to shoot higher than each other, but in the process, never able to be on the same plane. But so much had changed since then. I'd had to change my opinion about so many things, and learn how to put aside so many assumptions. I thought of how we'd been able to speak and hear each other in the debate round at Kent, at his house at Pemberley.

"Actually," I finally said, feeling unbearably shy, "my feelings are quite the opposite from that day."

"Really?" Darcy ran his hand over his eyes, a tentative smile forming on his lips. "I wasn't sure if you were just angry at Aunt Catherine, but when you shouted to the entire cafeteria this morning that you would date me if you wanted and there was nothing she could say to stop you, I . . . I couldn't help it. I started to hope."

"Oh, that *was* out of anger," I admitted.

Darcy's expression fell. "Oh?"

I met his eyes tentatively, surprised by the depth of feeling I found there. "But that doesn't mean it wasn't true."

Darcy stared straight ahead, nodding once, twice, and then once again. Then he beeped the horn for absolutely no apparent reason, making us both jump.

"It was an absolutely epic moment, you know." Darcy turned to me as he made his voice into a serviceable imitation of Professor de Bourgh's. "Obstinate, headstrong girl!"

"I am most seriously displeased!" I added shrilly.

"I take no leave of your coaches!" Darcy waggled his finger in the air.

"However insincere you may choose to be, you shall not find *me* so!" I intoned snootily.

We were both smiling at each other in the little private cocoon of his car when he reached out to touch my cheek.

"I don't know how to be anything but sincere," he said softly. "You were so witty, so fast-spoken when I first met you, I didn't know if I could keep up."

I leaned into his hand, his skin cool against my cheek. "I

was trying too hard, running from my own insecurities."

"And what I said—I only fed those hurtful thoughts." Darcy withdrew his hand, looking like he wanted to cut it off.

I wasn't sure what to say to that. My heart was racing wildly. And so I turned to humor, which was, as I'd once told him, a great way to discuss serious things.

"Be honest," I quipped. "I thought you were engaged to Anne de Bourgh."

Darcy chuckled. "Only in her mother's imagination."

"A shame; you would have made a magnificent Mr. de Bourgh," I said archly. "Stuffed on their mantelpiece, brought out for parties."

He brought his other hand to my hair, touching an errant curl. Then he brought his lips to my temple, pressing them there so gently it was like a whisper. "Did you actually call her a sandwich?"

"I couldn't help it," I said, feeling very distracted by what his lips were doing. "She is a bit of one. Not even a very tasty one. Like PB&J on white untoasted bread."

"Leela." Darcy's eyes roamed over my face with such feeling, I felt the heat rising not just in my cheeks, but everywhere. "What am I going to do with you?"

"Never let me take another elocution class again?" I offered.

"I'm pretty sure Aunt Catherine's not going to be asking either of us to a workshop anytime soon."

Our foreheads were touching now, and my eyes were closed. I was feeling the electric rightness of this all.

"And they give us Desis a hard time for arranged marriage," I drawled softly.

"A suitable boy and girl," murmured Darcy, moving his mouth gently over my cheek.

"Wait a minute." I pulled back, my hand on his chest. "What happened with Jay and Bingley?"

"Mmm?" Darcy was trying to pull me toward him, but my crumbling resolve managed to hold fast.

"Bay and Jingley," I repeated in a muffled voice as he did something delicious to my ear. It occurred to me I might not have said their names right, but I was so wonderfully distracted I didn't care.

"They're back together." Darcy was tracing my collarbones as if he was studying them to sculpt. "That's a good thing, right?"

"But what I'm asking you to clarify, Mr. Darcy, is if you have anything to do with it?" I untied the loose scarf at his throat and threw it into the back seat.

"Aren't you warm? I'm warm," he said as he started to unbutton my coat for me, fumbling a little with the big buttons. "This car has an excellent heating system, you know."

"A delightful heating system," I agreed seriously, scooching closer toward him as he threaded his arm around me, beneath my coat. "But what about Bingley and Jay?"

"It was always Ro, just making trouble for no reason. She convinced her brother that their parents wouldn't accept Jay if he wasn't exactly perfect. Which he seems like he is, at least for Bingley." Darcy ran a thumb as if experimentally across my now-warm bottom lip.

"Why did you let me think it was you who broke them up?" I asked, so distracted by his thumb I wasn't 100 percent sure what I was asking.

"I guess I can be pretty headstrong myself," Darcy said ruefully. "But to make up for it, I pointed out to Bingley that Jay was perfect for him, and nudged him in the right direction."

"Thank you," I said, letting my lips graze over his.

Darcy grinned wickedly against my lips. "Do you have any other friends whose love lives you'd like me to help coordinate?"

I leaned back, looking at him in the eye. "Why?"

"Well." He pulled me back toward him. "Because if I'd known this was the reward . . ."

I laughed, kissing him again, this time with more confidence. "Tell me about DebateStories," I said against his mouth.

Darcy straightened up a little, rubbing his hand absentmindedly over his lips. "It was Gigi's idea entirely; I just helped her with the logistics of setting the thing up."

"You stood by her," I pointed out, feeling ashamed at my own initial reactions to Lidia. "You listened to her."

He shook his head. "I didn't give her the support she needed for too long. I wanted to protect her in some kind of bubble, instead of encouraging her to speak, find her voice and her wolf pack."

I ran my fingers over his creased brows, easing his expression. He really was too hard on himself. "Well, you certainly made up for that now. She's not just found her wolf pack; her voice is giving a lot of other women strength to find theirs."

"That was the idea to setting up DebateStories," Darcy

agreed. "To create a space where people could tell their stories, have their voices and their truths heard."

I grinned. "You were listening."

"Yes, Ms. Bose, I always was," Darcy said formally, giving me a little bow from his seat.

I kissed him then, and he kissed me, rather heartily, back. When I could catch my breath, I asked, "When did you know? How you felt about me, I mean?"

"I wish I could tell you it was when you were singing to me at the Hartford High competition, but all I felt then was embarrassment," Darcy said, winding his fingers through mine. "I can't tell you the hour, or the spot, or the look, or the words that started it all."

"Well, that's rather disappointing," I began, but Darcy held up a hand to my lips, concluding, "Because I was already in the middle of it before I knew I'd even begun."

That, I had to admit, was very nice to hear.

"Come on now, you withstood my beauty," I insisted.

When he made a sound of protest, I smiled and shook my head. "So it must have been my impertinence, my rude behavior that attracted you to me?"

"It was your lively, brilliant, and, yes, *beautiful* mind," Darcy corrected me with a smile.

"Or was it my willingness to jump to conclusions about you?" My voice was laced with apology as I asked this.

Darcy's mouth twisted. "I hadn't given you any reason to think I was anything other than cruel, cold, and proud."

"You always looked so annoyed by me." I pushed a finger playfully into his chest.

He caught the finger in his hand, wrapping it in a kiss. "I was shy."

"You could have tried to talk to me more freely." I kissed his hand back.

"If I'd felt less, I might have said more," he admitted.

Then there were a few minutes when neither of us could speak. When we could again, I said regretfully, "We should probably go back. The awards ceremony will start soon."

Darcy tilted his head, sneaking in another kiss. "It was my understanding this *was* the awards ceremony!"

"Are you, good sir, actually making a joke?" I asked, feeling quite breathless.

"I do know how you love to laugh," he returned, behaving in such a way as to ensure we couldn't leave right away.

Later, as we left the warmth of the car to return to the building, Darcy stopped in the middle of the parking lot. As rapidly and fiercely as it had begun, the rain had stopped, and the sun was tentatively peeking out its face. The world felt reborn and fresh again, scrubbed clean by the passing storm. There were new stories being born, and possibilities everywhere.

Darcy put out his hand, asking, "Any chance you're free to dance?"

I took a big breath. Was I?

"Yes," I answered, feeling the joy bursting through my very skin. "Yes!"

And so we danced across the wet parking lot, our bodies

moving together beneath the shy new sun. When he kissed me, his breath bringing my lips to life, I couldn't tell anymore if we were standing still or swirling, our feet on or far above the ground.

"Mr. Darcy!" I protested when I finally could come up for air.

"Obstinate, headstrong girl," he muttered, pulling me toward him once again.

AUTHOR'S NOTE

Dear Reader,

It is a truth universally acknowledged that *Pride and Prejudice*'s Lizzie and Darcy are among the most iconic examples of enemies-to-lovers couples. In Austen's original 1813 novel, the pair bicker, fight, and debate their way into falling in love—so it made perfect sense to me to set my modern reimagining in the ultra-competitive world of high school speech and debate tournaments.

I am a huge Austen-head. I've read *Pride and Prejudice* umpteen times and seen every possible stage, TV, and movie adaptation. Maybe my love of Jane Austen comes from my being a daughter of Indian immigrants. There are certainly a lot of similarities between the way that Austen characters obsess over eligible matches and the central role of marriage in many Desi communities. Yet, although Leela and Darcy—the protagonists of this novel—are both South Asian Americans, that's not my central impulse for writing this story.

The themes of *Pride and Prejudice* I wanted to explore in this novel include the class conflict between private school Darcy and public school Leela; the importance of being willing to change your mind about someone and not give into prejudice; as well as toxic masculinity and sexism. Although Wickham, the lying, womanizing villain of Austen's *Pride and Prejudice*, preys on much younger women, there is no space in the original novel for those teenage girls to fight back in any public way. I wanted my modern, feminist characters to say all the things that their 1813 counterparts could not, and in doing so, honor the #MeToo stories being shared by many brave high schoolers, including speech and debate competitors, in an effort to make these spaces more welcoming, equitable, and just.

This is a novel that celebrates the power of finding your community and speaking your truth, even when it's scary. It's a novel about knowing we are all worthy of taking up space in the world. In between the wit and banter, the complex debate topics and funny musical theater references, this is ultimately a story about justice and honor, friendship and love.

So, dear reader, whether you have, like me, read and watched versions of *Pride and Prejudice* a zillion times, or really never heard of it until now, I hope you have found power, laughter, courage, and joy in these pages.

Words matter. Art matters. Debating the issues that affect our lives matters. Your voice matters. YOU matter. And love—in all its beautiful romantic and nonromantic derivations—matters most of all.

♥ Sayantani

ACKNOWLEDGMENTS

"My idea of good company," says Anne Elliot in Jane Austen's *Persuasion*, "is the company of clever, well-informed people who have a good deal of conversation." I have been lucky enough on this writing journey to have not just good, but the best of company. This includes my brilliant agent, Brent Taylor, my editorial genius team of Abigail McAden and Talia Seidenfeld, and the creative team of Elizabeth Parisi and Samya Arif, who imagined Leela and Darcy into being for the beautiful cover. Gratitude to Melissa Schirmer, my production editor; Jessica White, my copy editor; and to the rest of my Scholastic family including Ellie Berger, David Levithan, Rachel Feld, Lizette Serrano, Emily Heddleson, Danielle Yadao, Lauren Donovan, and Elisabeth Ferrari! Many thanks to Sahana Thirumazhusai for her invaluable insights on debate culture in forensics competitions!

Thank you to all those author friends I've made on this wonderful journey, including my We Need Diverse Books, Kidlit Writers of Color, and Desi Writers families. Thank you to the librarians, teachers, parents, and readers who have enjoyed and shared my stories.

A big shout out to my own brilliant and slightly chaotic high school forensics team—Alyssa, Beth, Geoff, Jen, Sharon, Tim, and of course our intrepid leaders Miss Hsieh/Elisa A.! Thank you for using your voices to make art and promote justice. Thank you for helping me to find my own voice.

As always, gratitude beyond measure to my beloved parents, Sujan and Shamita; my husband/one-man publicity team, Boris; and my not-very-therapeutic-but-still-adorable pup, Khushi. Particular love and thanks to my darling teen collaborators, Kirin and Sunaya, who helped me dream this book to life. How did I get so lucky to be your mama?